THE PLAY'S THE THING

Why did he have to ▮▮▮▮ ▮▮▮▮ former? Where did the ▮ ▮▮▮▮▮ disappear to when he took ▮▮▮ ▮▮▮▮ and hot-blooded Romeo ▮▮▮ ▮▮▮ sponding to him—and t▮▮ ▮▮▮ow, would be wrong.

As they danced, R.J. said softly to her, "Can you not pretend to be pleased by your Romeo?"

"Are you criticizing my performance, Mr. Hopkins?" Juliet stumbled over a step, which gave her next words less effect. "I remind you, I have participated in dozens of plays, and no one has ever faulted my performance before."

Smoothly, he compensated for her misstep. "Perhaps all you know are the false young women of your society, Miss Fenster. But Juliet is not false. She is young. She is passionate. She understands love in a way you never will."

"I have seen great actresses upon the stage play the role just as I do, sir," she lied. It was his fault she could not play the role properly. There would be true scandal if she were to respond to him as the bard's Juliet had responded to her own Romeo. "How dare you criticize my passion."

"I have seen fish hanging in the market with more passion that you, my fair Juliet." His whisper was inaudible to all but her, but as he spoke, he lifted her hand as if to kiss it, and his breath touched her skin in a warm caress. . . .

Dear Romance Reader,

In July last year, we launched the Ballad line with four new series, and each month we'll present both new and continuing stories set everywhere from medieval England to the American West—the kind of passionate, romantic stories you love best, written by the most gifted authors. At the back of each book, we'll tell you when you can find subsequent books in the series that have captured your heart.

First up is the second entry in Lori Handeland and Linda Devlin's wonderful *Rock Creek Six* series. This month Linda Devlin introduces **Sullivan**, a half-breed bastard with no place in the world—until he finds his fate in a special woman's arms. Next, Maura McKenzie continues the *Hope Chest* series with **At Midnight**, as a modern-day newspaper reporter tracks a murderer into the past, where she meets a Pinkerton agent determined not only to solve the case, but to steal her heart.

The passioante men of the *Clan Maclean* return in Lynne Hayworth's spectacularly atmospheric **Winter Fire**, as a widow with a special gift meets the laird of the proud but doomed clan. Will her love bring about his salvation? Finally, Kelly McClymer offers the fourth book in the charming *Once Upon a Wedding* series, introducing **The Infamous Bride** who begins her marriage on a rash wager—and finds that her husband's love is the only wedding gift she wants. Enjoy!

Kate Duffy

ONCE UPON A WEDDING

THE INFAMOUS BRIDE

KELLY McCLYMER

ZEBRA BOOKS
Kensington Publishing Corp.
http://www.zebrabooks.com

ZEBRA BOOKS are published by

Kensington Publishing Corp.
850 Third Avenue
New York, NY 10022

All Kensington titles, imprints, and distributed lines are available at special quantity discounts for bulk purchases for sales promotion, premiums, fund-raising, educational or institutional use.

Special book excerpts or customized printings can also be created to fit specific needs. For details, write or phone the office of the Kensington Special Sales Manager: Kensington Publishing Corp., 850 Third Avenue, New York, NY 10022. Attn: Special Sales Department. Phone: 1-800-221-2647.

Zebra and the Z logo Reg. U.S. Pat. & TM Off.

First Printing: October 2001
10 9 8 7 6 5 4 3 2 1

Printed in the United States of America

PROLOGUE

Boston, 1843

"Let me make certain I understand you, Father, Mama Annabel." R. J. Hopkins, from long practice, smoothed the bitterness out of his tone. "In order for you to have faith enough in me to turn over management duties, you require that I go to London and choose a bride?"

"Precisely." Jonathan Hopkins nodded.

"We will see the world, R.J.," his younger sister, Susannah, said with a tight smile. "That is the way I'm choosing to look at our trip to London." Apparently she was no more pleased at the news than he.

"And I must do this immediately?"

His stepmother ran her finger down the bright yellow feathers of the finch perched on the cuff of her sleeve. "You needn't make the trip sound like a death sentence, R.J. Every man needs a wife to keep his life in order. And London should be a pleasant change for you. You have never complained about travel before."

"I travel for business. I have no business in London."

"I always meant to establish stronger ties with those I deal with in London," his father said hastily. "Never fear, I shall keep you busy enough. Wouldn't want to send you over there just to have you come back as idle and worthless as some of those aristocrats, my boy. Just want you to find a well-bred wife and settle down to a sober life of business."

"You believe a wife will prevent me from becoming a libertine, then?" The finch ruffled its feathers, cocked its head, and fixed its bright, beady eyes on him. He lowered his voice. "I had not realized my behavior warranted such a worry."

"Your behavior is all that a father could ask." Jonathan Hopkins sighed. "A good wife is necessary to a successful businessman, R.J. You have seen how valuable Annabel has been to me. Sometimes I believe no one would come to dinner here if it were not for her charm and her skill at entertaining."

Annabel smiled as she scooped up the finch perched on her sleeve into one hand. She rose to place the bird back in the ornate gold cage that hung at the window behind R.J.'s father. "Nonsense, Jonathan. It is your head for business that they admire and respect."

R.J. privately agreed more with his father's assessment. While the men and their wives who attended their dinner parties no doubt respected Jonathan Hopkins's acumen, it was not his father's sober talk that kept the dinner table lively and the conversation keen. Annabel knew how to manage things, even men like his father, men with ledgers for hearts and black ink running through their veins.

Men who rarely doubted their own judgment.

"Your point is well made, Father." He knew there would be no profit for him to argue, not if he wanted to prove himself worthy of heading his father's business. So, he would take a wife. It was time, after all.

The little bird peeped once, but Annabel shushed it and closed the little door. R.J. did not like the disapproving gaze Annabel fixed on him as she sat down once again. He watched the caged bird hop on its perch and fix beady black eyes on the gardens beyond the window as if it wished to fly away free. Could a bird long for something never experienced? No matter. Escape was not a possibility.

He would marry. Still, there was one point he must argue. "I would rather ask Lucy Matthews to marry me. I see no reason why I must go to London for a bride."

For the first time, his father blinked, as if it took him a moment to find a ready answer. "Lucy is a biddable girl, though young, and would no doubt become a good wife in time. If you find no one else, you may ask her when you return."

"I would prefer to ask her now." He would prefer not to have to think about marriage at all. But if his father wanted him married, then he wished to choose a wife at once and be done with the business as soon as possible.

His father shook his head slowly. "Annabel has her heart set on a title for Susannah, and she believes a little English noble blood wouldn't hurt your line, either. I agree."

So that was it—an infusion of good blood to balance out any taint of his mother's legacy. "Do you believe venerable English blood will be of any more value to my children than that of the Matthews? I can think of no family more proper."

"Do you fancy yourself in love with the Matthews girl?" His father's shrewd eyes bored into him.

"No," he said honestly. "But she answers all the requirements for a wife, and her family has made it clear that she will have me."

"True enough." His father nodded approvingly. "Then what does it matter to you if you delay asking her until you have seen what is available in London? I am needed here. I cannot accompany Annabel and Susannah. While there, you might as well look for a bride. Marriage is an important matter, and you shouldn't settle for the handiest woman but the best suited to make your life pleasant and run smoothly."

He understood at last, his father did not want to go to London. So the job must fall to him. He allowed the fury at the interruption of his plans to settle before he asked quietly, "And if I do not find any suitable woman there whose family is willing to have me?" He would dare come no closer to alluding to the fact that no young London miss had been allowed to wed Jonathan Hopkins, who had come home with a miserably unsuitable Italian bride—R.J.'s mother.

His father's color grew hectic, but that was the only sign that he understood the reference. "Knowing Annabel, you will. Your stepmother is hard to divert when she has made up her mind." With a wave of his hand, his father's color receded from bright red to slightly pink. "My money's as good as theirs, and my blood better any day."

R.J. nodded his head. He was as firmly caged in this matter as was the finch. "Very well." He would accompany Annabel and Susannah to London, then. But he was determined to come home without a wife.

The plans he had made so carefully years ago were sound and needed no change. Ultimately, he would be responsible for running his father's business. His business one day. The disruption was unfortunate, but he was a businessman, and he understood that sometimes one must bear an interruption or two—just as long as it did not prevent one from ultimately carrying out one's own plan.

He did not believe he had to worry that Lucy would get another offer during the time he was away. Though her family was all that one could wish, she herself was plain, quiet, and shy. The perfect wife for him.

ONE

Juliet Fenster rapped her knuckles on the tabletop in front of her. "Kate, a lady does not bellow, she projects when she sings. Betsey, when playing the harp, the strings are plucked gently, not twanged." The pair of twelve-year-olds exchanged glances and giggled.

"Don't laugh or she'll make you sing that nasty high song only her voice can make sound beautiful," Rosaline, Juliet's seventeen-year-old sister, chided the younger girls.

Juliet's scowl sent Rosaline back to copying out her Latin lesson but did not wipe away the teasing smirk on the girl's face. Fortunately, Helena, Rosaline's twin, looked up from her own studies to give Juliet a look of sympathy.

However did their governess manage a full day with these monkeys? Juliet had to spend only an hour a day in music instruction, and sometimes that proved too much for her temper. She cut a sigh short when a maid hurried into the schoolroom, offering a welcome distraction. "What is it, Ann?"

"The button girl has arrived." Behind the maid, a shy, gangly girl of twenty dressed in country fashion entered the room carrying a large basket.

"Let me see." Kate abandoned her proper shoulders-back singing posture without asking for permission. She ran to the girl and tugged at her basket. "What have you brought us this month, Sally?"

"Kate!" Juliet reprimanded her youngest sister sharply but ineffectively. For some reason, the younger girls did not listen to her as easily as they listened to Miranda and Hero, their oldest sisters. When she was stern, they teased her and only obeyed her command if it suited them to do so.

"Here." Juliet took the basket from Sally and shook off Kate's hands. She pulled out the bundled roll and unwrapped it to reveal the oak chest nestled inside. "I won't open this until you are all still." She sat at the table and waited for the girls to settle themselves around her.

"Let us see, Juliet, please," Helena pleaded softly, even though Kate and Rosaline were still fidgeting.

Juliet opened the box, and they all gave an appreciative coo as they saw the buttons before them. "Doves! How beautiful."

"I like the swans." Helena smiled, reaching in to finger the smooth ivory of the gracefully carved buttons.

"The toads are my favorite." Rosaline was the first to move away from the chest. "Sally, when is your father going to carve swords? I have asked twice now."

Sally laughed. "He says, Miss Rosaline, that he will carve you swords to adorn your wedding gown."

Rosaline scowled as she returned to her copying out. "Then I shall never have any such buttons. I am determined never to marry."

Juliet shared a rueful glance with the smiling Sally and said to her sisters, "You may each choose a dozen for yourselves. But be careful not to lose any. I must send them to the dressmaker promptly or Sally's father will not get paid for his work."

She took out another chest identical to the first except that instead of buttons it held the money earned from the last batch of buttons Sally had delivered. Wrapping it carefully, Juliet placed it back in Sally's basket and handed everything back to Sally.

"Thank you, Miss Juliet." Sally said.

As Juliet walked the girl to the door, she spoke quietly so as not to draw her sisters' attention. "Was he pleased with the last shipment of stone? I found some excellent jade and ivory."

Sally bobbed her head quickly. "Indeed, he told me to thank you for it."

"How are his spirits?" Juliet did not want to dwell on his difficulties, but she knew that Sally's father, having had his legs amputated a dozen years ago, suffered from despondency at times.

"Excellent. And his appetite has picked up considerably."

"Is there anything he needs? Tools?" There was little work for a man who could not walk and Raster Booth had whiled away his time carving little wooden buttons and figurines for his eight children. He had often lamented to her brother Valentine that he was not much use as a tenant farmer without legs. Valentine, of course, would never have sent him away.

Sally beamed. "Miss Juliet, since you started him at making buttons of stone, he is a changed man. Why, just last week he laughed out loud." Tears came to the girl's eyes. "Mam said it was the first time since the accident."

"I'm glad to hear the work is not too taxing." And she was.

"No, miss, not at all. In fact, my father says you are a genius."

Juliet blushed. Hero was the smart sister; Miranda, the clever one. Such a compliment from Sally's father was nice but certainly untrue. All she had done was find one of his children's rabbit buttons on the ground. The button itself had given her the idea. Wooden buttons were too plain to adorn silks and satins. But Juliet immediately saw the use for the same carvings done in soft stone to enhance the fine silk or satin of a gown. She had made certain that others who enjoyed fashion as she did saw the beauty of such buttons as well.

"It is kind of you to see that the dressmakers buy them," Sally added shyly.

"See to it?" Juliet laughed in amusement. "Tell your father that there are two dressmakers who may come to blows one day over first choice of his buttons."

Sally shook her head, her sausage curls brushing along her narrow cheeks. "He wouldn't believe such a fairy story, Miss Juliet."

Juliet did not attempt to convince her that it was no fairy tale. She had become used to the reaction of her family to her odd stumble into business. Although she had been teased unmercifully by her brother, who seemed to think carved buttons an astonishingly amusing concept, her idea had proved successful so far.

She patted the girl on the arm and said, "Be sure to stop down in the kitchen before you go. I had Cook put a basket together for your family."

"Oh, Miss Juliet. You shouldn't have."

"Nonsense. It is nothing—a ham, some eggs, a few apples, treats for the younger children."

"You are an angel, miss."

Juliet glanced over her shoulder at the girls, squabbling now as to who would get which buttons. "Tell that to my sisters." She sighed and turned back to sort out the mess.

Just as Juliet opened her mouth to attempt to regain order, Helena let out a gasp and held out the society pages. Juliet knew she should scold her for reading the papers when she should be working on a lesson.

But Helena's face was paler than usual, and she seemed distressed as she said, "Juliet—didn't you say you expected Lord Pendrake to ask for your hand any day now?"

"Of course not. I am a lady, and a lady would not be so immodest." Pendrake had seemed on the verge of telling her something important yesterday, though, when they drove out.

Rosaline let out a bark of laughter. "Then you said you thought the poor boy would not be able to keep his heart's secret from you much longer. Which amounts to the same thing. Only said in a convoluted way, like a lady."

Why did her sisters never show her any respect? Juliet would have scolded her, but Helena's words made everything—buttons, Sally's father, music lessons—flee her mind.

Her sister held out the papers. "Lord Pendrake has just announced his engagement. To another woman."

Knowing he had another hour at this tedious dance before Annabel would allow him to escape, R. J. Hopkins leaned against a convenient wall and watched the spectacle before him. The musicians played so that their music filled every nook and cranny in the room. The wine and champagne flowed freely. The ladies' eyes shone as they whirled about the dance floor.

So much silk and satin, so many feathers. And the jewels that adorned the bared wrists and necks must have cost several small fortunes. All to show off a handful of eligible men to the girls—and their families, who wished to make a match. What a waste.

His friend Freddie Snow, alternately known as Lord Pendrake, poked an elbow in his ribs, discreetly but with force. "You're looking at them as if they were the most dangerous of lions."

"Who?"

"The young hopefuls." Freddie laughed, his snub nose crinkling with amusement. "Why don't you ask one of them to dance? I guarantee she will not eat you. And your stepmother will stop glaring holes in your back."

"Considering that you yourself just willingly stepped into the maw of one of the young hopefuls, I respectfully decline to trust your judgment." R.J. sipped the champagne in his glass, marveling at the excellent vintage and wondering at the cost.

Freddie's smile dimmed. "A man has to marry. And my mother has had her heart set on Elizabeth since the day the girl was born." He stretched his lips into a grimace. "You know our mothers are boon companions. They are set on the match."

"You would not have asked for her hand if you thought her wrong for you, Freddie. You are just suffering the natural jitters of a soon-to-be-caged man." He knew his friend was ambivalent about his engagement. Privately, R.J. believed Elizabeth would make his friend a perfect wife. She seemed to know what Freddie thought before he spoke a word.

The two were well suited—if Freddie would only forget the fascinating Miss Fenster, his latest obsession. R.J. had heard all he wished to about Juliet Fenster. Beautiful. Charming. Witty. Not one whit of Freddie's endless prattle could adequately explain his desire for the girl to R.J.

"I suppose I am—" Freddie broke off.

R.J. felt the tension suddenly coiling in Freddie as his friend's shoulders stiffened. R.J. looked for the source with idle curiosity. His stepmother and sister were bearing down upon them, a young woman in tow. Annabel seemed less than happy, but Susannah was glowing, obviously pleased with herself.

He groaned inwardly. No doubt Susannah had found yet another sacrificial lamb to parade in front of him. He loved his younger sister, truly he did. Though she had the same desire to run his life as her mother did, Susannah's heart was gentle and kind. He knew she wanted only the best for him. She had told him often enough that her one wish was to see him happy.

He wished, though, that she had not set herself out to introduce him to every unsuitable woman in London. Even at a distance he could see that the woman at Susannah's side had none of the qualifications he was looking for. She carried her head regally, and her honey-colored hair was artfully curled with a certain flair that suggested she might be impetuous. Other men's eyes followed her movements openly, which suggested she was a known flirt. The women watched her with envy, which suggested she was successful at capturing men's hearts.

R.J. sighed as he smiled at his sister. In this one thing, he wished Susannah had her mother's discretion.

"R.J., I have someone for you to meet," she said exuberantly. He saw the disapproving glances cast her way—the English seemed to wish every young woman to act as if she had no more energy than she would need for her deathbed—and instantly forgot about his own annoyance. "Miss Juliet Fenster, may I present my brother, Mr. R. J. Hopkins. R.J., may I present Miss Juliet Fenster." She added, "Her sister is the duchess of Kerstone."

The infamous Miss Fenster smiled at him charmingly. No wonder Freddie was so miserable. R.J. smiled and bowed politely, knowing that he would be expected to dance with the young lady in order to appease his sister.

Susannah confirmed this by saying sweetly, "I have told Miss Fenster how exquisite a dancer you are, R.J. You will not disappoint me, will you?"

"Not at all, Susannah." R.J. saw, to his amusement, that Miss Fenster had not intended a dance with him. Her startled glance at Susannah was utterly guileless. Unlike the expectant glance she bestowed upon Freddie.

But Freddie, almost visibly squirming as he spoke, said only, "Miss Fenster, I hope you are enjoying your evening."

"Indeed I am, Lord Pendrake." She lied quite charmingly, but the lie was evident in the way she leaned forward ever so slightly to encourage poor Pendrake to ask her to dance. "The musicians are playing well tonight, are they not?"

R.J. took pity on the cornered lord. "Indeed they are," he said as he held out his hand to the forward Miss Fenster. "You must dance with me or my sister will be most disconsolate."

She took his hand reluctantly, but her hesitation did not show as they walked swiftly to the dance floor and joined the dance. Indeed, the casual observer would think that she had become quite taken with the handsome Mr. Hopkins, considering how she smiled and batted her lovely lashes at him.

It would have been simple enough for him to return her flirtation as they danced, as was expected of him. She glided through the movements of the dance with him as if her feet did not touch the floor. Returning her charming smile was instinctive. For some reason, though, he wanted her to know that he was not fooled by her manner. "He is quite besotted by his fiancée, I assure you."

He was surprised when she did not pretend to misunderstand him. "Lord Pendrake? Well, I would hope so." Her smile was brittle, and he knew he had overstepped English propriety. But that was something he enjoyed in London; the one thing he enjoyed, perhaps. Americans were considered little better than barbarians and so could get away with the most outrageous pronouncements.

Still, he decided to push her a bit more. Apparently she had not been quite bored enough with Freddie to welcome his change in affections. He was curious to see how far the infamous Miss Fenster was willing to go to change Freddie's mind.

Next time, if he had any influence upon her, she would think twice before trying to reengage the affections of a newly affianced man. "I take it you are disappointed that you are not the one he asked to be his wife."

"Me?" She looked at him fully for the first time since Susannah had introduced them. "Certainly not." The intensity of her gaze contained a warning. Apparently she did not enjoy being trifled with.

For some reason, the warning glance goaded him to further rudeness. "No?"

"Really, Mr. Hopkins. I should think even an American would know this topic is most inappropriate."

R.J. had sympathy for the first time ever for what his father must have gone through. Miss Juliet Fenster's attitude dripped condescension. The sound of her words, magnified by the husky overtones of her voice, rippled through him. A beautiful sound to match her beautiful hazel eyes. Though her hair was almost gold in the light of the ballroom, her lashes were darker, framing her eyes in a most attractive way.

He blinked, reminding himself that she had gone through the whole charade of being introduced to him just to reach Pendrake. As for himself, he couldn't care less, but he did not like to see Susannah's friendship used so.

He said, "I do apologize, Miss Fenster. I had thought you would wish me to leave you somewhere near poor Pendrake so that he would be compelled to ask you for the next dance."

"My card is filled," she informed him frostily, flipping the dance card at her wrist. "I could not have danced with you had not Lord Turrington been taken suddenly lame just as we were to step out onto the floor."

"Just before you were introduced to my sister?" He let his gaze make clear that he did not believe her. He wondered if she used artifice to darken her lashes, the effect was so striking, with her otherwise pale blondness.

She frowned at him in rebuke but said only, "Exactly so."

To his relief, the music ended, and he quickly guided her back to her sisters. The duchess had been watching them dance with such worry in her expression that he felt as if she'd shouted an accusation of kidnapping against him aloud. Apparently she knew her sister's intentions toward Freddie. Given the duchess' expression as he bowed, he doubted the flirt's intentions were in the least honorable.

Juliet watched with intensity as Pendrake crossed the ballroom, although she pretended interest in the dull conversation between her sisters.

"It is not wise to stare so; you will invite gossip," Hero said softly. More loudly, she continued her conversation: "I don't believe I ever remember being warmer at a ball. The crowd is exceptional tonight."

Juliet turned a look of astonishment upon both her sisters that most likely would deceive neither of them. "I was not staring at him."

Miranda, her oldest sister and also the duchess of Kerstone, clucked softly. "He is engaged now, Juliet. I am sorry that he broke your heart, but you must hide it here or you will find yourself the subject of ridicule."

"He couldn't break my heart." The last thing she wanted her sisters to know was how badly Lord Pendrake's defection stung. Always before she had tired of a man long before he found another woman to adore.

This time, however, Pendrake had proposed to Elizabeth immediately after driving out with Juliet. She had had no hint that his feelings for her had changed. Indeed, she had expected to have to gently turn down his request for her hand any day. Instead, he had gone directly from her to ask for another woman's hand.

It was intolerable. "But he has made me a laughingstock, Miranda." She watched him, standing against the wall in conversation again with Mr. Hopkins, the American who had come to London to marry off his sister to a title. "Barbarian" would suit him better than American. His sister was a sweet girl, but Juliet would not mind when he left the shores of England to return home.

How dare he intercept her attempt to speak to Pendrake? The two men stood so casually as they spoke that she was certain neither of them gave her a single thought. The cad who'd practically jilted her didn't even show a bit of shame for his heartlessness.

She looked at her sisters, who were, as usual, treating her pain as if she were a child in the throes of a tantrum. "Humiliating me is a much worse offense than breaking my heart."

"Especially since you never gave it to him." Hero whispered, as if by her own lowered voice she could soothe Juliet's inflamed temper.

Juliet refused to allow herself to be calmed. "Pendrake will regret this; I promise you both."

Hero persisted. "It is only your pride wounded because he would not dance with you and passed you off to the American." With an affectionate light in her eye, she added, "Console yourself with the certainty that there are others who will take his place in your affections eagerly enough. Leave the poor boy alone."

"How easy for you to say such a thing. You have Arthur to adore you, just as Miranda has Simon." Juliet glared at her sisters. How dare they suggest she give up hope of one day having the same kind of love they had found with their husbands? Not that Juliet would want either of those men. No, the duke was much too stuffy, and Arthur preferred dusty old books to dancing. Still, the way they looked at their wives escaped no one's notice.

"That is not at all what I meant." Miranda sighed. "Obviously, if he could behave with such a lack of consideration for your feelings, Pendrake was not the man for you."

"How can I be certain of that now?" She had not entirely given up hope that he might have been the one to look so at her instead of seeing only the fact that she was beautiful and amusing. And now he had gone and engaged himself to Elizabeth Forsdyke.

She would not rest until she knew, from his own lips, why he had done such a thing.

TWO

"Do you think he will attend tonight?" The carriage bounced over a rut in the road, and Juliet clutched her beautiful new bonnet tightly to her head. Try as she might, no unobtrusive manner of approaching Pendrake had occurred to her in well over a week. She must contrive a way to ask him why he had abandoned her. And soon. Her patience was frayed to the edge of despair.

"I cannot say, Juliet." Miranda did not sound as if she were in sympathy with Juliet's concern at all.

"Sometimes I think he is deliberately avoiding me." Or his family was keeping him from her. But she would not voice that suspicion aloud. Her sister would only laugh at the thought. "He has come to none of the balls since he jilted me."

"Can you blame him?" Her sister's question was sharp. "Think how you would feel if one of your cast-off suitors demanded an explanation when you did not wish to give one, never mind accused you of jilting him when you had no formal agreement."

"Our hearts were in communion. I know it." Something, or someone, had stopped Pendrake from offering for her. Juliet could feel the truth of that in her bones. "And now we will never have that harmony that perfect couples have."

Miranda sighed and added, "You will see; in time you will find someone. Someone perfect for you."

"In time?" Easy for her sister to say. She had her husband. A duke, no less. "How many years must I wait? I am practically on the shelf, Miranda."

"You are no such thing." Miranda's laughter rang clear. "You will see—"

"I see too clearly, I fear. Pendrake wishes to forget my existence utterly and has not even thrown me the crumb of asking for a dance just once to show that he does not despise me."

"He does not despise you. He simply chose to marry another woman."

Juliet felt a wave of despair close over her head. "Perhaps the truth is that no sensible man would ever choose me for a wife. Perhaps I am thought of as an exotic bird, to be admired but of no real use other than for amusement and decoration."

"Don't be ridiculous!"

"Then I must ask. Next time I see him—"

Miranda snapped impatiently. "Juliet, you must stop pursuing the man! He is engaged. Why would he risk gossip by asking you to dance or even giving you more that a brief, polite greeting?"

True enough. "To demonstrate that he still holds me in regard, of course."

Miranda sighed. "Juliet, he is a man. He very likely has no idea of the depth of your distress. No doubt he believes he is doing you a kindness to stay away."

"Well, he is not. How can he not know that his wicked desertion has devastated me? I want him to beg my forgiveness for such cowardly behavior."

Hero shook her head. "You will have to satisfy yourself with holding your chin high, Juliet. If you pretend you are not hurt by his actions, everyone will believe it."

Knowing that her sisters would be of no assistance, Juliet left them at the entryway and entered the ballroom alone. She searched the faces of those already present as she quickly made a circuit of the ballroom. Her heart nearly stopped when she saw him, but she did not allow her expression to show anything more than polite indifference to the sight of him.

"I see he is here tonight." Miranda came up behind her. "Do not make a fool of yourself, Juliet. You will be the one to regret it."

For an hour, Juliet was able to smile and dance with every man who asked her as if her heart were not breaking. She was certain that Pendrake's presence meant he was ready to speak to her. Ready to face her and explain why he had not told her about his engagement himself.

As time passed, she realized he would not approach. In fact, every time she glanced casually to where he stood, she saw him in deep conversation with the American, Mr. Hopkins.

What difference did it make what everyone else believed? Foolish gossips. It was Pendrake's actions she wanted explained. "Why did he not warn me? I could have asked him directly if only he gave me the opportunity." But obviously he had no intention of approaching her, and silly convention prevented her from requesting a dance from him.

Though the idea intrigued her. Wouldn't the old crows buzz about that? Unfortunately, Miranda's husband was such a stickler for propriety, he would no doubt exile her back to Anderlin with her brother Valentine and his wife, Emily, if he were to hear of her having done something so bold.

Juliet wanted nothing more than to cross the room and ask him directly why he had humiliated her. She would have no peace until she knew. She sighed. Sometimes avoiding scandal was a tedious business. Perhaps if she simply bumped into him and exchanged a few words . . . Surely no one could object to that. She did not ask either sister, but began navigating a course directly toward Pendrake.

R.J. saw her steady approach and spent a few moments of inaction in sheer disbelief. Fortunately, Freddie's back was to the approaching Miss Fenster, so he remained unaware as R.J. quickly moved to intercept her. His friend was still uncertain enough about his upcoming marriage that R.J. deemed it best he not have to deal with an assault on his senses such as Miss Fenster would provide.

He took hold of her arm with a smile of greeting that he hoped would fool anyone watching them. Deftly, he maneuvered them into a shadowed alcove for a private conversation without a single objection from the woman in his grasp.

"I just want to speak to him. Is that so awful?" Apparently she had decided to throw herself upon his mercy.

"It is no use." Once again he was blunt. Somehow with Miss Fenster he had no patience for games. "You must set your sights on another lord."

To his shock, she raised her gaze to meet his and was equally blunt. "Why do you say so?" She searched his face, obviously seeking the truth of the matter. "He is not wavering at all—you are certain of this? You have not known him half as long as I."

"I am certain. I have known him since we were both in short pants. My father and his are good friends."

She looked crestfallen. For a moment he hoped she would accept his word and leave Freddie to pursue his fate with Elizabeth. He added, to cement the finality of the matter, "Lord Pendrake has made it plain to me that his marriage is a family duty. He knows the time has come to take it up."

He realized his error as soon as her expression sharpened with hope. "A family duty?" Her eyes shone like jewels, and he felt sorry for Pendrake and any other man who had come under Miss Juliet Fenster's spell. She whispered, "He does not love her, then?"

"Love her?" The scorn that thickened his voice made her flinch, and he felt a twinge of regret to see that he had touched a vulnerability he had not suspected. Still, it would do neither Miss Fenster nor Pendrake any good to leave her with any illusions on the matter. "Did you imagine him a fool who trusted his future to be decided by a fickle heart?"

She gasped with indignation, but he did not let her interrupt his lecture.

"Or perhaps you mistakenly believed you had twisted him about your little finger so that he had become one?" He shook his head sharply. "Let me assure you, Lord Pendrake is a sensible man who knows better than to let his heart lead his head in the matter of choosing a wife."

Her nostrils flared. "I hope you are not implying, Mr. Hopkins," she replied icily, "that only a fool would choose me for a wife. Surely even an American can recognize that as an unpardonable insult."

There was a tremble of hurt in her voice that made him soften what he had been about to say. "I make no comment on the sort of man who would choose to marry you, Miss Fenster." No doubt there were many fools blinded by a pretty face and a lively manner to the reality of living with such a creature day to day for the rest of their lives. "I merely say that Pendrake has wisely allowed his head to rule his choice of wife."

He could see that she felt the truth of his words keenly but intended to argue further. He added, sternly, in the hope that she would take his warning and guard her behavior in the future, "What man's head would direct him to choose a wife who would use another man to foster his jealousy?"

His blunt words at last left her speechless. For the first time, he could feel her attention directed fully at him. Her gaze swept him from head to foot, then returned to meet his. She smiled and tilted her head as she contemplated him, as if delving into his very soul. The glisten of her unshed tears made the intensity of her fury quite clear.

He understood why men such as Pendrake had been bedazzled. Even he, who knew better than to believe his words had hurt her, was tempted to reach out and comfort her. He stopped himself only by remembering that she was using the tears to manipulate him. No doubt she felt nothing but frustration that he was not responding to her wiles and offering to arrange to deliver Pendrake to her feet.

She was beyond doubt the most beautiful woman he had ever met. Giving her his most determined expression, he counted himself fortunate that he was a sensible man and immune to any and all blandishments she might contrive.

Juliet faced the severe American, striving for as innocent a look as she could manage. The dark blue of his eyes seemed to lend gravity to his words. Despite the pain of hearing her worst fears confirmed by his words, she knew she must convince him that he was mistaken. "I am afraid that you have completely misunderstood my concerns, Mr. Hopkins."

After all these years of disapproving looks and unkind comments, she should be used to the fact that other people thought her less than serious. She could not stop the slight tremble in her voice, so she smiled brightly to mask her hurt.

Apparently she succeeded, because he did not soften his tone at all when he replied, "I understand you completely, Miss Fenster. You intend to remind Lord Pendrake of your charms so that he will abandon Elizabeth for you."

"How absurd." The man was much too perceptive. But it wasn't as if she truly wanted to make Pendrake do anything against his will. No, she simply meant to ensure that he fully understood what it was he had given up when he turned from her.

"Did you, or did you not, intend to *accidentally* engage him in conversation just now?"

She did not deny it. "I merely wished to ensure that he was happy." Or, more properly, that he did not throw his happiness away foolishly. Perhaps he would come to his senses before it was too late. Not that Mr. Hopkins would ever understand that. The American had ice water flowing though his veins.

His lips pressed together briefly before he asked, "Or is it more likely that you wished to make him unhappy in his engagement?"

She brushed his suggestion away with a flick of her fan. "Of course not. I think of him very fondly, and I merely wish him to be pleased with his choice, not coerced by some family obligation." That was true enough. She needn't dwell on the fact that it irked her that Pendrake's family might have coerced him away from her in particular.

Annoyingly, her earnest confession did not erase the skepticism from his expression. Indeed, he continued to question her motives. "I am surprised you feel that way."

"Why is that?" She toyed with the idea of flouncing away from him and this tedious conversation. But then she reconsidered. If Mr. Hopkins conveyed her distress to Pendrake, surely he would realize that he owed her an apology at the very least.

Additionally, if he would not, the longer she stayed here in the alcove with him, the more chance that Pendrake would take notice. The American was a tolerably handsome man in a dark and solemn way. If he had smiled at her more than the one time when his sister introduced them, and once when he led her onto the dance floor, she might have been fooled into thinking he had a heart.

Fortunately, his lack of a heart was of no consequence to her. It was Pendrake's heart she was concerned with now. And she had long ago learned that nothing piqued a man's interest in a woman more than a rival for her affections.

"I had heard gossip—" He smiled down at her as if he were indulging her in a child's pretense, and she had a strong urge to kick him in the shins to see if he could be roused to any temper at all. But that would spoil the impression that she found his company interesting. "Perhaps it is my folly to have believed the idle chatter that many had expected Pendrake would break with his family wishes and make an offer for you."

"Where did you hear such drivel?" Could he be speaking the truth? Was she not the only one who had expected Pendrake to make an offer for her? Oh, how maddening that she had not yet found a way to talk to him directly.

He raised an eyebrow, and she feared he would scold her yet again for her forward nature. Instead, infuriatingly, he became the epitome of reticence. "Suffice it to say that I have heard it said by more than one person more than once." His harsh and unmusical accent grated on her ears, almost as unpleasant as his words.

"You should not credit gossip, Mr. Hopkins." Juliet could not soften the sharpness of her voice, for her disappointment in his ill-timed discretion was too great. "It is something we English have perfected throughout the centuries. You Americans are, perhaps, more forthright and not used to our ways."

Could it be that the gossips were right? Had Pendrake meant to offer for her but for his family's pressure? Would it mean that she did have his heart, then?

"I thank you for your concern, Miss Fenster." He bowed slightly, and she had the distinct impression he was mocking her in some way. "I assure you I do know better than to trust too much what I hear in such a way."

"From whom did you hear such gossip?" The question was forward, but he was an American and most likely would not realize it. Besides, he was being unpleasantly blunt himself. "Perhaps I can steer you away from those who would play unkind games with a visitor to our country." She wanted to know if the gossip had any roots in the truth. Finding out who had spread it would certainly lead her closer to the truth of the matter.

He leaned forward slightly, as if to whisper to her in confidence. To her frustration, however, all he said was "Even as a backward American, I have the discretion not to reveal my sources and cause them embarrassment."

"That is certainly commendable, Mr. Hopkins." She studied his closed expression, wondering if there was a key that might open it to her. Only when he smiled at his sister had he seemed in the least approachable.

She thought of her own brother. Perhaps she might find a key to him through his sister. A quick glance at the room led only to disappointment. Miss Hopkins was happily dancing in the arms of a handsome young man.

"Your approval of my discretion is all I desire." Again, she sensed the mockery, although the sentiment was not apparent in the controlled set of his features.

"I cannot give my approval if I do not know who has been whispering in your ear, Mr. Hopkins." She pressed him, presenting him her most charming and persuasive face, although she felt flirting was wasted on this backward colonial, since he seemed to have only two expressions—stern and sterner. "Can you not at least give me a name? Just one?"

At the very least she must know whether to risk scandal by approaching Pendrake and demanding an explanation. She would not want to look a fool if the gossip was wrong and he confessed that his heart belonged to Elizabeth Forsdyke. She found herself unable to believe such a thing, though. Pendrake, loving the drab Miss Forsdyke?

He shook his head. "I'm afraid I must live without your approval, then. For I will give no gossip a name."

Juliet considered trying again to draw him out, but his face was set impassively, and she could sense that her efforts would likely not prevail. "Very well, I commend your sense of discretion, sir," she lied, adding a more outrageous untruth; "I myself never indulge in gossip. Small minds, you know."

"I do indeed" was all he replied.

Frustrated, Juliet decided she would simply have to find out in another manner. The difficulty was in finding someone as forthright as the American to reveal gossip to her when she was the subject. She could think of no one, not even her own sisters, who would do so. Perhaps his sister, also being American and somewhat impulsive, had heard the same gossip and might be willing to reveal it?

She must find out the truth. She would not rest until she did. And if Pendrake had only succumbed to the pressures of family duty? Certainly that could be remedied. After all, hadn't her brother Valentine married his wife Emily even though it had caused a scandal and made her family unhappy?

Come to think of it, hadn't Arthur turned aside an expected engagement to another woman to choose her shy sister Hero as his wife? Perhaps that was to become a family tradition. Valentine and Arthur had followed their hearts, and they were happy.

Shouldn't she allow Pendrake the same opportunity to choose with his heart? After all, marriage was forever—and no one should enter such a sacred trust without absolute assurance.

THREE

R.J. glanced down at the smoothly beautiful face that concealed a mind he could nevertheless see working furiously. He could not help but wonder what she was planning for poor Pendrake now. So she never gossiped? He'd buy London Bridge before he believed that claptrap. He did admire, however, in a rather horrified way, her ability to cut to the heart of a matter. With another woman he might have never gotten a bald admission of her desire to ask Freddie to defend his decision.

The gossips had been cruelly accurate. This spoiled beauty hadn't liked being tossed aside so unceremoniously. He wondered if the other gossip he had heard was accurate. That her sister's marriage to a duke had turned the suddenly well dowered and well connected flirtatious younger sister into a fickle-hearted lady who thought only of her own pleasure.

Certainly he had seen little to contradict the malicious gossip. He noticed, now that they stood so close together, that the tiny buttons decorating her bodice were intricately carved mother-of-pearl. Apparently they served no purpose except for decoration.

He focused on the buttons, carefully averting his gaze from the swell of her breasts, just visible at the extravagant neckline of her gown. The buttons were unlike any he had seen before, carved in the shape of roses, just as the scent of her that wafted up to him was of roses. Expensive. Frivolous. Like the woman before him.

He saw her glance sweep the room again. No doubt searching for a glimpse of Freddie. Who would, he realized at that very moment, be jealous if he caught sight of R.J. with Juliet in a dark alcove.

Abruptly, he had had enough of being a pawn in a misbegotten game of hearts. "I think we should rejoin your sisters, Miss Fenster. I have told you all that I intend to. I am of no more use to you." He knew he should not be so blunt, but he could not help himself. There was something about her careless air that made him want to rein her in before she hurt someone badly.

She did not argue, but took his arm with a feather-light touch. "Really, must you be so unpleasant, Mr. Hopkins?"

He was tempted to shake some sense into her. For all that she had changed in her manner to him, his words of warning did not seem to have penetrated deeply. She still had not realized she would be better off to give up any foolish quest to assuage her wounded pride. At the very least, she was likely to embarrass herself.

"I cannot bring myself to believe you want to shame your family. I assume you have not thought of the consequences of your actions." He could not imagine the duke would be pleased if she did publicly corner Freddie. "I wish to make myself absolutely clear so that I can have no blame in this matter. I will be of no use to you in winning Pendrake back."

To his surprise, Miss Fenster blushed slightly as they moved away from the shelter of the alcove. Unfortunately, her discomfort was quickly overtaken by pique as she said in a low voice, "I assure you, I never thought of you as likely to be of any use at all. After all, you are an American."

He stopped her once again. "Miss Fenster. I have known Freddie well for years. He has made his decision, and you would do well to accept it and forget him."

"How can you profess to know him well when you live—"

He did not want to get distracted into more conversation, so he took her arm and began to move again as he interrupted her to say, "He spent months every year visiting his sister in Boston."

"Oh, yes, his elder sister. I had heard—" She stopped herself. "But then, as I said, Mr. Hopkins, I do not gossip." Changing her tone to one of bland neutrality, she continued: "I am glad to hear that you did not have to come to London knowing no one."

"I am most fortunate." As if it would have been possible to enter society without the entrée from someone powerful. She was glib with the expected polite fiction that he was accepted for anything more than his fortune.

For a moment he slowed, wondering if she was offering him an insult. No one in this room would deign to speak to him if his stepmother had not known a few of the right people and acquired the necessary sponsorship. Surely she was not unaware of such a thing. Even his business acquaintances would not necessarily have been enough for an introduction into society.

She slowed to match his slackened pace. Her glance was curious, but she did not seem to be searching for signs of offense from him. "Is your sister enjoying herself? And Mrs. Hopkins, too?" Her question was nothing but polite, yet it made him uneasy.

"Susannah finds London most entertaining. And my stepmother has told me more than once that the city exceeds her expectations."

"I am certain you will have much to tell everyone when you return home. Will that be soon?" At first, the question seemed artless, but then he realized it was beyond doubt a veiled insult.

He halted an equally insulting response as a realization dawned upon him: Miss Fenster had treated him more as he might have expected Susannah to do rather than as the matchmaking mamas and their daughters had. In an exasperating way, he found her candor refreshing.

And yet it was wholly unexpected. He wondered if she had somehow not heard news of the extent of the fortune attached to him. Certainly everyone else who had heard, including his stepmother's sponsor, the countess of Winchelsea, had practically salivated at the amount.

"I cannot say. If I find a bride here, I will no doubt have to stay to settle things with her family." He had been aware of speculative eyes upon him since he set foot into London. He realized, with some amusement, that his sojourn in the alcove with Miss Fenster could not have gone unnoted. Nor would it go uncommented upon. Her sudden dismay was ample evidence that she now clearly understood the gossip she had brought upon her own head. He felt very little sympathy. After all, he would bear the brunt of the talk as well.

"Are there many young ladies interested in leaving England for America?" Again, her question was quite proper, but underneath lay the implication that no sensible young lady would ever be interested in such a prospect.

"I would be most ungentlemanly to speak for those ladies, I am certain. I can say with assurance that you have convinced me you find me useful only to bedevil another man." He maneuvered them around a large woman in voluminous skirts and was rewarded by seeing her sisters. A few steps farther and he would be properly rid of this particular young woman.

"If I did not know better, sir, I would think you were jealous of the attention you believe I have given to Lord Pendrake." Again her voice was smooth and musical, almost hypnotic, the way it hummed through him. "Perhaps you wish I would give you the same attention."

He forced himself to ignore the inflammatory suggestion, although it was difficult when she was directing that low, musical laugh at him. She seemed to find the thought of desiring him highly amusing. It would be interesting to see if—once his wealth had been properly established in her mind—the attractive

Miss Fenster would be less inept at hiding her own motivations in talking to him.

He repressed a shudder. The thought of the full force of her charm used to captivate him was not a pleasant one. He would not like to be the target of her special interest. Given what he had seen so far, she headed for her goal without letting facts, figures, or the feelings of others distract her.

"Hardly, Miss Fenster," he answered more harshly than he should have. "I know better than to wish for the attentions of a young woman who would spend a fortune on buttons which serve no purpose but decoration."

He heard her sharp intake of breath, but at that moment they reached her sisters. With a short bow to both the duchess and her sister Mrs. Watterly, he said only, "My pleasure, ladies."

Before they could do more than smile and nod in response, he turned on his heel and gladly left Miss Juliet Fenster behind him. He had spent enough time indulging her foolishness.

He only hoped Freddie had not been caught up in the drama the way Miss Fenster had intended him to be. He searched the room for his friend, or for the young woman Freddie had asked to marry him, but saw neither immediately. Perhaps Freddie had come to his senses and swept Elizabeth off for a private tête-à-tête. Life would be easier for everyone if they were off together acting like lovebirds, oblivious to the scheming Miss Fenster.

There were a few startled glances as he plowed through the crowd, looking now for Susannah and

Annabel, but he met each glance or glare blandly, as if nothing at all were wrong with his ungraceful course through the room. As he traveled, he gradually began to regain his composure. He was worrying over nothing. It would be easy enough to warn Freddie, obliquely, of course.

Tomorrow he would put a word of warning in Annabel's ear as well. It would not do to allow the impressionable Susannah to spend any time at all with Miss Fenster.

Juliet stood stiffly, her back to the departing Mr. Hopkins. In deference to propriety and the fact that they were in a crowded room with many eyes upon them, she did not allow her expression to betray her fury. Her sisters knew her too well to be fooled, however.

Miranda said wryly, "I take it things did not go as you planned." Infuriatingly, there was not a note of sympathy in her voice.

"Everything they say about Americans is true!" Juliet spoke in little more than a whisper but with a great deal of force. "They are no better than barbarians and ought not to be let into polite society."

"Surely not." Miranda allowed herself a brief, discreet gaze at the rapidly receding man before she met Juliet's gaze again with concern. "He seemed polite enough, if in a hurry."

"That is only because you did not have to endure his ill manners, as I did."

"Did he make unseemly advances toward you?"

Hero, at least, was sympathetic. "It was quite ungentlemanly to take you into the alcove as he did."

Miranda, who was unfortunately more observant than Hero, said mildly, "If he did not do so to prevent you from disgracing yourself with Pendrake."

Juliet ignored the question implicit in her sister's comment. "Do you know what he accused me of doing? He said that I was using him to make Lord Pendrake jealous."

Miranda's solemn face broke into a wide, astonished smile. "He sounds like a perceptive man."

Juliet snapped back, "He is the one who took me aside to prevent me from speaking to Pendrake directly. What else could I do?"

Hero, who had been watching Miranda and obviously drawing her own conclusions as to the nature of the offense to Juliet, said softly, "You must admit it is hardly flattering to be used as a means of revenge."

She glared at them both in frustration, although the only sign she allowed to show was the rapid waving of the fan she held beneath her chin. "I did nothing of the sort."

"No?"

"He is not a true friend to Pendrake. If he were, he would let me speak to him." She remembered, now that she had vented her fury at the odious man, what he had divulged about the gossip surrounding Pendrake. "You will never guess what he knew about Pendrake's engagement."

"What?" There was a wary look in her sister's eye, but Juliet paid it no mind.

"It is a tragedy that must be righted at once. He does not love her." She added triumphantly, "Pendrake is marrying just out of family obligation."

"Juliet—" Hero began warningly.

"Just as Arthur almost did, Hero." She had no interest in hearing her most cautious, careful, boring sister lecture her on not letting emotion run away with her reason.

"You cannot know that." Both her sisters evinced identical expressions of astonishment.

But she was certain despite their doubt. "I feel it in my heart. He truly wanted to ask me, but his horrid family is forcing him to go against his desire. Isn't it terrible? We must do something."

Miranda pulled her own fan out and began nervously tapping it against her chin as she glanced about the room to see that no one else had heard the pronouncement. "There is nothing to be done. He is already engaged, Juliet. Surely you would not want him to cause a scandal by crying off."

Juliet didn't like the thought of a scandal. But if it were just a little one . . . "Valentine and Emily survived their scandal. I'm certain Pendrake and I—"

Her eldest sister's expression was at its most severe. Apparently even Miranda's penchant for happy endings did not warrant averting this tragedy. The fan at her chin made a tiny clicking noise with each emphatic tap as she spoke: "They are happy in the country with their children, fortunately for the pair of them."

"Exactly. James and Edward are wonderful babies. I doubt Valentine and Emily miss London at all."

Juliet had seen this incomprehensible happiness demonstrated by her brother and his wife whenever she went home to Anderlin for a visit, so she knew she spoke the truth even if she couldn't fathom how anyone could fail to be bored bloodless in the countryside.

Miranda continued her lecture relentlessly: "However, I would not want to be Emily and have to endure the snubs she must face whenever she comes to town. Would you truly want to be put in that position?"

Again, Juliet put the unpleasant thought from her quickly. "That is because she not only broke her engagement, but she eloped with Valentine before she had properly informed the marquis. And I suppose many hold it against her that she affianced herself to the marquis when he was such an evil man. Pendrake is not evil."

"Neither is Elizabeth Forsdyke."

There was that. If Pendrake were to follow his heart and marry Juliet, there would be no way to avoid hurting Elizabeth. "I shall find someone else to marry her. She would not want a man who does not want her. No self-respecting woman would want that."

Hero raised an eyebrow at that. "Isn't that what you want, Juliet?"

The words stung, but she rejected them immediately. "He never said he did not want me."

"No. But he has made his decision. And his decision was to marry Elizabeth Forsdyke, not you."

Juliet wanted to curl up in a little ball and cry. It was so unfair. Miranda always looked for the happy ending—for everyone else. "What about my happiness? What about Pendrake's happiness? Doesn't that matter?"

"Of course it matters, you goose. But your situation is nothing like Emily's or Hero's. Pendrake was free to make his choice without hindrance. Valentine swore an oath not to marry Emily. And Arthur did not think himself worthy of Hero or he would have asked her no matter what his grandmother had arranged."

Juliet looked at Hero, who was blushing but not denying such an odd statement. How could Arthur have considered himself unworthy of plain, shy Hero? She sucked in a breath in excitement. "Perhaps that is why Pendrake allowed his family to browbeat him so?" It would explain much if that were so. Poor boy. He did not believe himself worthy of her.

"He cannot be allowed such a noble sacrifice." Juliet's heart melted at the thought. Somehow he must be shown that she wanted a man who truly loved her, as he did. "I must let him know that I am not of the same mind."

Miranda's voice was firm. "No, Juliet. You must not interfere. He did not offer for you, and that is all there is to it."

Hero added softly, with a puzzled expression, "It is not as if you do not have a dozen more suitors willing to lay themselves at your feet if you but give them the word."

"But they do not treat me like he did."

"When did you first feel this?" Hero prodded, "I have not seen you treat him any differently than the other men who pay you court. How many times have you said to choose one man among all your suitors would be impossible—as well as condemn you to a lifetime of boredom?"

When had she known he was different? She could not say. "I had not wanted to make it obvious until he spoke."

"Why would you not tell us?" Miranda was watching her closely, with the penetrating look only an older sister could give.

Juliet looked away. She did not want to admit that she had not understood until tonight how much Pendrake meant to her. "These matters are tender, as you both know." She could see that that argument swayed her sisters to begin to believe her. "You would have merely teased me that I would yet break another heart."

"I am sorry," Hero said quietly in sympathy. "I had not realized you held any more affection for Lord Pendrake than you felt for the others who called upon you."

"Well, I did not like to announce it in case he did not return my feelings." She quickly brushed aside the thought that he had professed himself several times and she had only teased him for it. "And I have never encouraged any of those men who come around," she protested. "I just seem to be the kind of woman who men like to call upon."

Miranda looked across the ballroom. "With the exception of Mr. Hopkins, apparently. One man you have failed to charm."

"He must be a rock," Hero teased.

Juliet glanced over to see that the American was in earnest conversation with his sister. He chanced to glance her way, and their gazes caught for a moment. She felt a distinct chill down her spine.

She shifted her attention back to her sisters, dismissing the thought of Mr. Hopkins. "He is a man, and it would be easy enough to turn his head." She didn't know why it was true, but she knew it was. Men enjoyed her company, and she enjoyed theirs as long as there was no demand beyond a playful flirtation. He would be no different once she found a way past his stony façade.

Sadly, as she mentally reviewed the men who had courted her, she realized that there had been none of the richer, soul-deep communication her sisters shared with their husbands. She craved that connection. Somehow, though, she had believed she was not clever or good enough to deserve a love so deep.

Now, in retrospect, she knew that she and Pendrake had shared that communion of souls. Not in words, of course, but in the silences between them. And thanks to people like Mr. Hopkins, who thought only of practical matters, that connection could be lost forever. It fell to her to counter those who would counsel a man to take a wife as practical as a button that actually fastened, it was up to her to convince her true love that they were meant to be.

"I believe turning Mr. Hopkins's heart soft would be beyond even your formidable charms," Miranda said with a soft laugh.

Juliet frowned at her sister. Who cared about Mr. Hopkins when Pendrake might be lost to her forever? She thought again of the rude American who had dared to chide her. "I could have him at my feet inside a month if I wished it."

Hero glanced over at the Hopkinses, brother and

sister, where they stood, heads together in a heated
conversation. "Then I suppose we are all fortunate
that you do not wish it."

Juliet would have made a scathing retort except that
Lucius Fairmount approached her for the next dance.
Within a moment, she was swept away into the midst
of the other dancers.

The rest of the evening passed miserably. Although
she danced every dance that she wished to and was
brought in to supper by a handsome and entertaining
young gentleman, Juliet had no more opportunity to
speak to Pendrake.

Catching sight of a knot of young women who
glanced at her and giggled, Juliet determined that she
would behave more circumspectly until she had won
back her true love. No doubt the gossip involved her
time in the alcove with Mr. Hopkins. It was unfortunate that she had to suffer for what had been a fruitless
attempt to communicate with Pendrake.

She shrugged the thought away. The gossip would
pass quickly if she gave no more fuel to it. And she
had no reason to speak to Mr. Hopkins ever again. He
had made it plain he would not help her win Pendrake
back even if it meant his friend would be forced to
marry a woman he did not love and live in a cold and
unhappy home forevermore.

She frowned at the horrible thought. No. She had
no more use for the American. His sister, however,
might be willing to advance the cause of true love.

FOUR

In the carriage, as they traveled home, Juliet looked to where Miranda sat, swallowed by the shadows. "We must have Miss Hopkins to tea tomorrow."

Her sister did not answer her immediately, and when she did, it was in a voice heavy with worry. "Whatever for? The girl is only here for a husband. We have no eligible men left in our family now that Valentine and Arthur are married."

Hero interjected with sleepy amusement, "Perhaps she means to give away those suitors she no longer wants to the American, Miranda."

"What is so odd about my wishing to invite a young woman to tea?"

"You have never done it before; I suppose that is what makes me question you."

Juliet blew out an impatient breath. "Only because I have not found any who might be congenial before."

"And you find Miss Hopkins congenial?" Miranda's voice held a tinge of astonishment. "You did not spend above five minutes in her company tonight."

"It was enough time, I assure you." The girl was a

breath of fresh air, if the truth must be told. She was not so versed in the etiquette required of a young woman and therefore had not been judgmental of the way Juliet bent the rules of social nicety. "I find her delightful."

"Are you certain it is not her brother you wish to invite?" Miranda asked.

"It could not be Mr. Hopkins," Hero said with a laugh. "After all, he is an American barbarian. Juliet would not want to deal with him again if she could help it."

"I certainly would not." Juliet's sentiments were heartfelt. If she never saw Mr. Hopkins again, she would not be sorry. "However, despite her odious brother, she herself is quite charming." And she would no doubt be less shy about revealing the source of the gossip that had Pendrake at its center.

"I imagine that Mrs. Hopkins would be delighted to receive an invitation from us. I confess I am curious to hear about the northern part of America. Simon's mother has not traveled from the southern region, although she professes a desire to do so once her daughter is older. I will invite Miss Hopkins."

"Excellent. Thank you." Juliet sat up against the plush of the carriage set, buoyed by excitement despite her evening of music and dance.

Miranda added, "But Juliet, I expect you to be kind to her, since we are inviting her at your express whim."

"I shall treat her like a sister."

"Oh, dear, then she will run away and never visit us again." Hero laughed. Miranda joined her. Juliet did not find her sister's joke at all amusing. She consoled herself with the thought that tomorrow she would be able to enlist help to win Pendrake back.

Unfortunately, Miss Hopkins declined the invitation to tea. And the invitation to ride that was sent the next day. A supper set up especially to entice her into the household also garnered only her regrets. Juliet began to think that fate might be against her this time.

"Why can I not go?"

"Because your mother does not wish it."

Susannah was furious. "Mama is being quite unreasonable. I found the duchess and her sisters to be quite amusing. Especially the youngest of them, Miss Juliet."

"No doubt you did," R.J. said dryly. "I advise you to be grateful not to have to compete with Miss Fenster for eligible beaux."

"I do not mind." Susannah looked at him solemnly. "You know that I do not wish to marry an English lord."

He touched her cheek briefly in sympathy. "I suspected as much. But your mother has her heart set on it, so I do not think you will escape your fate."

"Do not joke with me." She brushed his hand away impatiently, and he was forcibly reminded that she was no longer a child. "I have no intention to marry here. I want to live in Boston, not London. Mother does not understand." She looked at him searchingly and then sighed. "But I think you do."

"I can understand." He could even remember when

he had been as young as she and had thought there might be some way to break from the future so carefully planned for him. "However, withstanding Annabel is a feat I do not think we can perform, even together."

"R.J.—" She hesitated and then shook her head. He had the sense that she might fly away at any moment.

He asked in sympathy, "Is there not one young lord who meets your standards?"

She met his gaze with her own, and he was uncomfortably aware of the force of her objection. "Not one."

Wisely, he refrained from reminding her again that no matter how strong her will, against her mother she was not likely to prevail. He said lightly, "I think you search as diligently as I."

She did not laugh. Instead, she leaned forward, turning her gaze toward the window that looked out upon the garden. "That is why I am asking for your help."

He frowned, thinking of what might cause such a serious conversation. Perhaps she had hoped to marry someone else. "Is there a suitor back in Boston I had not heard of?"

She looked at him directly, and he realized with a shock that she intended to prevail in whatever battle she was now waging. "If there had been, I would not be here now. I would have made certain to be married even if I had to create a scandal to bring the wedding about."

Would she heed a warning from him? No, not with the light of determination he saw glinting in her eyes.

He contented himself with saying mildly, "You know your mother much too well."

She rested her cheek against the wing of the chair and sighed. "I do indeed."

"I'm glad you can be sensible." He smiled, wanting to encourage a smile upon her face again. "Is there anything I can do to help—short of bustling you back to Boston?"

She did not smile, but she sat forward once again with a more congenial expression. "Let me go to call upon Miss Fenster."

"I cannot." Especially not with the sentiment she had just expressed. Put those two heads together and no telling what scandal would brew up around them. He shuddered at the thought. "I am sorry. But you must find another young flirt to befriend."

She rose and crossed to the window impatiently. Again he had the sense that she might take flight. Then she turned, and he was relieved to see his little sister with the light of innocuous mischief in her eye. "If I did not know better, I would suspect that you object because you do not wish to put yourself in her company. Could it be that the practical businessman R. J. Hopkins has had his heart pierced by Cupid's arrow and is trying to fight the effects?"

"Sister, you speak nonsense."

"Do I? Then why are the tips of your ears turning pink?"

"Because you are suggesting something I find most appalling, I assure you."

"Why? She is beautiful. I saw the way she looked at you, R.J."

He bit his tongue to avoid blurting out the truth—that he had been nothing more than bait in a trap set to snare Freddie. He stood up, determined to escape this conversation. "I have business to attend to, Susannah."

He sighed. Perhaps his sister would have returned to her senses by the time his business was finished and he was again home. To aid in that event, he leveled a parting shot at her as he left the room. "Don't you have a husband to avoid catching, little sister?"

She laughed but got the last word. "None as persistent as Miss Fenster."

"How long is she going to be under the weather? I saw her myself at the theater yesterday when I accompanied Rosaline and Helena there," Juliet fumed.

Miranda raised her head from the letter she was reading from the dowager duchess, Simon's mother. "The dowager says that little Sylvia has acquired the most appalling accent despite all her efforts to convince her to speak English properly."

Juliet did not care one whit about the dowager's daughter right now. "If she sounds as harsh and unkind as Mr. Hopkins, I pity the child's chance for a good marriage."

"She is only five, after all." Miranda laughed. "And Mr. Hopkins is from Boston, Juliet. Sylvia's accent, so the dowager says, is soft and slow, like those born in South Carolina—not so nasal as the northern Americans, such as Mr. Hopkins."

"Well, I never did understand why she married Mr.

Watson and moved to America in the first place. Not to mention she was much too old to be a mother again. What was she thinking?"

"She was thinking she wanted to spend the rest of her life with Mr. Watson no matter where he was, I expect." Miranda turned back to her letter with a faraway expression in her eyes.

Juliet could understand that emotion. Wasn't that what she wanted with Pendrake? And she certainly didn't want to wait until she was an old woman, like the dowager, to make it happen. Which reminded her of her initial complaint—yet another invitation rejected by Miss Hopkins. "Obviously the Hopkins girl is more particular than she seemed upon first acquaintance. We shall have to find some invitation that will intrigue her enough to accept."

Miranda put her letter down with a sigh and gave Juliet a serious look. "Have you considered that perhaps her brother has forbidden her to visit us because he found your behavior too forward?"

"Preposterous! Not accept a visit to the duchess of Kerstone simply because he is a starched shirt of the worst sort?" The thought was quite worrying. Could it be true? If Miranda thought it, even without knowing the true nature of the conversation between them that evening—"Surely he would not."

"I have heard that he is quite protective of her, even though she is the daughter of his father's second wife and quite a bit younger than he." Miranda softened her expression, and Juliet could see the sympathy her softhearted sister held for her as she said, "I don't think it would be wise to continue to invite her when clearly, for whatever reason, she will not accept the invitation."

The truth, even spoken as gently as Miranda had, hurt badly. To have her behavior faulted by an American was the worst indictment short of outright scandal. "It is so unfair."

"Unfair or no, you must be careful, Juliet. Over-stepping propriety too often or too far can bring you disaster. Even Simon's reputation cannot protect you."

Juliet pictured the shame she might bring to her family should she cause a true scandal. "I know. I am a horrible person. How could I—"

"Nonsense." Miranda smiled dismissively, as if Juliet's problem were of no importance. "You are passionate and young. Wisdom always comes hardest to people who are saddled with both qualities in large measure."

"I suppose you are right," she conceded, though the words came with difficulty. She might have argued that she was not, at twenty-three, young. But her eldest sister, who had turned thirty and was still childless after seven years of marriage, would hardly agree with her.

No doubt Miranda, and all the rest of her family, believed Juliet should be sensible and turn her attention to a more available suitor. After all, it was only Juliet's heart that would break.

She forced a smile onto her lips in counterpoint to her thoughts. It would be of no use to have her sentiment dismissed as melodrama.

As if to judge her sincerity, Miranda watched her

searchingly for another few moments and then, with another sigh, turned back to her letter.

Which left Juliet with the same dilemma as before. How was she to find out Pendrake's true feelings? Perhaps she should simply follow her instincts and find a way to allow him to speak his feelings directly to her rather than trying to enlist Miss Hopkins to find out the bent of his heart. Miranda's warning was still too fresh in her ears. If he did not return her feelings, she would not like to look the fool, or worse, be subject to public shame.

Perhaps Miss Hopkins could be approached at a less private function. Juliet discarded that thought. She did not know how difficult it would be to pry the information from the girl. How unfortunate it would to have her questions overheard, given that the topic of conversation would be Pendrake and his engagement.

An idea popped into her head, one so delicious she could not resist it. The one difficulty was that Miranda would never agree. Perhaps it would be better not to tell her until the matter was accomplished.

Miranda glanced at the clock on the mantel. "Hadn't you better go up to give the girls their music lesson?"

"I suppose." Juliet wondered how she could instruct the girls in the proper technique to accompany themselves on the piano when her thoughts were consumed by this new plan of hers.

When Miranda looked up at her and tilted her head in surprise that she had not yet moved, Juliet rose. Her plan would work, she could sense it. Only she could not go alone.

Hero might have done except she had headed back to her estate yesterday—who had ever heard of calling a home Camelot? Of course, it did suit both Hero and Arthur. She sighed and for a moment considered trying to persuade Miranda before accepting the fact that her first assessment had been accurate. Miranda would forbid her.

As she climbed the stairs to the schoolroom, she realized the answer was literally right in front of her. Rosaline and Helena were the perfect companions for her scheme. They were not to be brought out in society until next year, but they were not too young to accompany her upon a call to the Americans.

She smiled to herself. Surely Miss Hopkins would not refuse to offer wise counsel to two girls who would be in the same situation next year.

Trying not to show her impatience with the tedious details of the day's music lesson, Juliet just barely managed to keep her temper under control as she corrected Helena's fingerings, counseled Kate not to bellow her words, and forbade Rosaline ever again to sing the bawdy ditty she had gleaned from eavesdropping on the servants.

As she suspected, the girls were willing enough to be taken from their lessons, though Katherine, the governess, objected at first. "This time of day is for the improvement of the mind, Juliet."

"I do understand the schedule," Juliet, without a moment to consider, blurted out quickly. "I thought a visit to the museum would qualify as an improving exercise for the mind. Don't you?" Surely that would be an educational-enough excuse.

She held her breath, awaiting the governess' answer. Katherine agreed, after a moment's consideration and a glance that suggested she knew a visit to the museum was not Juliet's true objective.

Another moment of uneasiness passed as she noticed Kate and Betsey paying close attention to the conversation. It would be a tricky proposition should the youngest girls wish to go along.

Fortunately, Kate and Betsy both made faces at the suggestion. Apparently they thought the museum a most boring outing and quite willingly agreed to return themselves to their geometry lesson.

Everything worked out well until they came to the steps of the Hopkins's residence. There, their card was accepted, but they were told, with only the most cursory delay, that the lady in question was not at home.

Juliet wanted to argue. There was a cold air about the footman's message that made her suspect that Miranda might very well be right in saying Miss Hopkins had been forbidden her company. But then she dismissed the urge. If she was considered an unsuitable influence, she was not likely to change that perception by demanding to be admitted to the residence.

"What shall we do now?" Rosaline asked, her hands on her hips. "I have no intention of going home before I must. I am dreadfully tired of conjugating Latin verbs."

"We can try again tomorrow, Juliet. Perhaps she will be at home then." Helena had always been the kinder twin.

"I must think of something." Juliet began to walk hesitantly toward home. For one foolish moment she considered calling upon Pendrake's mother. Even as she imagined it, she realized that would not serve at all.

In the end, her sisters persuaded her to go to the museum, as they had told the governess they would do. Rosaline always enjoyed the exhibition of swords and weapons of war; Helena, the sculpture and paintings.

There, to her great delight, Juliet spotted Miss Hopkins. The girl stood before a large marble sculpture, examining the work as if she intended to duplicate the lines and form once she returned home. For once Juliet used forethought. She checked her forward movement and stopped to observe the crowd. R. J. Hopkins was nowhere to be seen.

FIVE

The fates had spoken; Juliet was sure of it. Eagerly, she approached the girl. "How delightful to find you here, Miss Hopkins."

The girl looked startled and a little uneasy. Her gaze surveyed the area nervously as she replied politely, "Miss Fenster, how kind of you to remember me."

"How could I forget you? You were so very kind to introduce me to your brother." A slight blush appeared upon the girl's cheek, but Juliet ignored the sign that her words had been unwelcome. "Let me return the favor and introduce you to my sisters. Rosaline and Helena, this is Miss Hopkins. She is visiting from America."

"Hello." Miss Hopkins's naturally outgoing nature took over at that point as she glanced at the girls briefly and then returned her gaze to them more fully. "My, you are remarkably alike. Are you twins?"

"Yes, we are," they replied in unison.

Her gaze traveling from one to the other of the pair, the American said in a tone of wonder, "I don't believe I have ever met twins who resembled each other so greatly before."

Rosaline answered dryly, "We may have similar looks, but our natures are very different."

Miss Hopkins took a step closer to them, obviously forgetting any warning she might have had from her brother. "How fascinating."

Juliet, rejoicing that the ice was now broken and Miss Hopkins was as open as she had been when they first met, said, "We have two sets of twins in our family."

"Indeed?"

She nodded. "Yes, the duchess and my brother Valentine are twins as well. But they do not look at all alike, to the relief of our family."

Their laughter was cut short by a curtly snarled "Susannah!" The voice, with its harshly unpleasant accent, was familiar.

Juliet turned to face Mr. Hopkins. "How nice to see you again, Mr. Hopkins," she lied with as much gaiety as she could manage. "I was just explaining to your sister that my family boasts two sets of twins. May I introduce my younger sisters, Rosaline and Helena Fenster."

"Miss Fenster." He nodded politely at her sisters, but his glance came back to her and held, focused for a pointed moment on her buttons once again. She had an urge to apologize for the carved ivory elephants. She quelled it. It was no business of his if she chose to use a few pretty buttons to decorate an otherwise-plain outfit.

Only a man without a heart or soul would concern himself with whether a button actually has a useful purpose.

"I am delighted to see you," he said, although his expression did not match his rather wooden words. There was a fury burning in his eyes that she very much feared she had caused.

With a quick glance of warning to his sister, he grasped Juliet by the elbow and said, "I have seen a sculpture that I believe you would enjoy viewing." He nodded to the openmouthed girls and said, "Excuse us just a moment, please."

Juliet thought briefly of refusing to follow him. The grip on her arm did not allow her the option, however.

Juliet found herself in front of a realistic but otherwise rather unremarkable carving of a tiger before she could formulate an objection. "Really, Mr. Hopkins, I do not see this piece being worthy of your dragging me across the floor like this."

"Miss Fenster, I remember from our last meeting that you do not mince your words, so I will not mince mine." She was caught by his eyes, which shared the same cold ferocity as those of the carving by which they stood.

Juliet could see that she would not like to hear whatever it was he felt compelled to say. She attempted to disarm him with a smile. "Why Mr. Hopkins, I—"

He leaned in toward her slightly, exhibiting, as he moved, a menacing grace that quite took her breath away. "I do not wish you to make a friend of my sister."

"Surely—"

He did not wait for her to finish her thought before

he growled, "I do not wish you to speak to my sister again."

Her heart was beating erratically, and her thoughts were jumbled by his barbaric candor. Still, she knew she must protest. "It would be rude—"

Yet again he interrupted. "I would rather you cut her than use her for whatever scheme your clever mind is hatching at this very moment."

She did not like his accusations at all. Carefully, she stepped away from his suffocating closeness before she retorted, "I would much rather cut you, Mr. Hopkins."

His gaze, which had not left hers, narrowed. "I assure you, I will not mind one whit, Miss Fenster. I warrant that even in London a cut from you would be no more substantial than one I might receive from mishandling a sheaf of paper." His eyes dropped to linger on her buttons again—only until she took a deep breath to answer him—and then he raised his eyes to capture hers once more.

The protests bubbling within her died. There was something powerful in the dark glare of his eyes that scrambled her very thoughts. The silence between them stretched long, but she could not seem to tear her gaze away from his, could not seem to speak, could not even turn and flounce away, as his appalling behavior deserved.

At last, he looked toward where their sisters stood ostensibly admiring a painting of some sort. "I believe we are missed." The girls were sending puzzled glances over their shoulders, which suggested that their attention was not fixed on the painting in front of them.

Once again he took her arm without so much as asking permission. As they crossed back over to the girls, he said sharply, "I do not want to be rude to you in front of my sister, Miss Fenster—or in front of your own. Please, let us pretend that you were indeed interested in the statue."

"Of course," she agreed, wondering if she still might somehow spirit his sister aside.

As if patiently instructing a child, he continued, "I will then take my leave, and you will wish us a pleasant good-bye."

Juliet tried one more time to change his mind. "Your sister will wonder—"

In the same patronizingly paternal tone, he cut over her objection to say, "I will tell my sister that she is not to speak to you again, Miss Fenster. So may I suggest that you not approach her again if you would find it unpleasant to be cut by an American."

"As you wish." Juliet could see no benefit in challenging him. She had never had a man so angry at her before—except perhaps her brother Valentine. She did not know how to deal with him, how to make him see how unreasonable he was being.

Quickly, politely, but clearly, the Americans said their good-byes and departed from the museum. Juliet was no more informed about the subject closest to her heart than she had been before. She wanted to stamp her foot but, noticing that she was attracting the attention of other patrons, decided to control her natural impulses in such a public place.

"I think you are outmatched, Juliet," Rosaline said with a wicked smile as they walked home. "For once, there is a man in London who does not fall at your feet."

"It had to happen sometime," Helena said in answer.

Juliet did not care that Mr. Hopkins treated her as if she were a snail to be stepped on. She did, however, seethe with fury that he would deny his sister her company. "Stuffed shirt!" She looked at her gleeful, mocking sisters and said recklessly, "I will ooze charm until I have him at my feet if it's the last thing I do."

Helena frowned doubtfully. "He doesn't look vulnerable to anyone's charms, Juliet. Not even yours."

Rosaline shook her head. "You've just thrown oil on the fire, Hellie."

Juliet gave them both her most quelling look. "I must find out what Pendrake feels for me. It would be a tragedy to find too late that he and I were made for each other."

Rosaline made a most unladylike sound. "So, you will show your undying love for Pendrake by making Mr. Hopkins fall in love with you?"

Juliet blinked. The thought of Mr. Hopkins's face suffused with affection and love was a bit much for her imagination despite her assurance that she could win him over. "I said I would have him at my feet." She suspected that he was more the tiger than she had earlier supposed. Not a creature it was safe to drop one's guard around. "But I will win him as my friend and admirer, nothing more."

Her sister's voice was ripe with disbelief as she asked, "And how will you do that?"

For a moment Juliet could think of no answer. And then she realized what she must do. "I will find out what kind of woman he desires, and then I will be that woman, of course."

Helena frowned. "You musn't set out to win his heart if you don't want it, Juliet. That would be wrong."

Rosaline laughed. "Never tell Juliet she musn't, Helena. You know that only makes her more determined. Now, no doubt, she'll have him proposing to her."

Juliet felt a twinge of unease. "Nonsense." She didn't want the man to propose to her. She just wanted him to look past her fancy buttons to see a woman who would not harm his sister. Perhaps then he might even help her win Pendrake.

She continued: "I will ensure that Miranda invites them to the duke's annual house party."

Rosaline, as usual, raised an unpleasantly acute question. "What makes you think they will accept the invitation? If Miss Hopkins honestly wishes to snag a husband quickly, why would she leave London for two weeks?"

"Every year there are two or three engagements that come about between those who spend a quiet fortnight in the country with the duke and his fairy-tale bride." Juliet smiled. "Susannah Hopkins's mother will not resist."

"And no doubt you hope that you will be one of the engaged couples this year?" Rosaline shook her head in wonder. "Do you suppose Pendrake will come?"

"I know it." Juliet smiled. "He has never missed a year. He told me himself a month ago that he looked forward to winning the lead role in the play we will perform."

Helena said hesitantly, "A month ago he was not engaged to Elizabeth Forsdyke."

"You worry too much, little sister. We shall let fate decide who Pendrake shall marry." Fate would bring them all together, and she could not doubt she would end up with Pendrake. She would simply have to find someone else to console Elizabeth Forsdyke.

"Do not be a fool, R.J." His stepmother was thin-lipped with exasperation. "Everyone who is anyone will attend. I refuse to allow you to lower Susannah's chances to make a match."

R.J. regretted that he had been so vague when telling her that Miss Fenster would not be a good companion for Susannah. He was still reluctant to reveal his own bad manners, which would be necessary were he to tell her the details. So he merely said, "I have explained—"

Annabel sailed over his objections. "And quite sensibly, my dear. Juliet Fenster is much too much of a flirt, and I don't want Susannah emulating her. But this is a different matter. The earl of Blessingham will be in attendance. You know his interest in your sister is very serious."

"Blessingham will be there?" He had known the

man fancied Susannah, but he did not know if Susannah returned the interest.

No wonder Annabel wished to accept the invitation. Blessingham was the Holy Grail to her. The earl could make Susannah a countess. Suspicion tickled at the back of R.J.'s mind. He wondered if Miss Fenster had known—but no, even she was not capable of such deviousness. He could not believe it of her. There was more vulnerability than malice in her scheming, he was certain of that. Although he remembered the look in her eyes as he took his leave of her in the museum. It had not been defeat.

Annabel nodded, wearing the satisfied expression of a cat who'd caught a bird. "Indeed he will. There will be no better venue for Susannah to attach his feelings more permanently."

"Does Susannah favor his suit?" He asked the question cautiously, wondering whether Annabel had somehow divined her daughter's reluctance to marry.

"How could she not?" Annabel looked momentarily puzzled, and then her eyes lit with enthusiasm. "He is an earl, after all. And he has a lovely castle—with turrets." Turrets in disrepair and debts that Susannah's settlement would take care of, but he did not say so aloud.

"Turrets would sway any young woman's head," he agreed, certain that Annabel would not understand his undertone of sarcasm. He saw no indication in his stepmother's satisfaction that she harbored any doubts that Susannah would indeed soon be a bride. It seemed his sister had said nothing more of her unhappiness.

"The duke's estate is said to be magnificent, R.J.

It is not everyone who is invited." Her voice firmed. "We must go."

"I suppose we must," he said hesitantly as he cast about for an irrefutable reason to refuse.

As if she did not hear the reluctance in his voice, she said happily, "Just imagine—boating on the lake, walks through the gardens. I hear they are stunning."

He groaned inwardly at the thought of more idle days and nights spent in pursuit of amusement. He could see her there. Juliet Fenster. She would look as if she belonged, perched on a marble bench surrounded by blooming rosebushes. He wondered if Pendrake would be there? If she were wise, his fiancée would find an excuse to keep him away.

He sighed. "Do you think this party will make that much difference to Susannah's chances?"

She nodded. "I have it on good authority that several marriages are made there each year. It seems the duchess has a penchant for bringing about happy endings."

He forbore to mention that Susannah's happy ending would not involve an offer of marriage from the earl of Blessingham. Annabel would not understand. But he tried one more time to dissuade her from the idea. "I have it on good authority that scandal seems to shadow that family."

She looked up, her nostrils pinched in distaste. "I am not speaking of ill-formed unions. I speak of good marriages, made with honor and not a blemish caused by scandal. The place is perfect to bring Susannah's earl up to scratch."

"Still—"

"R.J.—" She hesitated a moment, as if unsure

whether she should give her worries voice. But then she said quickly, "Have you formed an attachment to Miss Fenster that I should know about?"

He was shocked speechless for a moment. "Of course not."

"I know you say not, but you were huddled in that alcove for much longer than was proper." She looked at him as if she had a question she was unsure of asking. So very unlike Annabel that he dreaded her next words. "I know that your father would not approve. He wishes you to have a quiet, biddable wife. Miss Fenster seems the sort who might cause a great scandal if she does not find a husband strong enough to keep her in check."

"I assure you I do not harbor any sentiment at all regarding Miss Fenster. I simply think it unwise to expose Susannah to someone with her rather flighty nature."

An expression of relief flitted across her features. So his father had sent her to make certain his son did not do something reckless in London. The thought was unpleasant but not surprising.

"Well, then. As long as you are not falling under her spell." His stepmother stood up, signaling that she was tired of the argument. "Between us we will have no difficulty making certain that your sister is not influenced by the frivolous Miss Fenster."

R.J. could see that the matter was settled as far as his stepmother was concerned. He had the authority to refuse the invitation, but to do so would only cause her to put her back up in a fury and find a way around his dictate. "As you wish."

"Perhaps you will find yourself a bride there as well." She added absently, "As long as we are both agreed that Miss Fenster is not to be considered."

"On that we are agreed." Upon his finding a bride, he would not emphasize that he would rather choose from the women in Bedlam. She would not understand, and she might relay his sentiments to his father.

"I shall have to accept at once and make the preparations for the journey, then." She left, an air of determination about her. When it came to Susannah's future, there was nothing she would not do, he reflected. And he supposed she was right. Susannah was close enough to an engagement that it would be foolish to throw away this chance.

He felt a touch of guilt at his easy acceptance of the pressure put upon Susannah to make a match. He had refused to allow it for himself. But he could not help think their two situations very different. No doubt, once the time came, his sister would see the sense in accepting Blessingham. Women were made for marriage, after all. As long as, he reminded himself, she had told him the truth and there was no man waiting for her back in Boston.

Restless, he gazed out the window. He wanted to be home again. London was full of idle and frivolous rich people. Not one of the men and women he saw each evening spent a moment in honest toil.

No, he forced himself to be charitable. Their system of aristocracy not only encouraged, but lauded them for idleness. He had met with men who wanted to grow their fortunes, who watched over their lands and riches with care. But they fled from any taint of "work" because their society would then treat them like fallen gods. He was grateful he was American.

He had to agree with Susannah. He wanted to be back in the bustle of Boston. He wanted to hear familiar accents, not the crystal condescension of the aristocrat or the docile, flat voice of servants. He could not imagine bringing a wife home who had belonged to this place.

He closed his eyes against the vivid memory of Juliet Fenster dressed in pale lawn, with the lamplight making a false halo in her hair as she sang at the Southington's musical gathering last week. A visit here was not utterly intolerable. But Boston—indeed, any state in America—was preferable to this ancient homage to a long-dead feudal system.

What he had seen in London had only made him more determined not to take an English wife. Only an American wife could appreciate a husband who believed in honest work. Only an American wife would understand that hard-won wealth should not be wasted on an excess of gowns—or buttons.

How could Annabel worry that he might have a secret desire to make Miss Fenster his wife? Though she was beautiful and sang like an angel, he had no doubt she was incapable of constancy. He had seen what harm a passionate, beautiful, and inconstant woman could do to a man. He was determined never to marry a woman he might come to hate so bitterly that he could not speak her name aloud—or bear the sight of her child.

SIX

"He has accepted our invitation." Juliet was astonished at how her heart beat so rapidly at the thought of Mr. Hopkins coming to spend two weeks with them. Or perhaps it was merely the result of her mad dash up the stairs to tell her sisters. She had interrupted Rosaline and Helena at their fencing lesson to deliver the news.

Rosaline, not one to concede defeat before absolutely necessary, raised her face guard and asked, "Will he bring his sister, then?"

Juliet glanced down, hesitating, but she already knew the answer. "Yes, his sister and his stepmother will also attend." She glanced back up triumphantly. "I told you he would not refuse this invitation."

Unwilling to admit that she had been wrong, Rosaline flipped her face mask back down and replied, "No doubt he will still keep his sister as far from you as possible, Juliet."

"Only until I win him over." She was careful not to let her uncannily observant sister see how the thought of turning the stone-hearted Mr. Hopkins into an ally made her knees weak.

Helena lifted her mask and shot a worried glance at Rosaline before asking, "What plan lurks behind those wicked eyes?"

Juliet needed their help, but she sensed now was not the time to ask. "No plan, only fate itself."

Helena persisted. "What fate?"

Rosaline said dryly, "Better to ask whose fate, Hellie."

Juliet made a face to quiet her sister's laughter. "Do we not perform a play every year at this house party?"

"We do."

"And do we players not practice for hours and hours to get everything right?"

"Yes."

"Then don't you imagine, with so much chance to get to know me, that Mr. Hopkins will see that he has completely misjudged my good sense and judgment?"

"Or he shall learn that all his suspicions were correct," Rosaline teased her mercilessly.

Juliet shook her head. "Master Shakespeare's play is just the thing to bring him around."

The girls leaned forward eagerly. "What play?"

"Romeo and Juliet, of course." Juliet was proud of her scheme, certain of success.

Helena frowned. "Will the men participate in such a play? Or will we end with all women doing the manly parts?"

"Why ever would we?" Juliet could not imagine the men refusing to participate in her play. They had never done so in previous years.

"No man enjoys the swooning, lovesick Romeo."

Rosaline shook her head as she lowered her face

mask again and raised her sword to Helena. "You forget, sister, there are battles aplenty to be fought." She added with another laugh, "In addition to the one Juliet will fight for Mr. Hopkins's heart."

Helena nodded, dropping her face mask into place. "True enough."

She raised her foil to engage with Rosaline again but then hesitated and turned back to ask, "I suppose we needn't ask who you will choose to play Juliet."

Juliet smiled, pleased that Helena had seen her cleverness. Surely if her sister could see that no one else could play the role, so would those she must entice to act in her play. "It was fate, my sisters. Fate that made Father give me the name Juliet."

"What part will you give Mr. Hopkins, then? Romeo?"

Juliet shuddered at the thought. "I want to make a friend of him, not a lover. He shall be Tybalt."

Rosaline saluted with her foil. "I suppose poor Lord Pendrake will have only you to thank, then, for being cast as Romeo."

"I did promise him last year a lead role in our next production." Uncertain of whether he would still wish the role or, indeed, if he and his fiancée would attend at all, Juliet was determined to believe that all would be well. She did have a solution if things did not go the right way at first, however. Mr. Hopkins would no doubt dislike acting. If she persuaded him to take the part, he would fail miserably at portraying a passionate, love-struck young man. Then she would be free to prevail upon Pendrake to take the role over with no one gossiping about her choice.

Rosaline and Helena looked at each other, then at her. Rosaline's tart answer was obviously meant to be from both of them. "I know that you have not always paid close attention to your lessons. You are aware that Juliet ended up dead at the end of the play?"

Helena added, "And Romeo as well."

Rosaline said softly, "Hellie, I don't think our present-day Juliet cares much about the fate of Romeo so long as he died loving his Juliet."

"My thoughts exactly, my wise young sister."

"Not so much younger—twenty minutes."

With muffled giggles, they engaged in their mock sword fight, giving Juliet no further notice.

Juliet dismissed them—and their comments—as childish. Ancient tragedies indeed. The play was just the thing to bring Mr. Hopkins around to become her friend and to help her straighten out the muddle with Pendrake. The American might seem unmovable, but she would find a way into whatever softness his heart held. She knew that she could convince his sister to help her cause. She had to.

For a moment she was troubled thinking of Helena's worry that the man might actually fall in love with her, and then she shrugged the thought off. She would never let it go further, even if the foolish man turned out to be capable of more than the brotherly affection he had shown his sister—which she very much doubted possible.

In the end, she realized, he would be much too sensible to allow himself to become overly attached. After all, Mr. Hopkins was well aware it was Pendrake's heart she meant to uncover, not his.

* * *

R.J. had no idea it would be so exhausting keeping Susannah from Juliet's company during their visit. He had made an excuse not to go on the hunt yesterday, but today he could find no reason to refuse. That would leave Susannah vulnerable to the impetuous Miss Fenster.

Or perhaps not. His stepmother did seem capable of taking care of the matter, focused as she was on ensuring an engagement for her daughter during the visit.

It was himself, he found, who could not seem to escape Miss Fenster's company. She had been seated near him at dinner. No amount of taciturn response stopped her chatter. He wondered what it was she wanted from him, only so that he could deny her. Unfortunately, in company he could not ask her.

"Do you Americans hunt?" she asked in yet another attempt to draw him into conversation.

"For food, not sport." His answer was not completely truthful. Some Americans still had the habit. Those who wished to be as idle as the English aristocracy. "In America we value hard work and discourage wasteful excess." Her buttons today, he noticed, were jade teardrops that clustered about the low neck of her gown. A neckline he would have insisted be raised if he were the one paying for her gowns.

She pouted at him prettily. "Do you consider plays and other such entertainment wasteful, too?" He could see no sign that his words had offended her as he had meant them to, considering their previous conversations.

"No. A play, properly performed, can be an uplifting experience for the spirit and good for the mind as well." Annoyed that he had allowed her to goad him into more than a monosyllabic response, he added, "I prefer lectures to plays, of course."

"It is a shame that my sister Hero and her husband, Arthur, are not here this year, then," she said. For a moment he thought his sally had missed its mark. Then she added, "There is nothing those two enjoy more than sitting for an hour or two listening to someone drone on about some obscure culture or ancient history."

"You make it sound stultifying." He could not help but add, "But I assure you, to the properly trained mind, it is not."

She wrinkled her nose at him, and her voice rose slightly in mockery, though he did not think any casual listener would recognize it as such. "Give me a good, rousing play any day, Mr. Hopkins. Movement, laughter, tears."

"That reminds me," said the gentleman on her other side. "Miss Fenster, what play have you chosen for us to perform this year?"

"One of Mr. Shakespeare's greatest tragedies." She seemed much too pleased with herself, and he felt an uneasy sense that he was about to find out how she meant to get what she wanted despite all his determination to thwart her.

"Excellent. Then there will be sword work?" The young fop who asked the question barely seemed hardy enough to raise a sword. "I do so enjoy sword work."

"Enough bloodshed for Attila himself," Juliet assured him, but her eyes darted quickly to R.J., as if she had something planned that involved him. He was certain whatever it was, he would not enjoy it.

"You will have a play performed here?" The decadence appalled R.J. The duke was a wealthy man, but he thought him wiser in the expenditure of his fortune than this.

"We will perform a play for our own amusement, Mr. Hopkins. We have done so every year since my sister married the duke. It has become a tradition to honor our late father, who saw fit to name us each after a favorite Shakespearean character. Surely you will participate."

He opened his mouth to assure her that he would not waste his time playacting, not even in a Shakespearean masterpiece that had been esteemed by her dearly departed sire. He was not given the chance.

She laughed coquettishly. "You cannot object to the frivolity of a Shakespearean tragedy, now, can you?"

"I admire Mr. Shakespeare greatly," he admitted grudgingly.

"Wonderful." She clapped her hands with delight, and he felt as if she had closed the bars on an invisible cage. "I have just the part for you, then."

"Which of the tragic plays do you perform? *Julius Caesar? King Lear? Hamlet?* Surely not *Othello?*"

She shook her head and laughed with a soft musical sound that nevertheless sounded ominous to him. "None of those; we have ladies to please." She hesitated with a theatricality that would have served the greatest actress upon the stage and then announced, "This year we will perform *Romeo and Juliet.*"

She smiled directly into his eyes as if expecting some reaction from him. Dread settled in the pit of his stomach.

He had been prepared to find that she had concocted some foolish scheme, but not even his imagination had supplied this.

Was she mocking him? Could she know about his misbegotten name? Impossible.

Annabel would never let the truth past her lips; it embarrassed her almost as much as it did his father. Certainly Susannah, who found it an amusing fact and one to tease him about mercilessly, had not spent enough time in Miss Fenster's company to exchange such information.

"Who will be Romeo, then?" He could see the eager attention from all at the table as a young woman at his right asked the question. He did not want to hear the answer but could think of no way to interrupt her without bringing attention to his own unease.

"I had promised Lord Pendrake last year that he might do the honor of the leading role." She seemed not to notice the hush that followed her pronouncement. But he felt strongly that she knew the line she trod so finely.

He saw her plan clearly; he could not doubt that others who knew her better saw it as well.

He could not help goading her. "A promise is a promise. However, he might not insist upon the point now that he is to be married."

"I do not know. I shall have to ask him." Again,

the collective breath was held, and the glances flew down the table, where Pendrake was mercifully oblivious of his fate.

"I'm certain he would be honored," he said, enjoying the surprise that widened her eyes for a moment. Until he added, "Only if Elizabeth might be Juliet, I suspect." How far would she dare go?

"Elizabeth does not like our amusements. She prefers the hunt, with the gentlemen," Juliet said brightly, though he fancied he saw a flash of pique in the hazel depths of her eyes.

He could not tell for certain, because she swept her lashes down and quickly hid any signs of irritation. To his relief, she showed no indication that she had chosen the play because she knew his secret and wished to torment and humiliate him. As long as he spoke to Susannah and warned her to say nothing of it to anyone, he should be safe enough.

Feeling on safer ground, with a careless shrug and a sip of the duke's excellent wine, he baited Juliet again. "Then I suspect Lord Pendrake will choose the hunt as well."

To his satisfaction, her lips pinched together just slightly. He wondered if she knew that made them eminently kissable and then chided himself for the careless thought.

He glanced at the men around him, young and old. They could not take their eyes from her face. No doubt she was well aware of every effect her movements had on men and used her beauty to utmost advantage.

He hoped she would drop the matter now. Then Pendrake would be safe from her designs for yet another evening.

Perhaps not, he realized, when she smiled and said, "True. No doubt I shall have to endeavor to find a smaller part for the pair of them—one they can manage even if they do spend a great deal of time at the hunt."

The young lady who had started the conversation joined in again. "Who else might perform well?"

A young man to her right suggested, "Shapleigh has a thespian bent."

Another added enthusiastically, "He made a marvelous Macbeth, didn't he."

"Certainly he did." He could see in her eyes that Juliet wanted to avoid the pressure to name a Romeo.

He wondered if he could force the conversation to such an extreme. No doubt it would greatly curtail her ability to convince Pendrake to take the part if she chose to pursue the matter. To that end he said, "I confess I am intrigued at the thought of watching Shapleigh spouting words of love below Juliet's bower." Though he was not ancient by any means, Shapleigh looked at least ten years older than his actual years. The thought of him as a lovesick boy was ludicrous.

"Then—" began one of the others.

Desperate not to commit herself, Juliet glanced at him, and he felt a chill of warning before she said, "I believe Mr. Hopkins to be an excellent choice."

A small, shocked silence followed her words. She glanced around at the astonished faces and laughed. "Do you not think he would be perfect—seeing as, being American, he is the Montague among all of us Capulets."

There was a clear challenge in her eyes when she captured his gaze with her own. "Can you not see the similarities, Mr. Hopkins?"

Surely she knew he would refuse. "I'm afraid I have not one drop of thespian talent, Miss Fenster."

She was not disappointed in his answer; he would swear it. But still, she argued with him. "You would not deny us, would you?" She pouted, pushing her full lower lip out and putting a false note of despair in her words. "We are not professionals, sir. We consider the effort much more important than the actual talent."

"I am desolated to admit it, but I shall have to refuse on the grounds that your reputation would suffer if I were to play even a corpse in your play."

He could see the light of battle in her eye. "But Mr. Hopkins, I think you would make a most excellent Romeo." Her plan came clear to him at once.

She would not let him refuse gracefully. Perhaps later, when it suited her purposes, she would be so very understanding of his lack of talent.

But not now.

Of course not; she was much too used to getting her own way, and she had every intention of putting Pendrake in the role of Romeo.

Romeo. Could she know? There was mischief in her eyes again. No, he could not believe—

Mercifully, at that moment, the duke gestured for the servants to begin clearing. It was time for the gentlemen to retire for cigars and brandy; a custom R.J. found eminently civilized, as he did not want to offend his host by lifting his wife's sister into his arms and shaking her like a rag doll for taunting him.

The one person who would most delight in wounding him with her knowledge had merely stumbled close upon it. There would be no danger as long as he made it clear to Susannah that she could tease him as she wish, with the privilege of a younger sister. But she was not to make him an object of ridicule in London society.

He had enough difficulty in this foreign land. He did not need to add yet another oddity for the society crows to pick over and caw about.

SEVEN

Mr. Hopkins had not been even slightly flattered at the thought of playing Romeo. Why?

Juliet rose with the ladies, following Miranda's lead into the white drawing room. She could see that her proposal that the American play Romeo had generated whispered conversation. No doubt she would be questioned again once the ladies had settled to their cards or their conversations.

She wished his sister had been close enough to overhear the exchange. Perhaps she might have given a larger hint as to why he would refuse the idea of playing Romeo so quickly. Perhaps he was as stuffy all the way to the core as he was on the outside. She shook her head at that incomprehensible thought. But no, he had almost seemed insulted . . . or threatened. In fact, now that she considered the conversation again, he had turned a trifle pale when she suggested he might make an excellent Romeo.

The play itself was unexceptionable; even Queen Victoria and her Albert did not disapprove of the bard. Did Mr. Hopkins have something against Shakespeare? Surely the playwright worked hard for his living.

She tried to see it from the perspective of a man who was offended by buttons with no useful purpose. Shakespeare could be said to have worked so hard that his work outlived him by centuries. Centuries of making people laugh, cry, and sigh. How could even a man as bloodless as Mr. Hopkins disapprove?

As she had predicted, Juliet found herself the focus of many eyes. She could tell by the quick stares and muted giggles that her idea was quickly being spread around the room to those who had not been close enough to hear her propose Mr. Hopkins as Romeo.

Within ten minutes, she was surrounded by young women who wanted a part in the performance. "Oh, please, let me play Juliet," said one starry-eyed young girl.

Elizabeth Terwilliger, the woman Mrs. Hopkins had apparently handpicked as the future bride of her stepson, interjected: "I just know that Mr. Hopkins would wish me to play opposite him."

"Do you think so?" For a moment Juliet considered the thought with pleasure. Though neither Miss Terwilliger or Mrs. Hopkins seemed aware of it, she had seen Mr. Hopkins duck into empty rooms simply to avoid crossing paths with that particular young woman. Perhaps, if Pendrake could not be persuaded, she would relinquish the role to Elizabeth.

"We have a, shall I say, special understanding," Elizabeth said with a chuff. It was a most unfortunate habit she had, chuffing to emphasize her sincerity.

"I shall have to think a bit on that suggestion. I had assumed someone else in the part, I confess." Juliet pictured the two of them together in the balcony

scene with wicked glee. He would not thank her for
the honor, which would, ironically, be thanks enough.

"Who would you wish to play Juliet, or need we
ask?" inquired another woman, who was much better
acquainted with Juliet. "Or do you not want the part
now that the American is taking the role of Romeo?"

"He is handsome, though. Those dark eyes. Why
would anyone mind playing opposite him?"

"His accent is rather grating." The young lady who
made that comment had a voice like a squeaky door
hinge.

Juliet agreed. He would no doubt do an appalling
job. She wondered if it was time to confess that Mr.
Hopkins would be a most unsuitable Romeo.

It amazed her that there were not more objections
being tossed about. The man had the passion of a turnip. A desiccated turnip, at that.

"It is not a professional staging," said Matilda Durham, who was most definitely on the shelf, and dusty
at that. "After all, he did come to the country looking
for a wife. Who knows whose heart he might capture,
given the chance to recite those passionate lines." Her
eyes almost sparkled at the thought. "I say, give him
his opportunity."

"Perhaps it is you who want the chance," Hetty
Barker teased Matilda, who apparently also had hopes
of snaring the title of Mrs. Hopkins.

Matilda sniffed and gave Juliet a jealous glance. "I
would play Juliet—if I didn't think the part was already claimed."

Juliet smiled, hiding her surprise at the number of
women interested in playing opposite the American.

"I confess, I thought I would this year. After all"—she smiled, knowing that all would acknowledge that fate had decreed her the role—"my dear father saw to it that I have the name already."

"But not the youth." Matilda said.

The unexpected rake of unsheathed claws hurt, but Juliet kept her temper, just barely. "If we were to go by age, we would have to raid the nursery, I fear."

"True." Matilda no doubt did not realize it, but one of the reasons she was still on the shelf was her ability to find a complaint in every situation. "Nevertheless, it is so unfair. You always keep the best parts for yourself."

"It was my choice of play, after all," Juliet said, defending herself. "I shall play director, and costumer as well. Why should I not choose the part I like?" And the partner fated for her as well. Pendrake. But she would not reveal that. Not here. Not yet.

As if it had only taken her saying it aloud to convince the others that she would play her namesake, the women fell into the discussion of which parts they would take now that the plum role was decided. There were few good parts for women in the play. The nurse. Juliet's mother. Some of the more daring young ladies wanted to play young men and wield swords, at least, if they were not to have a speaking part.

Juliet smiled at that, thinking that Rosaline would most definitely approve. Accidentally, her gaze fell upon Miss Hopkins, who had been dragged into the corner to play cards with her mother and her mother's set of friends. She smiled absently, wondering once again if Miss Hopkins would know why her brother

had reacted so strongly to the suggestion of playing
Romeo. She wondered if either of the women had
heard the rumor. She suspected they had, because earlier Mrs. Hopkins had sent a thunderously disapproving frown her way as she swept back to her chosen
card table, her daughter close behind, like a duckling
in dangerous waters.

To her surprise, Miss Hopkins set down her hand,
smiled in apology to her mother, and stood. Her voice
was clear even from this distance, though it could not
be called loud. "I am afraid I shall have to be the
silent hand again. I am not as skilled at this game as
any of you. I think I shall warm myself by the fire."
With that, she left the table and crossed to the fireplace.

Juliet felt that her moment had arrived. Casually,
as if she had not noticed the movement, she stood and
crossed to the fireplace. She reached out to warm her
hands as if that were her sole aim. She took no particular notice of Miss Hopkins in case her mother
watched them.

Before she could think of what to say, Miss Hopkins, without turning her head, whispered to her, "I
think it will be perfect, you as Juliet and R.J. as Romeo."

Juliet felt a flush of guilt. The girl thought her
brother would play the role.

There was no graceful way to tell her that he could
never play such a passionate, emotional role. At least
not without sending the audience to sleep.

But all thoughts of who would become Romeo in
her play fled when the girl said with a guileless sweet-

ness, "I confess, I am silly. I harbor the unfounded hope you will be my new sister, not that tart-tongued harpy my mother prefers."

"Has your brother suggested—?" Juliet was appalled at the idea and did not even know how to phrase the question politely. "He could not possibly—"

"Oh, no. I don't suspect even he knows that you could make him a wonderful wife." She said shyly, "He thinks about business so much, I don't think he seriously believes he'll find a woman to marry here. In fact, he has one all picked out back in Boston. But she's all wrong for him."

"She is?" Despite herself, Juliet was intrigued to hear the answer.

"Oh, yes," she answered a bit loudly, and hesitated. Juliet sensed a quick movement beside her and guessed that the girl was checking to make certain her mother had not noticed. Evidently not, because she continued in a whisper; "She is so meek and mild, and everything about her is dull. She would let him have his say about everything and never give him a moment's worry."

"I think that is what a man is looking for in a wife, at times," Juliet said dryly at this bit of naïveté.

"Perhaps what a man is looking for is not what he needs. Have you considered that?"

Juliet laughed again. "No, I confess I had not." The girl's comment was perceptive, if irrelevant. Still, she was surprised to see one who was in the market for a husband to be so unaware. "Nor, I suspect, would any man admit to such a thing."

"Of course not. Each man looks for a paragon."
Susannah sighed.

Juliet thought of R. J. Hopkin's definition of the
perfect wife. "I am definitely not such a paragon, as
your brother knows all too well."

"No doubt." The girl sighed, making the leaping
flames dance close for a moment. "He needs someone
to make him laugh. I believe you could do that."

Juliet considered the frowns, glares, and freezing
glances she had suffered. She could not recall one
time when he had smiled at her except with utterly
frigid civility. "I'm afraid you must look elsewhere if
you want someone to make your brother smile. If,
however, you wish to give him indigestion—" She
broke off, realizing that she would be better off making a friend of Miss Hopkins.

"I don't think so. I think fate has spoken in the title
of the play."

The girl's words so surprised Juliet that she forgot
herself and turned to stare at her.

She was smiling in delight. There was a mischie-
vous look in her eye as she leaned forward toward
Juliet's ear.

Juliet bent her head to catch the whisper from Miss
Hopkins. "After all, his first name is Romeo, just as
yours is Juliet. What could be more destined?"

She was so stunned, she could say nothing for a
moment. From the corner of her eye she saw Mrs.
Hopkins rise in agitation from her chair. No doubt she
would call the girl away. There would be time for none
of the questions that suddenly bubbled within her.

With a worried glance at her approaching mother, Miss Hopkins whispered a plea, "Tell no one."

"I will not," Juliet reassured her even as she wondered why anyone else would be interested in the man's name.

Susannah leaned forward to say confidentially, "R.J. does not think the name fitting a proper businessman, and he would be mortified to have it become common knowledge."

Juliet replied softly, smiling at the unhappy Mrs. Hopkins approached them like a mother protecting her child from wolves. "I will say nothing."

Miss Hopkins turned to toss a thank-you back to Juliet as her mother towed her away to join a safer corner of the room.

With a sigh born of chagrin, Juliet realized that she had forgotten to ask about Lord Pendrake and the true state of his heart. Drat.

Well, perhaps after the rehearsal for the play began she would no longer be a forbidden companion of Miss Hopkins.

Certainly the girl herself had no reservations about Juliet if she wished her to marry her brother.

Juliet shivered at the thought. Being embraced by Mr. Hopkins must no doubt be a cold affair, even if his Christian name was Romeo.

She would keep her promise, though the thought of seeing everyone's reaction to such delicious news was tempting.

Why ever had he kept it secret? His sister must be exaggerating.

Romeo was a name that might cause a few odd

looks, but it was nothing to be ashamed about. It was a romantic, beautiful name even if it did not fit him one bit.

No, he should have been named Horace or Humphrey if his name was to match his demeanor.

Still, she would say nothing of it. To anyone but Mr. Romeo Hopkins. When the time was ripe.

To think of him in the play was absurd, however, no matter what his sister thought. He knew it; she could see it in his eyes when he tried to refuse earlier. And he was absolutely correct.

That part should rightly go to Pendrake.

Miss Hopkins aside, fate did not intend the role for a man with ledger ink in his veins.

"To lower yourself to make a fool of yourself in a play is bad enough, but one with that unfortunately named character in it . . ." Annabel swept a hand through her hair, adjusting a jeweled ornament and raising her parasol to block the sunlight from reaching her complexion.

She leveled a warning glare upon him. ". . . Your father will not be pleased to hear of this, R.J."

No, his father would find acting in an amateur production most frivolous. Still, for Annabel to invoke his father's name, she must be truly furious.

He shifted on the warm marble of the garden bench, feeling a bit like a schoolboy caught in a foolish prank. "Father will not hear until long after the play has been forgotten. I hardly think it will matter to him at all." A bit of leftover schoolboy devilment made him hold off telling her that he was not actually going to play the role of a lovesick swain.

"That is not the point I am making, R.J." Annabel was assessing him shrewdly, and he realized that she still believed he was enamored of Miss Fenster. "I just don't think it is rational to allow yourself to be caught up in these goings-on."

His neck muscles clenched at her use of the word. Rational. As long as he could remember, she, or his father, had used it to mean that he was in danger of allowing his mother's emotional and unpredictable blood to control him.

If anything would ever convince them that he had no more self-control than his mother had possessed, it would certainly be mooning after Juliet Fenster. Something the role of Romeo would require of him.

Susannah laughed. "Oh, Mother. It is just a bit of fun. Why, even Lord Blessingham will be joining in as Mercutio."

"He will?" Her fury abating as suddenly as it had arisen, Annabel Hopkins sighed. "I will never understand these young men. They should have more serious things to occupy themselves with. Such as finding a wife."

"I agree, especially now with the lower classes making their discontent known."

Annabel frowned. "Malcontents plague every society."

R.J. shook his head. His visit to London had been enlightening. Times were changing, and practices must change with them. Industry was revolutionizing the world. And crushing a segment of the population.

"It is time for the leaders to lead, not sit idly by, fiddling while Rome burns."

"Odd, then, that you chose to play." Annabel frowned.

R.J. answered, feeling as if his sister had given him a reprieve he did not deserve. "As Susannah has said, everyone is joining in. And I would not want to be shamed by refusing." He looked hard at his little sister, who had the grace to blush before she smiled back at him.

"You will be wonderful," she teased him. "I have little doubt that you will find a wife among the admiring audience for certain."

The teasing did not surprise him, but the hint of true hope in her eyes made him worry that she had decided one of the women here at this lavish house party would make him a good wife. He hoped it was not Matilda Durham, his stepmother's candidate for daughter-in-law.

Annabel raised a brow. "Indeed, that would be a miracle. There has been no one to his taste in a thousand young misses until now." Again, her look was searching, but she said nothing aloud about her suspicions, and he did not want to mention them in Susannah's company for fear that his little sister would think the match an excellent idea.

"But fate has cast the die, Mother." Almost as if she read his mind, his sister turned to tease him. "R.J. will soon be smitten; I can feel it."

"Can you?" Annabel frowned, then schooled her features into a motherly smile. "I admit I have hopes that Lord Blessingham will have decided to ask for your hand by the end of this visit. But even I cannot bring myself to believe your brother will ever choose an English miss for a bride."

Susannah glanced down into her lap evasively and blushed. "I feel Lord Blessingham will speak soon." She looked up into her mother's gaze, such sincerity blazing from her eyes that he wondered what true emotion lay beneath.

"Lady Blessingham. I see you making your curtsy to the queen when I say the name." Annabel's eyes shone.

Susannah shivered almost imperceptibly. He would not have noticed if he had not been able to see the trembling surface of the silk shawl resting upon her shoulders.

He wondered if her chill came from anticipation, distaste, or fear as she added, "I endeavor not to hope it too forthrightly for fear he will hear my thoughts and turn away from me." Her words sounded insincere to his ears, but evidently Annabel herself did not hear the false note, for she merely beamed in motherly pleasure.

"Never worry, sister," R.J. teased her in retribution for her earlier taunts. "If anyone can bring a man to have the nerve to beg for your hand, Romeo can ask it of brave Tybalt."

"Thank you, dear brother." There was no thanks in her eyes, though, he noted. More fear that he might actually deliver Blessingham to her, unwanted though he was.

His tone more sympathetic, he said, "You shall

have fate decide before our visit is done, I am certain of it."

She frowned at him. "Then I wish the same of you." But her unhappiness with him disappeared as she glanced over his shoulder, and her face broke into a genuine smile.

When he turned, he saw Juliet Fenster approaching, dressed as usual in the stylish manner that no doubt cost the duke a pretty penny. He had learned enough of her circumstances to know that her brother did not have the wherewithal to outfit her lavishly in the high fashions that she favored. No, the funds for her wardrobe came from the duke, and the ungrateful woman seemed to delight in finding expensive frippery to beggar her sister's husband with.

He wondered if he should put the idea of his playing Romeo to her Juliet to an end now. It would please Annabel, he knew. But even as he had the thought, he knew he would not. It would make Miss Fenster entirely too free to manipulate Pendrake into the role—if she had not already done so.

She navigated the garden in a gliding swirl of cobalt blue skirts, her unseen feet seeming not to touch the ground. She was followed by a few of her young admirers, one of whom had an armful of papers.

As she reached them, he caught a whiff of a perfume that was not from the garden but from Miss Fenster herself. She smiled at him and gestured so that the young man handed him—with a jealous scowl—a sheaf of papers with "Romeo" scrawled on the top.

For a moment he thought his secret out on display

for all to see, but then he realized that these were his lines for the play, copied out in a neat, flowing hand.

The chance to end this nonsense was at hand. He could return the papers to her. Leave the role to someone else, even if she chose Freddie.

He clutched the sheaf of papers in his hand. Feeling as if he had stepped off the edge of a cliff, he made his decision. He would play Romeo.

EIGHT

Still reeling from the idea of himself as an actor, R.J. looked into her smiling eyes and could not resist sharing his misgivings by quoting the bard:

> ". . . for my mind misgives
> Some consequence yet hanging in the stars
> Shall bitterly begin his fearful date
> With this night's revels, and expire the term
> Of a despised life clos'd in my breast
> By some vile forfeit of untimely death."

She laughed at him. "I hope, my dear Romeo"— she hesitated, her smile widening, and his heart missed a beat at her casual use of his name. Was there knowledge in her eyes that had not been there before?— "that you do not say your performance will be so poor as to require your death of shame?"

She knew. He could see the knowledge of his given name in her eyes. A knowledge that had been missing before. Only Susannah could have told her. But when?

All were smiles as they awaited his response, none

aware of her appalling breach of manners. "I can only say that I hope I have more of consequence to do than playact in my life, Miss Fenster," he answered stiffly.

The smiles dimmed, but more at his poor wit than at her forward behavior. She, however, merely tilted her head and laughed at him.

Frustration filled him at this vulnerability. None of the others understood the daring intimacy or that she had been bold enough to call him by his first name. Except, of course, Susannah, who was smiling as if she were much too pleased with herself.

Whatever did the girl think would happen? Had she, he wondered with dread, decided that this Miss Fenster was suitable wife material for him? Heaven forbid!

He glanced at his stepmother. She did not seem in the slightest uncomfortable to hear him called Romeo. No, wait, there was a perceptible purse to her lips, now that he looked more closely. If she knew that Juliet was fully aware it was his true name, she would be furious.

Of course, he realized with a start, it was the first time she would have heard him addressed by that name. He had not heard it since his mother died when he was five.

His father had always called him R.J. Everyone but his mother had called him R.J. But no, it was not a name to be forgotten. Which was why no one ever dared say it aloud. Until Juliet Fenster.

He glanced down at the script and felt the stir of unease. He must look at her and say these words of love? He had forgotten Romeo's youth and impetuous nature. This had never been his favorite play. He had preferred *Macbeth* or *Hamlet.*

He stood quietly, ignoring the urgent desire to hand the misnamed sheets back to her. To concede defeat and watch her lure Pendrake wherever she would. In the end it was her smile and the amused look in her hazel eyes that decided it for him. He was no coward.

Let her declare his name for all to hear; he would protect his friend. No other would play this part. Only he could show the mocking Miss Fenster that there was still one man alive who could see beyond her wiles and resist her charms.

Knowing that she alone would understand his meaning, he said softly, "The play's the thing. Is it not, fair Juliet?"

There was a tiny gasp of surprise from Annabel, which he ignored. It was the dawning spread of realization upon Miss Fenster's features that he relished.

She understood he would not relinquish the part now. Imperfectly concealing a frown, she said, "Truly, my *Romeo.*"

Looking down at the sheaf of papers in his hand, he thumbed through the lines as if he hadn't understood the threat implicit in the subtle emphasis of her angelic voice reciting the name his mother had given him.

For the first time, he understood how his mother could have considered it beautiful. He bit back a groan. How was he to survive nine days of rehearsal, listening to Juliet's soft, sweet repetition of his despised name?

* * *

"Please deliver your line, Mr. Hopkins," Juliet said curtly. She knew she should not be too obvious, but after three days of rehearsals, her unhappiness was great. She had pictured approaching Pendrake to offer him the role of Romeo. She had been certain in her heart that he would see the true nature of her offer— that she would rescue him from a loveless match if he could only bring himself to think of his own happiness first. Unfortunately, Pendrake had managed to elude all her attempts to offer him the role.

Indeed, she had not had a chance to speak to him when his fiancée was not glued to his side. Their behavior was disgraceful, the way they spent every moment in each other's company. One might even imagine they were in love. And now she was stuck with Mr. Hopkins. Mr. Romeo Hopkins. What was she to do?

As if in answer, he said his lines,

"O speak again, bright angel, for thou art
As glorious to this night, being o'er my head,
As is a winged messenger of heaven . . ."

She was captured by his eyes, by the power of his voice. Not the voice of a boy but of a man who knew what he gazed upon. Who knew what he wanted. She shivered. As the silence grew around them, she forced herself back to sense. Back to the realization that her line now waited to be spoken.

Stiffly, she said,

"O Romeo, Romeo, wherefore art thou Romeo?
Deny thy father and refuse thy name;
Or if thou wilt not, be but sworn my love,
And I'll no longer be a Capulet."

He did not speak his next line; instead, the heat of his Romeo retreated back into the ice of the real Mr. Hopkins. "Miss Fenster, may I suggest that Juliet has not yet spied her Romeo and so it would be more appropriate if you were not staring into my eyes?"

Juliet glared down from the crate she stood upon, which would serve as a makeshift balcony until Rosaline had finished overseeing the production of the appropriate scenery. "We are merely rehearsing, Mr. Hopkins. I assure you, I find it necessary to watch you deliver your lines. I am also directing this play, if you would be so good as to recall." She would not have him believe she had actually been captivated by him.

"Please forgive me." There was a smile upon his lips that told her that he understood she was flustered. And told her as well that he enjoyed having caused her discomposure.

She said crossly, "I cannot do the balcony scene without a proper balcony. We shall practice the opening scene again. I will not be so distracted then."

Obediently, everyone gathered for their parts. She instructed them where to stand, how to move, when to exit. For a moment she thought of him only as a performer, hers to command.

But she had forgotten how he looked at her—even though she was out of the scene, offstage—when Lord

Crabsley, playing a somewhat dyspeptic Benvolio, tells the love-struck Romeo that his fair Rosaline is not as incomparable as he imagines her to be. He looked directly at her and recited his lines of faithfulness to the fair Rosaline, even though Romeo was destined to desert his passion for Rosaline and fall fatally in love with Juliet in the next scene.

This time, she turned her head and whispered directions to the stableboy, who had been borrowed to keep the players supplied with food and drink and run to fetch the players as needed so that none would become bored with the endless hours of practice. He ran off, and she watched his wiry little body until he disappeared around a hedge and she was forced to look back at the players.

Too soon it was time to bring Juliet onstage. And too soon it was time to allow Shakespeare's young lovers to meet. To become the young woman meeting the young man who would change her life forevermore. She would have halted practice yet again, but she feared he would take it as a personal triumph. Blast the man for not simply refusing the part, as he should have done!

"Beauty too rich for use, for earth too dear!"

The line, as he recited it, made her grit her teeth. Though he portrayed a hot-blooded youth, she heard the cynical overtones of the true Mr. Hopkins in his recitation of the words. He was mocking her.

Despite her sense of cowardice, she was set to halt rehearsal again. Perhaps even for the day. And then, suddenly, he was a young man in love again, whispering words of love such as no woman ever heard before. His eyes were soft; his lips were soft. Soft enough to kiss. And the words didn't even matter, because he spoke with his eyes. She shook herself back to awareness as he finished his speech.

It was time for her line. *"Good pilgrim . . ."* She knew her Juliet was stiff; she was more careful than she had ever been. Her smile wider, more false. Her gaze more moon-eyed than that of a cow. She tried to step outside of herself and see herself as she wished the audience to see her. But she could not seem to do so. Not with his eyes upon her as she spoke her lines and moved upon the stage.

Why did he have to be such a passionate performer? Where did the cold, controlled Mr. Hopkins disappear to when he took the stage to play the young and hot-blooded Romeo? Juliet found herself responding to him—and that, she knew, would be wrong. It was one thing to make Pendrake jealous enough to do the right thing. But to have her affections for him divided—it was simply not done.

He said softly to her as they danced in what the studious dance master had assured them was a historically accurate medieval Italian dance, "Can you not pretend to be pleased by your Romeo?"

"Are you criticizing my performance, Mr. Hopkins?" She stumbled over a step, which gave her next words less effect. "I remind you, I have participated in dozens of plays and no one has ever faulted my performance before."

Smoothly, he compensated for her misstep. "Perhaps all you know are the false young women of your society, Miss Fenster. But Juliet is not false. She is young. She is passionate. She understands love in a way you never will."

"I have seen great actresses upon the stage play the role just as I do, sir," she lied. It was his fault she could not play the role properly. There would be a true scandal if she were to respond to him as the bard's Juliet had responded to her own Romeo. "How dare you criticize my passion."

"I have seen fish hanging in the market with more passion than you, my fair Juliet." His whisper was inaudible to all but her. But as he spoke, he lifted her hand as if to kiss it, and his breath touched her skin in a warm caress.

How was she to survive this? She had not meant to arrange things so intolerably. She had meant to make him a friend. To find out where Pendrake's heart truly was. A simple endeavor, no harm done.

And now, after three days of rehearsal, fickle, just as he accused her, she found she no longer cared a whit about Pendrake's heart. All she could see when she closed her eyes were Mr. Hopkins lips and the passion in his eyes when he played Romeo Montague on her makeshift stage.

And what had precipitated her change of heart? One brush of his lips—a brush that was yet a promise to be kept on the night of the performance. Somehow she became a mindless thing when he looked at her through the eyes of Romeo. She became, much to her chagrin, his to command.

Rehearsal continued on with no one the wiser, so

far. She had to regain a measure of control over her own emotions. They had not yet practiced the balcony scene straight through. She had avoided it, she admitted to herself. She was afraid.

Afraid that he would see how her feelings had changed, that he would laugh to see her heart in her eyes. She struggled to keep control of her performance, but she courted failure.

Just now she had barely been able to restrain herself from completing the kiss before the performance commanded it. Was that a gleam of comprehension in his eye? Would he kiss her in front of everyone? No. He did not. But there was extra heat as he recited his lines.

She must find a way to play her part and conceal the truth from him as well. She must make herself whisper the words of love and of longing with all the passion of a young Juliet. And she would. But not until the night of the performance.

Then she would play with such passion that she would set him afire. Would he be able to feel how much she wished she could touch him? How much she wished their little play could be done as it would be onstage, with lips touching lips rather than brushing the air a hairbreadth apart? She would deny it if he dared accuse her.

What if he did not accuse her? What if he simply faced her with the knowledge shining in his eyes? Would he laugh at her longings? Could he share them? No, she would not allow her thoughts to wander that path.

Sometimes she thought he did share her feelings:

when she looked into his eyes and heard Shakespeare's words in his resonant voice. At other times, she hoped not. Because his dislike of her was all that kept her from closing the gap between their lips and stealing a kiss. And what scandal if she slipped and allowed her lips to touch his?

Juliet had fought such feelings before. For some reason, she seemed to be unduly attracted to men. Sometimes it would be the way a man's eyes followed her. Or a dimple in a chin that produced butterflies in her stomach. Or even the shape of a man's hands, that brought a flush to her skin.

Aware of the consequences, she had never given in to the compulsions that boiled within her—at least not to more than a kiss or two. This time her attraction was suffocatingly strong. Even when he glared at her buttons, she wanted only to run her fingers along his jaw and up under the hair at the back of his neck. It would be soft; she was so sure of it, she could almost imagine that she had touched him there.

She did not like this at all. To gaze into his eyes, to utter words of love should not feel so real, so true. There was only one solution: she must continue to behave in so vile a manner that he would not know how she truly felt toward him. There was no other way for her to maintain her dignity. Her composure. How could he make her wish to throw both dignity and composure to the wind with a few words, a long glance? What fatal flaw had she been born with that made her vulnerable to a man like R. J. Hopkins?

She realized that all stood quiet, watching her. The

scene had come to an end while she was deep in her own thoughts.

"Let's take a break." She pointed to the picnic being brought out by the duke's servants. "I think we all deserve a good meal." Everyone cheered. Everyone but R. J. Hopkins.

As she watched the many couples courting under the watchful eyes of their mamas, she wondered what was wrong with her. Why did she always find herself attracted to the wrong type of man, one who could never truly satisfy the needs of her heart?

No answer came to her on that often-asked question. But at least she had one answer on another matter—ironically from the play itself. She and Pendrake were not destined to be together. If they had been, no man on earth could have turned her head, especially not the dry bones Mr. Hopkins.

R.J. approached her cautiously. The rigid way she held herself as she gazed with unfocused eyes over the picnickers suggested that her thoughts were not all pleasant. He did not want her to snap at him as she had been wont to do more and more as the days of work on the play had progressed.

"Rehearsals are going well, Miss Fenster," he said, hoping to ease the frustration that he could sense boiling within her.

"Despite my lack of abilities, you mean, Mr. Hopkins?" She did not turn to look at him.

"I think we would be wise to rehearse the balcony scenes after the picnic." He dreaded the idea of having to look into her eyes and speak those words of love. But he dreaded more having to do so for the first time on the night of the performance. The way rehearsals had been going, he was afraid that he would.

"No." She did not turn toward him to meet his eyes as she spoke. "I believe the day's work is done for us."

The day's work done? Did she not comprehend how much more work was needed? "We have not yet—"

"Tomorrow, Mr. Hopkins." She turned then. He could see she had no intention of being reasonable. "We shall do it then."

"Those scenes are critical to the success of the play." Critical for Romeo and Juliet, who would spend most of their time onstage during those scenes.

"And so they are. But they will wait for tomorrow all the same."

"Miss Fenster—"

She held up her hand to stop him. He sensed that she wanted nothing more than to turn and run from him, but she said coldly, "Mr. Hopkins. This is my play. But this is also my sister and brother-in-law's gathering. Their guests must not be worked like dray horses."

"Hear, hear!" One of the young men who seemed to gather around her like bees on a flower came up to her carrying a drink and a plate just in time to hear her last words. He handed the plate and cup to Miss Fenster and said, "Life is meant to be savored, don't you think?"

She smiled at the boy as if he had brought her gold and jewels instead of a few slices of apple and cheese.

"We must be understanding, Lord Ellsworthy. After all, Mr. Hopkins is an American and does not believe in enjoying life."

They laughed at him. He might have been more infuriated, but he was still marveling over the amazing transformation she had undergone, from the tense woman lost in thought to the flirtatious girl who teased Ellsworthy.

"May I escort you down to enjoy the picnic, Miss Fenster?" Ellsworthy brandished one of the wooden swords Rosaline had made for the play. "I assure you I can keep you safe on the journey."

She took his arm with a laugh.

R.J. said again, "The play, Miss Fenster?"

She gave him a playful smile, but there was no amusement in her eyes. "Tomorrow, Mr. Hopkins." He watched as Ellsworthy led her to a seat in the shade of the garden, where she was promptly surrounded by admirers. Not for one moment did he believe that the guests' comfort was behind her refusal.

What reason could she have to avoid rehearsing the balcony scenes? They had very little time before they must perform for their audience. Did she want him to make a fool of himself? Absurd, for that would only make her look ridiculous, since she would be on the stage with him.

He could think of no other reason for her to behave so irresponsibly. But there must be one. Could it be that she disliked him too much to say words of love to him? Certainly in the scenes they had rehearsed she had been wooden, almost perfunctory, in her performance.

He could not say the same for himself. He had thrown himself into the role with surprisingly good results. He had been complimented by the other players. At times, he was almost glad that he had accepted the role. Had his unsuspected ability as a love-struck Romeo made her jealous?

Still, he had underestimated the torture that rehearsals would be. The role compelled him to make love to her as Romeo did to Juliet. That he had found surprisingly easy. It was not difficult to tell her she was incomparably beautiful and mean it.

Somehow, despite all their earlier encounters, he had managed to miss the smooth silk texture of her skin. The incredible shape of her ears. The curve of her jaw and the sweet dip between her collarbones at the base of her slender neck.

Now, forced to spend his time close enough to kiss her, he noticed far more than he should. If he had to endure too much more of this, he would be as mad as his father feared he might become left to his own emotions.

His gaze sought and found her down in the garden, laughing at some witty remark or other. Two of her admirers leaped to their feet as she laughed and engaged in a mock sword fight with their wooden weapons.

He sighed. Unfortunately, he had also been forced to watch her flirt with an army of young men wielding swords in such a dangerous way, he was relieved they were only harmless wood. At least that way no one would die on the night of the performance.

NINE

Soon it would all end. The play. The visit. Perhaps even Annabel's hopes for Susannah's titled marriage if his sister continued to put off Blessingham. The day after tomorrow they would leave the dust of this place behind them. R.J. would do so gladly.

But first the play must go on. From a corner protected from the last-minute rush of getting the stage ready for their performance, R.J. watched Juliet act the general.

She was good at it, he reflected in surprise. To look at her, at the casual way she seemed to respond to responsibility, one would not guess she could organize a drawer of cravats, never mind the performance of a play. Of course, she did have help. Her younger sisters made excellent men-at-arms.

He admired the work they had done. Though it was no Drury Lane, he found himself impressed. This would be no amateurish performance to put the select audience to sleep. His thoughts skipped uneasily from the reality of an audience. He could not imagine the rows of critical eyes watching as he made a fool of himself.

So far he had been acting for only one person—Juliet herself. He had been more than satisfied with the results. For the last few days she had stayed away from Freddie, even when opportunity threw them together. Somehow his presence, his counsel, or perhaps his willingness to protect a friend had convinced her to give up pursuing a lost cause.

As he watched, Juliet began to lose her battle with a large chest. Typical of her, she did not call for help, but struggled silently and valiantly. No doubt she expected some young swain to materialize and help her without the need to ask.

Quickly, he crossed the stage area and lifted it easily from her grasp. "Where would you like this, fair Juliet?" He knew he should not tease her, not tonight, when all her work would be on display. She must be nervous. He certainly was.

She frowned at him, her cheeks pink from exertion. "I could have handled it."

He shrugged and the chest shifted onto his shoulder, emphasizing his movement. Her eyes widened for a moment, and he prodded her by saying, "I have it now. Where would you like it to go?"

She pushed back a tendril of hair that had drifted from the jeweled net that caught it back and sighed. "Over there," she answered, pointing to a corner.

He put the chest where she indicated. "Is there more I can do?"

She arched a brow at him. "It is a bit late to ask. I do believe that was the last item to be moved."

He glanced around to see that she spoke the truth: The frantic movement of moments ago had settled.

The twins had put together shapeless wooden objects that, assembled, became remarkably like a balcony of an Italian villa.

The youngest two girls, released from their studies for the day, had spent the previous hours draping scarves and linens seemingly at random. When examined, the effect created an atmosphere of impending doom. A table here, a door there, and all was set.

Around him were the trappings of medieval Italy. No one gazing upon the stage area would doubt that they were to see a tragedy performed tonight.

The Fenster sisters, including the duchess herself, were standing, hands on hips, surveying the scene with a somewhat cautious approval. He knew the feeling well. No matter how certain you were that you had remembered everything, there was always the slightest fear you had overlooked a critical item.

He smiled at Juliet as he indicated her sisters. "Your family, should it ever find the need, would do well running a theater."

He had thought it was a great compliment until he saw her grow suddenly pale and draw back as if he had slapped her. For a moment he could only stare at her in puzzled confusion. Oh, yes, he had forgotten the foolish aristocratic prejudice against honest work.

Recovering herself, she glanced around, no doubt to make certain that no one else had overheard the unfortunate remark. Once she had consoled herself that no one had been within earshot, she turned back to give him a glare. "We have no need to ply a trade, Mr. Hopkins," she answered frostily.

"I do apologize for the insult, Miss Hopkins."

Though he still did not think it one. "Please remember I am only an American, and in my country we think a man is worth more for what his sweat is made of than for his blood."

Her lips pressed together into a pale pink line. "A fine thing to say when you and your sister are both over here for a bit of our blood, and a title, too."

The duchess's slightly alarmed voice called out, "Easy, children. Let the blood spilled on this stage be only the false blood of the bard's characters."

"I apologize again, your grace. Miss Fenster. I think it may be my nerves are tender at the thought of the audience who will soon attend my poor debut performance."

"Nonsense, Mr. Hopkins." The duchess spoke briskly as she crossed to him, insinuating herself between the feuding Juliet and Romeo. "You are an excellent player."

"You are too kind." He rather agreed, though he would never admit it to a soul, not even to Susannah.

The duchess smiled. "And well you know it, I don't doubt." He had the stray thought that she would have made an excellent Nurse if only she had consented to join the performers.

But to do so would have required neglecting her guests. He suspected she would never do such a thing. There had been many times this week when he had wondered how two such different sisters had come from the same family.

"We are all excellent players," he said generously. He suppressed the uncharitable thought that her Juliet would have been better played by stiff and obvious

Matilda. It was only her own disappointment that Pendrake was not her Romeo that made her performance wooden and passionless.

"Indeed." Juliet's agreement was tart. He wondered if she realized that her own performance was sadly lacking. But he had no desire to risk losing his head by asking when she was at her most frazzled.

He left the sisters to their last whispered plans and retreated to his quiet corner to watch once more. To be truthful with himself, if not with anyone else, he was glad to see the high-spirited Miss Fenster subdued.

Perhaps it was not just Pendrake's loss, he conceded. Apparently her sister Hero had been the director of the previous family plays. This was her first year in charge of direction and sets as well as acting a major role. She had taken the task on with energy. Had she found herself unequal to it?

Certainly the enthusiasm of her performance was lacking. For which he should be grateful, for it was that lack of passion that ensured that he did not make a fool of himself.

Of course, there had been a certain pleasure in exchanging barbs with her. No matter her delight in inconsequentials, Miss Fenster had a most biting wit when she was put out. But the sharpness ensured a distance that kept him from revealing just how closely his feelings had come to echo the impetuous Romeo.

To his surprise, he'd enjoyed playing the melodramatic Romeo. Not that he would want to carry the character's predilection for tragedy into his own life. Not at all.

But for playacting he had to admit it was quite enjoyable looking into Juliet's eyes and telling her how beautiful she was. No one could argue with him. He was speaking lines written two hundred years ago. Lines spoken by more men than anyone would ever know. Probably some who had never set foot on a stage.

What he would never admit was that he would miss this heady license. Freedom to tell a woman that she was the sun and moon and stars. Tell her how she made him burn inside. How he wished to kiss her. He had never let himself utter such nonsense words to a woman before.

He could only wish the words were less true in reality. But some madness had overtaken him, and a part of him wanted to take her in his arms and kiss her breathless. To have the privilege of calling her Juliet in front of the world and not be referring to the bard's young beauty but to the spoiled and faithless Miss Fenster, who somehow inflamed all his senses in a way he had never experienced until now.

Accursed play. It should never be allowed to be performed again, for the safety of lovers everywhere. Fortunately for both, it was nearly over. Tonight they would perform the damned thing. He hoped his performance didn't make Annabel faint.

All was ready. It was a miracle. If she survived this night, she would post a letter to Hero first thing tomorrow. Her quiet older sister had always made the plays seem like an easy and amusing event to manage. But the work was astonishingly difficult and never-ending. If it were not for Miranda, she might never have stood here, seeing that everything looked nearly as perfect as she had planned.

Of course, her plans had included Pendrake as Romeo. But Mr. Hopkins had stuck it through, and she had no doubt he would garner nothing but admiration for his work tonight. Given how sanctimoniously he preached the virtues of hard work to her, he should be pleased with himself.

She sighed. Her own performance would have to change tonight, though. Her plan to treat him as rudely as she could manage had worked to keep him far from her except when they must say their lines and pretend to be young lovers eager for the future and unaware of the disaster that awaited them a few short scenes later.

However, her reckoning had come. She could not perform so woodenly when all eyes were upon her. At least she hoped she would not. She never had before. But then, she had never had to deal with anyone like the American before.

She looked at him, lounging casually, watching everyone else run around. Why did he not look nervous? It was his first performance. The audience would not all be friendly to an American taking the title role.

There would be those who would dine out for a week in London on the mistakes made by the players tonight. But perhaps he did not realize that. He was not of her society really, as he continued to remind her.

The one consolation she clung to was that this was the end of it all. She watched as those guests who had chosen not to participate in the play seated themselves in the audience. They were dressed as they would for the grandest of theater evenings. It had always been part of the fun before.

Indeed, the other players seemed to feel nothing amiss in this performance as they milled about offstage, waiting for their turn to stride onstage and play their roles. When it was his turn, the American strode onto the stage as if it were the finest in London. As if he owned it. She took a breath, again in awe of his ability to portray unbridled passion, and felt the audience draw in a collective breath as well.

Now, realizing that she would have to put aside her defenses and act the part of Juliet as it should be played, she swallowed hard and fought a cowardly urge to flee. She could do it if she didn't think too hard about what she was doing. Tonight would be the last time she must gaze into his eyes and tell him she loved him. And then it would be over.

Surely once he was back in London, or—perhaps she ignored the twinge of dismay the thought caused her—home in America an ocean away, she would no longer feel this connection to him: this need to have him near despite the fact that he drove her mad with his disapproving comments.

"Juliet, the audience is ready; it is time for you to go on now!" Kate, perfect as the stage manager despite her tender years, as bossy as she was, glared at her, hands on her hips. "Hurry!"

Juliet swept onto the stage, her eyes focused only

on Romeo. She knew, in a small corner of her mind, that Lord Forsby lisped Capulet's lines well. That the whispering, tittering group of gentlemen and gentlewoman were making the most of their brief appearance onstage. That the audience had ceased its impatient rustle and leaned forward.

His eyes met hers as he said his line:

"What lady's that, which doth enrich the hand
Of yonder knight?"

Within moments, he was addressing her, asking for permission to kiss her. It was time to say her line. For a moment no words would leave her throat, and she thought she would not be able to do the role justice. But then she saw the gleam of amused query in his eyes, and a flood of assurance filled her.

She let all the passion of her twenty-three years show in her eyes and was pleased to see him respond. With her head tilted in fascination, she made her voice husky, used the training her song master had taught her to send her voice in a thrilling rush over the crowd.

"Good pilgrim, you do wrong your hand too
much,
Which mannerly devotion shown in this,
For saints have hands that pilgrims hands do
touch,
And palm to palm is holy palmers kiss."

He said his line and leaned in to kiss her. She felt a coil of hope that he would touch her lips in truth.

But he did not. The warmth of his breath was all she felt. The coil of hope knotted into disappointment.

In a dream, she moved through the play, following his lead. The brushing of his lips, so near and so far. The words of love as she looked down from her balcony. The vows of forever taken by young lovers who would have no future. The look in his eye, the passion that was only playacting.

She had not thought he had it in him, and now she wished it were real so that she could bask in its warmth herself.

It took no real artifice to say her last lines. No effort to force tears to her eyes as she knelt over his supine, lifeless Romeo.

> *"O churl, drunk all, and left no friendly drop*
> *To help me after? I will kiss thy lips,*
> *Haply some poison yet doth hang on them*
> *To make me die with a restorative."*

She kissed him. Not a brush. Not a feint. But a full kiss.

With wonder, she said softly, *"Thy lips are warm!"*

He did not move after the first surprised quiver when her lips came down warm upon his.

She felt a fool, but she played her part as if she truly were mourning over a newly wed and newly dead lover. Indeed, she had the thought that he was a corpse, so still did he lie as she finished her death scene.

Her body lay near his, but she did not dare to touch him as she had originally thought.

The other players gathered around Balthasar for the final moments of the play while she lay as dead and still as he, yet still achingly aware of him, close enough to touch and yet so far away.

Would he condemn her for the kiss? Could she explain it so that he would not know her heart? An accident. Yes. She would claim she had dipped too low in her desire to make her performance worthy of the London stage.

He would not doubt her. He had already made it abundantly clear that he thought her frivolous enough to have no heart. He would never suspect that she had lost it to him this last week.

As the audience began to clap and stomp their feet on the grass, the players onstage sprang up, those off-stage converged, and they all took their bows.

Kate and Betsey, dressed like the little angels she knew they were not, handed her two bouquets of roses, from the duke's gardens. Kate's were red; Betsey's, white. She knew she should feel triumph. And part of her did. But another greater part of her felt defeat. He already thought her an incorrigible flirt. What would he think of her now?

She dared not look at him. It was all she could do to accept the congratulations from the audience—including Pendrake and Elizabeth, who suddenly looked so right together that Juliet was tempted to let the tears that pressed behind her eyes fall. After all, she could claim they were tears of joy. No one would ever know her heart was breaking.

Was there never to be a man who would love her? Who would be right for her? Was R. J. Hopkins right?

Was she too fickle, too full of easily spilled and lost passion, to ever deserve the devotion of another heart?

And what did it matter, anyhow? The only heart she seemed to want anymore, the only regard, was that of Mr. Hopkins. And there was no possibility that she would ever win that.

She could just imagine what he would say if she were to confess her feelings. No doubt he would remind her that she had felt just the same way about Pendrake not weeks earlier. And he would be utterly right.

Except . . . except this did not feel the same. This ache, this depth of longing, was more than she had ever known. But would it last, or would she find that she was indeed truly as fickle as he accused her of being?

She must explain about the kiss before he took it into his head to believe the worst. She took him aside and said softly, "I do apologize."

"Apologize?" A remnant of warmth, left in his gaze from his performance, set her heart beating fast again as he regarded her with puzzlement. "For what?"

"I . . ." She felt her cheeks heat with a fierce blush. Afraid that she would stammer, she said slowly, "I lost my balance, and my kiss, which was meant to be pretense, was real. I hope you will forgive me the trespass, as it was not meant."

"No?" Again there was that flash of warmth, but this time it was quickly suppressed. His smile was wry. "For a moment I had imagined that you thought me truly Romeo and wanted to taste the wine from my lips."

She did. She did so— But she would die before she would let him know that. "I did not—"

He looked at her kindly. It was worse than if he had chided her as usual. "I am certain you did not, Miss Fenster. Do not worry. I took no note of the kiss. And no offense at a clumsy mistake."

She bridled at the thought that he had considered her kiss clumsy. "I was not—"

"No, you were not. Your lips were very . . . sweet."

Sweet? Not passionate. Of course not. So why did she feel as if she had been patted on the head? And why did she so badly wish that he would take her up and kiss her properly, with a passion matching the one that raged inside her?

Juliet passed numbly through the gauntlet of guests wishing to congratulate her, hoping that her smile was not too obviously forced. With a hurried whisper to Miranda, she excused herself from the crowd and rushed for the privacy and silence of her room, where no one would remark upon it if her expression should happen to show her unhappiness.

She should be relieved, she reminded herself ferociously. She had not wanted him to recognize her feelings. And he had not. He had willingly believed she had kissed him by mistake. A clumsy mistake, at that.

TEN

A clumsy mistake. How had he come up with that barb? But what choice had he had when she was looking up at him with that same shining look her face had held during the play? The look that begged for him to embrace her. To kiss her. He had expected her performance to improve. But he had found himself forgetting the audience. Forgetting Annabel and his father. Seeing only Juliet. Wanting only Juliet.

He could only do them both a favor by reminding her that they had been playacting. Thank God it had worked, sending her away to the company of young men eager to cluster around and compliment her passionate Juliet.

Let her kiss one of them. Let one of their hearts—let all their hearts, damn them—be burned by the fire in her until nothing remained but cinders.

Passionate indeed. He was burning inside as if he had already been damned for his thoughts, though his actions were above reproach. He had not kissed her despite the opportunities, despite the desire. No. She had kissed him as he lay dead on the stage.

She had kissed him.

A kiss so unexpected. A kiss so sweet. A kiss that had taken his breath away. If she had pressed her lips against his for even one or two moments longer, he might have forgotten the eyes of the audience upon them and risen from the dead to return her kiss in full.

His mind was full of images of her as she had played opposite him: Juliet curtsying deeply, looking up into his eyes as if she had truly found her Romeo; Juliet smiling in invitation as they danced; Juliet in passionate wonder upon the balcony. . . . He did not want to think about such visions.

"If your business interests do not prosper, you could go upon the stage, Mr. Hopkins."

He turned to see who had addressed him so rudely and was shocked to see the mother of one of the young women who had been vying for his attention in the hopes of becoming his bride. Lady Dandridge, was it? He couldn't say for certain, so he merely nodded and smiled coolly. "You are too kind, my lady."

"Not at all." To his shock, she took his arm and pressed against him so that her bosom nearly escaped the confines of her bodice as it was forced upward. "I mean it most sincerely. Why, I found myself wanting to rush up there and rescue you before you could drink that fatal poison."

"As you see, it has done me no lasting harm." He pulled away from her.

She reached up with a coy glance that did not suit her years or her dignity. Her fingers brushed his lips. "Are you so certain? Perhaps you need someone to rub your lips free of any lingering poison."

"I am quite certain I do not." He gave her his best frozen stare, and at last she drew back from him, her bosom returning to its rightful place. He was puzzled as to why she had thought he would tolerate such familiarity in the first place.

She sighed in disappointment. "Very well, sir. I cannot help but think you must be a very fine actor if you could portray the passion of Romeo when you yourself are cold as an iced mackerel."

"That, my lady, was playacting," he assured her. He fervently hoped that no one else in the room had made the same mistaken assumptions she had. He was not a passionate man.

She smiled and fluttered her lashes at him. "If you ever feel the need to playact again, please remember me, sir. I can assure you I would greatly enjoy the performance."

He watched her go, careful not to let his mouth gape open in astonishment. He would have thought that the woman had simply lost her mind if not for the dozen or so propositions mingled with the sincere congratulations he received on his ill-considered performance as he passed through the crowd.

Only fortune—and society's quick censure—kept the young women still looking for a husband from making equally obvious plays for him. They contented themselves with dropping scented handkerchiefs at his feet and gazing up at him adoringly when he returned them with utterly correct civility and not a whit more encouragement.

Even gentlemen with whom he had been perfectly friendly treated him differently as he moved through the room restlessly. Some gave him glares befitting rivals in the battle of love, while others gave him the admiration reserved for rakes of the highest order. He found himself plied with brandy and compliments that would have turned the head of a less sensible man.

Once he glimpsed Annabel's frowning countenance. Once, Susannah's affectionate one. But there was one person he did not see. Juliet had disappeared from sight.

He told himself it did not matter if she had most likely been whisked away by a young man overcome by her passionate performance tonight. She could certainly handle any advances an eager swain might make.

She might even welcome such admiration, he decided uncharitably. After all, she had kissed him in public, had she not?

He could not bring himself to worry about whether Freddie was safe from her clutches now. Not the slightest sense of relief eased through him when he caught sight of his friend and his fiancée happily in conversation in a quiet corner of the crowded room. There was, however, no sign of Juliet.

At last, afraid that the extravagant compliments, mixed with the brandy, which made his head spin, would cause him to shout his displeasure aloud, he escaped the crowd. Perhaps a walk in the fresh air of the gardens would clear away the dizziness. Bring a touch of sanity back into his life.

He had been walking for only a few minutes when he heard what at first could have been mistaken for an angel come down to earth to soothe the troubled ears of those still trapped in their mortal coils. After a moment of listening in muddled wonder and staring at the stars in the night sky, he recognized Juliet's voice.

His pace took on a more purposeful speed as he searched the garden for her, wondering, with a rush of jealousy, which of her young admirers had captured her interest enough to be gifted with such a hauntingly beautiful song.

But he could not catch sight of her until he raised his eyes again, to the stone walls of the east wing, and saw that she stood high upon a second-floor balcony. After a moment's observation, he realized she was singing to no one but the moon.

Propriety called for him to turn his gaze away once he saw that she had retired to her room and thought herself private. But he did not. Nor did he turn away.

R.J. savored the sight, feeling as if fate had meant it for his eyes only. He gazed up at the balcony, mesmerized by Juliet standing there in her nightdress. There was a pensive look in her eyes as she gazed upward and sang her clear, sad song. Her voice was low; the song was for no one but herself and the moon.

He did not recognize the tune and could not make out the words. Still, he could sense the sadness, and it stirred something unnamed yet restless within him.

What made the flirtatious, shallow Miss Fenster sad this night? She had her triumph. The feel of her lips were still imprinted upon his. Did she carry the imprint of his mouth upon hers, upon her soul?

No, of course she did not. She claimed it had been an accident. But he had seen in her eyes that was not the truth. Perhaps she had for one moment allowed herself to forget that he was not Freddie? Such a thought made his head ache.

He called up to her, striking a pose that he thought would have done the real Romeo proud, if there had been a boy so foolish ever in the span of time.

*"But soft, what light through yonder window
breaks? It is the East and Juliet is the sun."*

Her song stopped abruptly. She peered down at him, a frown marring the smooth skin of her forehead, which he could imagine would be silken under his fingertips. Her eyes searched the darkness, reminding him that he stood in the shadow of a yew hedge. What would she say if he were to reveal himself? Would she know that he had been spying on her?

He stepped into the moonlight.

Her searching gaze caught him as soon as the moonlight struck him. "Mr. Hopkins?"

Her voice was flat with disappointment, and he held the fleeting hope that his appearance was not the cause. "Indeed. Were you expecting another?"

"I was expecting no one." As if she realized her dishabille, she drew her arms across her chest protectively. "Least of all you."

He had his answer. He was not welcome. He should leave, he knew, but he could not make himself walk away. He asked, though he cared nothing for the answer, "Why are you not celebrating your triumph?"

"My head thrums with pain, to be honest." For a moment her shoulders dropped with genuine weariness. But then she shrugged and added lightly, "I will never undertake such an enterprise again. I am only grateful that the play is finished."

He wished he shared such a sentiment. Instead, he felt empty. Hollow. Almost mournful. She was so far away, yet he wanted to touch her. "Your performance was magnificent."

She paused before answering, until just as he was certain she would end the improper conversation, she asked, "Not passionless, then?"

He laughed aloud. "No. Master Shakespeare would have allowed no one else to play the part if he had seen your performance."

She smiled but said in return, "Should I be flattered that you have changed your opinion? Or should I be wary that you speak falsely?"

He remembered then that he spoke to an accomplished flirt. A woman who knew how to pry a compliment out of a stone. Some of the joy of the moment faded. "Your admirers must have reassured you that I speak nothing but the truth when you came from the stage."

She hesitated before she answered, moving so that the moonlight no longer shone full on her face. "A compliment from you is worth hundreds from any of them."

"But you no doubt received thousands tonight." He might have known she would seek out some sign that he was now one of her smitten beaux. "I saw the eager flock surrounding you."

He had expected her to laugh, but she did not. "You did not seem to lack admirers, either." Surely that was not a touch of jealousy he heard in her voice? Impossible.

He thought of the married women who had approached him licking their lips as if he were a plump éclair to be coveted and devoured. "Why do you think I sought the peace of the garden?" All he wanted was to escape their unwanted attention.

"Then you understand why I am here, too." The confession surprised him. He rarely saw her when she was not surrounded by admirers. Did she not crave the attention she received? Or did it wear on her more than she allowed to show?

He had tired of it after no more than a few minutes of lascivious looks and guarded invitations. Could she feel the same about the young men who surrounded her? Nonsense.

Juliet Fenster had made a practice of displaying her nectar to attract the buzzing bees that followed her. She had not discriminated between gentlemen of sixteen or sixty. With the solitary exception of himself, he recalled. Until tonight's performance she had done little to win his admiration.

He shrugged. "But you knew from our rehearsals that I would play the part well. I had no such inkling that you would be as magnificent as you were."

"Magnificent, you say?" She looked down upon him, and he felt a shiver pass through him. The moonlight shone bright ivory on half her face and shadowed the other half. "You have used that very word twice tonight." She appeared ethereal and unreal. "Even if I choose only to believe you hold the sentiment half-true, that would still be a far cry from passionless, I give you that."

"Is that all you will give me, then?" He had meant to speak wryly, but some devil in him threw the words out with the same heat that coiled within him as he stood on the ground beneath her balcony.

"You would dare . . . just because I . . ." With a sniff of disdain, she pulled back from the balcony until her entire face was shadowed. "A thousand times good night!" she answered in anger, as if he had spoken aloud his wish that she come down from her balcony and couple with him in the soft, sweet grass of the darkened garden.

He did not want her to withdraw. "Nay, say it is not so, maiden. Can you not see it is I, your Romeo?" He wanted the two of them to stay this way forever. He wanted to imagine her in his arms, only the thin lawn of her nightdress between his skin and hers. He would never admit such a thing aloud, though. Perhaps she had read the desire in his face? He stepped out of the moonlight, back into the shadows of the yew.

She came to the edge of the balcony again then, still shielding herself from his eyes with her arms. Her chin was tilted high, but there was a bud of a smile on her lips as she replied, "I can see nothing, but I hear a jackass braying in the dark." Her voice vibrated .with emotion through the darkness of the night. But was she more amused or annoyed? He could not tell.

She had not retreated inside. He would take that as encouragement. He sighed theatrically. "That sounds more like Kate in *The Taming of the Shrew* than sweet Juliet speaking to her Romeo."

Her eyes shifted restlessly as she searched the darkness of the night. "Perhaps I sound so because you, sir, need to be taught how to treat a lady."

"I am certain you are mistaken." He had never been accused of offending a lady before. Had his words been improper? "Let me prove myself to you."

"Prove yourself to me? What do you think you have done all these weeks? Keeping your sister from me as if I carried the plague? Chiding me for my pretty, useless buttons? Calling me passionless? Just how could you redeem yourself?"

She had dropped her arms and leaned upon the balcony, looking down into the darkness, which no doubt made him as shadowy to her as she was to him. Only their voices had substance here. Which was why, perhaps, he dared say what he did. "I would kiss you as you were meant to be kissed."

"A kiss?" Her laughter should have wounded his pride. Instead, the blood rushing through his veins increased with every mocking word she spoke. "Your success has made you mad. I assure you, you are no Romeo to turn this Juliet's head."

He knew what the true Romeo would do. But he was R. J. Hopkins. Practical. Sensible. Rational.

Which was why he was startled to hear himself proclaim boldly, "If I were to climb up to you—to press a kiss to your lips as you did to mine earlier—perhaps you would not be so quick to stab me with your tongue, my lady." His words provoked an unexpected image of her tongue stabbing sweetly at his mouth in passion, not anger.

She leaned over the balcony's edge and spoke softly into the night. "What makes you think I want your kiss?"

"Are you not Juliet? Am I not Romeo?" For the first time, he said his own name without a twinge of shame. His mind was filled with an image of himself kissing Juliet. Was an image like that what had fueled Shakespeare as he penned his passionate lovers?

"Are you, Mr. Hopkins?" R.J. closed his eyes and gave himself up to his own imagination for the first time since he was a small child in his mother's arms. Perhaps, as she said, he had gone mad. Surely it was madness to continue to dream of sliding his lips down the silken skin of her neck until his head was cradled on her shoulder and he inhaled the warm scent of her skin.

He opened his eyes again and moved into the moonlight beneath the balcony. Madness. After all, she stood so near and yet so far away. Why didn't he end this torture? Why didn't he walk away? He reached for the ivy-covered trellis and shook it as he stared up at her. It would hold his weight.

She leaned over farther to gaze down at him. At his hand on the trellis. "Will you dare it?"

"Tell me if you wish a kiss from me."

"How can I?" She laughed softly. "I won't know if I want you to kiss me until you do."

He began to climb. "Tell me you want me to kiss you, Juliet."

There was only the rustling of the ivy and the raggedness of his own breath in his ear as he continued his climb. And then she asked, "Do you think I want a kiss from a man like you?"

There was a sadness in her voice that echoed within him and made him answer boldly, "I think you need a kiss from a man like me."

"What makes you think such a thing?" He could hear the tension that built in her voice as he climbed.

"The moon hanging in the sky tells me so." He looked upward. He could nearly touch her face where she bent toward him over the balcony railing. Only a few more steps and he would really touch her, as he had in his mind. But did he dare? He felt as if he, like the moon, were hanging on the edge of something momentous. But what? Reason? Passion? Madness?

The lawn of her nightdress made a soft sound as she pulled away from the railing and backed out of his sight. "The moon hangs so every month." He could hear no disapproval shading the husky tremor in her voice through the silken black of the night.

"I have never noticed it before, then." He climbed the last few feet of the trellis, the ivy crisp and springy under his hands as he grasped the firmly nailed latticework.

The balcony was narrow. She stood as still as the night air. Her feet were bare, he was surprised to notice, as he grabbed onto the railing to pull himself over.

ELEVEN

A large part of Juliet did not believe this was happening. Did not believe that R. J. Hopkins, staid and sober Boston businessman, was climbing the latticework to her balcony. For one moment, she considered retreating to the safety of her room rather than stand her ground against an uncertain enemy. Was this the man who had the heart of deadwood? Had Shakespeare's play somehow transformed him into an impetuous lover—or a madman?

No doubt the wise course was retreat. But her heart beat faster as he climbed higher, as his hand reached the railing and the top of his head moved near enough to touch. She wanted to look into his eyes and see for herself whatever was there to be revealed by the moody moonlight.

While she debated her decision, the lattice cracked under him. Instinctively, her heart in her throat, she reached out to grasp the cloth of his jacket. "I would never have expected this of you, Mr. Hopkins," she said as she helped him scramble onto the narrow iron balcony.

He was breathing hard, and his hand closed tightly

over the iron rail as he stood straight. With one glance
at the moon, he focused on her. He seemed more puzzled than passionate. "I have never done anything this
absurd in my life, Miss Fenster."

The scent of brandy was strong, and she felt overwhelming disappointment. "Fool. You have been
drinking."

He blinked, and the puzzlement left his eyes. He
moved a step closer, crowding her to one end of the
small balcony. "If I have, it is only because you have
driven me to it."

His body was between hers and the doorway to her
room and safety. Still, she had no intention of letting
him know that he had discomposed her. "That is a
poor excuse."

"Everyone was so pleased with my performance. I
could not pass someone that he would not put a drink
in my hand. Or that she would not look at me as if I
were a Christmas treat." Apparently realizing that he
had forced her to press uncomfortably against the cold,
hard railing, he stepped backward.

She inched nervously toward the doorway. Who was
this man?

As if he could see her dawning disapproval, he
added in a more conciliatory tone, "And I could not
find you. What would you have me do? Waste the
duke's fine brandy?"

She stopped. The moon illuminated the planes of
his face but shadowed his eyes from her examination.
"You were looking for me?"

He hesitated, his lips pressing together first, before
he answered her. "I was."

"Why?" Did he seek her out because he thought since she had kissed him once during the play, she would kiss him again? Should she be flattered or insulted if he had thought such a thing?

"I . . . I can't say. I just needed to see you." Uncertainty radiated from him. He reached a hand out to her tentatively but dropped it when she instinctively stepped backward. He glanced down to the ground where he had been standing moments ago.

If he had wanted to see her, he should at least be looking at her, not formless shadows, she thought testily. After a moment, when he made no move toward her, she said restlessly, "Well, you have seen me. Are you satisfied now?"

"No." His gaze, hungry and wild, caught hers. "What have you done to me?"

"What have I . . ." she whispered, her mouth dry. At any moment she expected him to take her in his arms as he so obviously desired to do. But he did not. With blinding insight, she realized he was as off balance emotionally as he had been physically a moment before on the broken latticework. Apparently R. J. Hopkins was as unsure of why he was on this balcony as she was. The thought was unexpectedly heady.

She sensed his struggle, waiting for him to reach his breaking point. Suddenly, the hunger left his eyes, and he looked away from her. He had not completely won his battle. No. She could feel his desire just as she could feel the cool night air against her skin. Could he feel hers?

"I shouldn't have climbed the trellis." The smile he

threw her was almost boyish. Almost disarming. But he didn't dare meet her eyes.

"Then why did you?" Half of her was afraid to awaken the hunger again. The other half . . . the other half frightened her so that she shivered.

"You needed to be kissed. I thought I should do the job." Was it only the brandy that had made him climb up to her? Had the night air cleared his head sufficiently that he would leave her without a kiss?

"How improper of you, Mr. Hopkins."

He answered in his familiar starchy tone, but the smile still lingered on his lips. "Improper of me? That you should need me to kiss you?"

Juliet didn't know how to answer him. He was teasing her, and she was used to being teased in such a way. But not in such circumstances—standing practically outdoors in her nightdress, with the moon shining much too brightly. If she wasn't careful, he might actually follow through on his threat to kiss her. She might see that hunger in his eyes again, and then where would she be? She decided the only safe answer was a complete denial, even if she wasn't certain how she felt about his wanting a kiss. "I most certainly do not want you to kiss me, Mr. Hopkins."

Her flat denial seemed to take him aback. He turned his face up to the moon and sighed. After a time, still looking at the moon, he said softly, almost as if to himself, "Then perhaps it is I who want to kiss you."

"Me?" She faked a start of shock, although in truth his words had raced up her spine like fireworks. He wanted to kiss her. It wasn't the brandy. He wanted to kiss her.

He turned his gaze from the moon to her once again as she asked, "You wish to kiss me? The inconstant Juliet?" She moved toward him, just one step.

He stepped backward, only to come up against the railing, as she had earlier. "Yes." He struggled again to suppress the hunger. And then it flared again in his eyes as he said huskily, "I believe I do." Still, he did not.

She stepped closer until she could detect the warm, masculine scent of wool and peppermint emanating from him. "Me? The woman who would give my heart to any man who paid me the right compliment and take it away again as soon as I tired of him? Who would never be content with one man?"

"Yes. You." He watched her as intently as if she held his life in her hands. And still he did not kiss her.

Words were not possible now. Not when she felt so powerful, as if she could command the moon if she wished it. And yet she did not know what command to give. A sudden intuitive fear that she had stepped off safe ground urged her to retreat now. Back to her room. Back to safety.

Instead, she moved forward to touch his chest lightly with her hand. She looked into his face and simply stood, staring up into the odd play of shadows and light along his head and shoulders. Still no words, only a sigh as soft as the night air.

"So you believe you want to kiss me? And yet you make no move toward me. Lips cannot touch without one of us moving. Or so I have always believed."

He said nothing. Did not move. But she could feel

the rapid rise and fall of his chest against her palm. The moment shimmered between them, all possibility. But what would be wise? Or better yet, what did she want from him? "Perhaps you are mad, then, as well as without passion, my Romeo."

His lips tightened, and he moved into a shaft of moonlight that showed her all too clearly that he had taken her words as a challenge. The set of his features clearly demonstrated his silent struggle with desire. She saw the moment his will lost to his hunger. As he bent toward her, she felt a thrill of wonder.

But wonder warred with trepidation as he leaned over her slowly, ever so slowly. Even now he left her an escape if she wished it. She was caught between retreat and surrender. What matter? She sighed once again, giving herself up to the uncanny notion that fate had already decided the matter for them as finally as Master Shakespeare had done for his lovers two centuries ago.

His sigh mingled with hers. "I am tired of words after all these days of practice." He bent his head. "Master Shakespeare should have written in fewer words and more kissing." His lips touched hers lightly where she stood motionless, waiting.

Amazement drowned the last remnants of fear as she felt the warm satin of his undemanding and yet compelling kiss. Juliet pressed her lips against his and stepped into the shelter of his arms. Why had she told him she did not want to be kissed? Why had she not known how she craved this? Her body vibrated like a fine tuned harpsichord with the sheer need to feel him pressed against her.

Pleasure and comfort in equal measure filled her as his arms came around her and his lips, soft and warm, touched hers. He wanted to kiss her. Her. And she wanted him to more than she had ever before wanted anything in her life. Instinctively, she parted her lips under his gentle demand.

"Juliet." He groaned her name as he claimed her mouth and pulled her tightly to him. She sensed he had, at last, stopped trying to control the hunger inside him. Hunger for her. His hands touched her where no other man had ever dared. His lips left hers to kiss her shoulders, her forehead, her neck, until she used her own hands to guide him back where she wanted him—his mouth against hers.

They might have stood there locked together in their embrace all night had the fireworks not blasted noisily and brightly over their heads. Simon and his guests celebrating summer.

Juliet did not mind that she had missed most of the display. She was enjoying the private fireworks R. J. Hopkins had set off inside her much too much to regret anything. For a moment, when he tried to break their kiss, she resisted. Gradually, however, she was unable to ignore the realization that they were outside, in full view of anyone who might wander far out into the gardens.

Without warning, he lifted her off her feet and brought her just inside the doorway, where they would no longer be visible. "We've missed the fireworks," he said, his breath ragged in her ear as he put her down.

He tried to push her away from him, but she resisted, sliding her arms around him, holding tight. "I don't think we have."

The heat of his hands burned through the thin lawn of her nightdress, and his whisper was a half-groan. "You are not even decently dressed. This is unwise." But his hands slid from her waist to her hip in a restless caress that urged her nearer even as he spoke.

Perhaps they were unwise. Yet surely not as much as their namesakes. "It is only a kiss. Nothing more." A kiss was not so shameful, was it? How would it be possible to ever regret this feeling?

"Just a kiss." She shivered at the feel of his lips trailing from her jaw to the cleft of her collarbones. He sighed against her neck, "Juliet, I'm afraid this is not just a kiss . . ." He groaned softly once again. She could feel his struggle to control the hunger inside him. He raised his head to gaze at the moon, still visible through the half-open balcony doorway.

"Nonsense. What harm in one kiss?" Stretching on tiptoe, she took his head between her hands and brought his gaze back to her own. "Indeed, what harm in a dozen."

She allowed the fingertips of her right hand to trace along the tight line of his jaw. "Better yet, ask what pleasure to be found." She cupped her hands at the back of his neck and pulled him gently and surely down until he groaned again softly and brought his mouth down upon hers.

With a shudder of surrender, he deepened the kiss, demanding more than gentle acceptance. She responded willingly, slipping her hands beneath his jacket to run her fingers along the firm muscles of his back, evident through the fine lawn of his shirt.

He broke for a moment, leaning his forehead against hers and struggling to master his breathing enough to whisper, "I should not do this."

Should not? Who had the right to say that? He wanted this. She wanted this. This—she didn't even have a name for what she wanted. This thing that her sisters felt with their husbands. That had made her brother willing to die for his wife. She would not lose her chance now, not when she held the answer to the secret in her very grasp.

She could feel the distance he was trying to put between them like a shield. "I should go."

"Don't." She buried her face against his chest, pulled on the loose cravat, grabbed at the unfastened halves of his shirt. Had he unfastened the clasps, or had she in feverish mindlessness? How could any person be so consumed by feelings that the mind ceased to work properly?

He worried that jealous tongues would criticize. What did that matter when her whole being demanded that he continue? She tightened her arms on his shoulders. "If it eases your conscience, I should not want you to do this, yet I will die if you do not."

"Juliet. We can't." He gave a ragged, whispery laugh that made her shiver with want. *"I* can't. I am only a man. I cannot keep you safe, not even from me. Not if we continue this." He felt as she did. His voice, as he said her name, told her so. It was truly madness. A magnificent madness. And he knew it as well as she did. So why did he fight so hard to deny the feeling?

She whispered, afraid if she spoke any louder, she would break the spell that held him to her. "Stay with me. Show me what passion truly is."

His laughter rumbled in his chest. She could feel the movement on her cheek, and she rubbed against him until he held her away. His eyes met hers. The hunger was still there, but caged. There was uncertainty in his whispered question. "What makes you think I know anything about passion?"

"These last days I saw the part of you that you have buried deep inside. I saw it tonight in your Romeo. I see it now, in you—Romeo."

She could feel him pull away. Not physically. No. He moved not a fraction of an inch from her in reality, and yet she felt she no longer touched him. He said gruffly, "Don't use that name."

"Why not?" She liked saying his name. "Romeo." So much better a name than R.J. "It is your name." She repeated it, rolling the *R* sound. "Romeo."

"That cursed name was a mistake." His voice held a harsh note. As if he heard the sound and feared what it revealed, he added, more softly, "My mother was— not the most sensible of creatures."

"Neither am I," she confessed, though at the moment she felt blessed by her lack of sense. Women with too much sense must never feel what she did now. "I want to know what passion is. I have never felt this strongly for any man before. My mind is whirling. My skin is all feeling and my heart so full that it could burst."

He seemed startled at her statement, his arms tensing under her fingers. "You have never felt this before?"

"Never," she assured him.

He touched his lips to hers, gently, without demand, as if testing them somehow. "You have been kissed before?"

"Many times." At her answer he moved away, this time physically. She protested. "What does that matter? I am tired of having the admiration of a dozen men who mean nothing to me. I don't want to kiss anyone else. I want you."

His gaze caught hers, and she could see he still had his hunger under control. Barely. "You don't know what you ask."

She would have argued but then thought better of it. He was a man disarmed by honesty. "No, I don't. So how can I judge what I want until you show me what it is I can have?"

He closed his eyes and stood very still. "Juliet—" She sensed the battle being waged inside him, but there was little to show on his tightly controlled surface how fiercely he fought. His jaw was clenched tight; his hands played along her shoulders and down her arms. After a moment, his hands came to rest upon her shoulders. "Perhaps you are right. Let me show you."

She expected that he would pull her close for a kiss. But he did not. Instead, his hands moved to cup her breasts. She could not help the gasp of surprise that escaped her. No one had ever touched her breasts before, though some foolish men had tried, much to their regret.

She watched his face as his fingers stroked her breasts. The sensations that coursed through her somehow coursed through him as well. She had never guessed such pleasure existed from the simple touch of a man. Then again, she had never been touched by a man before when she wore only her nightdress.

He opened his eyes and gazed down at her. His thumbs brushed her nipples. His breathing had grown ragged once again. There was a storm in his eyes. A storm she had caused. "See what you ask? Now do you understand why this is not wise?"

Intuitively, she understood that the power she held over him at this moment was so strong that he would not leave her unless she directed him to. "Wisdom is sometimes overrated," she said, her mouth dry.

He closed his eyes, but his thumbs continued to incite the delicious sensation flooding through her. "I should go."

She said nothing.

He offered once more. "Ask me and I shall leave you here and now."

She could not. She would not. She closed her eyes and placed her hands over his where they cupped her breasts. She lifted one heavy hand to her mouth and pressed a kiss to the pad of his thumb. "Don't go."

R.J. knew the moment he lost the battle with his good sense. Perhaps if she hadn't kissed his thumb— her lips warm, her breath against his palm ragged. Perhaps . . . Reason deserted him in a rush.

As if her words were all he needed to take the final

plunge off the edge of sanity, he lifted her into his arms and carried her into the lamp-lit room. Her bed looked virginal, lace and silk and ruffles no man would allow. He sat her gently upon the counterpane.

Slowly, knowing that the only thing that could stop him now was her protest, he removed his jacket. His bedraggled cravat. His collar. He undid the studs in his shirt one by one, putting each neatly into the pocket of his jacket.

He made each action deliberate. He watched her eyes, certain that she would call a halt. When the last stud was removed, he thought he saw a flicker of doubt cross her face. "This is not wise," he forced himself to say.

"No, it is not," she agreed to his sharp disappointment. And then she rose from the bed and pushed his shirt down over his shoulders. It fell to the ground in a soundless crumple he did not bother to remedy as she began to undo the fastening on his trousers.

TWELVE

He must be dreaming. That was the only explanation for what was happening. R.J. fought against the urge to crush her to him, to make love to her with a savagery he had never known before. What had she done to him that he could ignore a lifetime of self-control? He shuddered as her fingers brushed against him.

She looked up at him with a question in her eyes. As he pushed down his trousers and carelessly left them behind, she turned and doused the lamp. The darkness surrounded them, pierced only partially by the moonlight from the balcony's open doorway. He welcomed the dreamlike air of moonlit darkness.

"Juliet . . ." He could not have said whether he meant it as plea or protest.

But he rejoiced when she returned to him. Her fingers traced across his chest and said in a voice that vibrated with nascent passion, "I want to learn the shape of you in darkness tonight. The light saps my courage."

"And no wonder. The light reveals the truth. This is insanity."

"If it is, let us thank the moon for such wonderful madness." Her hands touched him gently, hesitantly, then more boldly.

He did not bring her to the bed at first, somehow believing she might still change her mind and stop this madness. For he could not. He would not. He stilled her questing exploration. Gently, slowly, he pulled the ribbons of her gown until the neck gaped loose enough to push from her shoulders just as she had pulled his unfastened shirt from him. He felt the gown brush his bare knees as it glided to the floor.

She pressed herself full against him, pulling back in momentary surprise when she felt the full measure of his desire for her, for this moon-driven, misbegotten dream she shared so generously with him.

Like a child with a new toy, she reached for him. He sucked in a startled breath at the firm touch of her fingers. She laughed softly and continued her gentle, insistent caress.

For a moment he gave himself to the sensation. He copied her earlier actions, putting his own hands over hers and guiding her in the motions that gave him the most pleasure. To his chagrin she learned so quickly, he had no choice but to divert her or he risked disappointing her altogether.

He pulled her close and brought her hands up so that he could kiss each finger and the palm of each hand. At last, acknowledging that neither of them would call a halt, he lifted her into his arms and carried her the short distance to the bed. His arms shaking ever so slightly, he brought himself as gently as possible down upon her trembling body.

When she would have arched up into him and ended things between them, he pulled away from her to whisper, "Wait." The gift she offered him was too great for him to take it before she knew the full pleasure she had asked of him.

"I can't," she pleaded, moving restlessly against him. "I can't wait."

He stroked her gently. "You will not regret it, I promise." She moaned a soft protest but allowed him to explore every inch of her with his mouth, with his hands. And when he could feel that she was on the edge, he pushed her over with a brush of his thumb. The same thumb she had kissed so sweetly earlier. As she cried out in release, he stretched himself over her and joined with her in one swift motion.

His kisses muffled her cry of surprise, and then her kisses muffled his as she arched up to meet him and his control shattered into a thousand brightly colored lights. Fireworks of pleasure followed all too closely by a firestorm of regret as passion drained from him and reason flooded back.

"I had. no idea . . ." She breathed into his ear. "Thank you, Mr. Hopkins . . . thank you . . . thank you . . ."

He braced himself for the recriminations. For the tears. But all she did was press a kiss to his chest and arrange herself comfortably against him. He knew he should go now, before they were discovered together. But he could not leave her to face the aftermath alone. He must wait a little, until she realized what they had done. What the inevitable consequences of their actions were.

Incredibly, as he waited for the tears to come, her breathing became even and shallow. He shook her slightly, but she only moaned and burrowed against him more snugly. She had fallen asleep. Without a single tear. And she had thanked him.

As long as he lived, he would not forget that thank you. "Thank you, Mr. Hopkins." He held her close, pushing aside a burgeoning sadness to enjoy the feel of her, warm and sated, in his arms. Recriminations would wait until tomorrow. Regrets always waited patiently. But they would not disappear.

His arms tightened around her. He had shown her the pleasure she had wanted to know. A part of him felt a fierce, primitive triumph for that. He had surprised them both with passion he had never known possible.

But at what price?

Juliet came awake abruptly to the birdsong that heralded the coming day. The brief hope that she had merely experienced the most vivid, detailed dream in her life gave way to the realization of exactly what she had done. There was no denying reality.

For another moment she tried. With her eyes closed, she lay snug against him—against the solid warmth of the American, Mr. R.J. Romeo Hopkins. Gradually, she had to admit that he was more than a figment of her imagination. One of her hands curled around his shoulder. Her cheek rested against his ribs.

As he took each measured breath, she could feel the rise and fall of his chest. Just like a man to sleep as deeply as if his life had not been changed by the night. But then, his hadn't. How could she have been such a fool?

The play. All the fault of the play. Damn Master Shakespeare. Damn his headstrong lovers. Damn the moon.

Strong language, but she was mightily vexed. She should have known better. She should have—her life was ruined. Unless—if no one found out—he was to go back to America, after all. An ocean apart, she would not have to chance upon him in society. To know that he had seen her at her weakest and most vulnerable.

An entire ocean would certainly dampen the fear that his careless words might make yet another scandal for her family to live down. Or, worse, that she might allow him to make love to her again. If he were across an ocean, she could not be tempted as she had been last night.

With a sigh, Juliet opened her eyes. She did not precisely concede that she regretted the experience. She could not. If he had vanished from her room with the morning light, she would have cherished the night forever. But he was here, solid and real, with all the attendant realities and problems that must be faced in the harsh light of day.

The difficulty was that she simply did not want to face them. She did not want to face him. How could she, without remembering how much pleasure his lips could bring her? Perhaps she could sneak away and return to Anderlin?

That way she need never see him again. Their limbs

were such a tangle, she was afraid to breathe too deeply as she pulled first her leg free and then her arm. She moved slowly to leave the bed without waking him as her mind began to work feverishly on how to accomplish a hasty return home without raising Miranda's suspicion.

The operation required that she look at him closely in the light so that she could stop all movement if he seemed about to rouse. She stopped a moment with surprise. She had not realized that men had hair on their chests. Her fingertips had tickled against it last night, but to see hair so dark on his skin was rather shocking. A closer look revealed that the hair was dark and silky where it curled against the skin around his nipples—so flat compared to her own.

His nipples were rather shocking to look at as well. They were dark brown and wrinkled, and for one horrifying moment she thought she would not be able to resist the urge to taste one—something she had not thought to do last night.

"I'm afraid to say that your idea, as enticing as it may be, Miss Fenster, is not at all wise."

She glanced up in dismay to see that his eyes were open, though he had not moved except to speak. Though his words were intended to have a dampening effect, the heat in his gaze and the rapid increase in his breathing betrayed him. The half-formed idea sparked into full life, and she ran her hand lightly over the firm muscles that banded his ribs. "What would it matter? I am ruined, after all."

"You are no such thing." He sat up briskly, shaking

off her fingers. His gaze had turned brisk as a winter breeze as soon as she uttered the word *ruined*.

"Of course I am." She turned away, acutely aware that neither of them wore a stitch of clothing. Last night it had seemed the most natural thing in the world. Now she found herself suddenly unwilling to be exposed to his sharp assessment.

"There has not been a maid in the room as of yet. No one but the two of us know what madness we were about. If we are quick, we will keep it so." She heard him slide from the bed and begin to dress, but she did not turn around to watch him rescue the clothing they had left in a sorry heap on the floor last night. Not even when he tossed her nightdress to her.

His words made sense. If no one knew, then it would be as if last night never happened. Beneath the covers, she struggled to put on her nightdress. "You must leave at once."

"First we must decide what to tell your family."

She turned to him, too startled for modesty. To her disappointment, he was almost completely dressed and just fastening his collar. His clothing, however, looked sadly rumpled. "Why tell them anything?"

He gave her the look she hated most, the one that implied that she was utterly brainless. Her younger sisters had perfected the expression, but Mr. Hopkins managed to convey his meaning very well as he said sharply, "They will ask questions, and we must give them satisfactory answers."

She wondered if he was the muddled one, not she. She asked impatiently, "What questions would they think to ask regarding an event that never happened?"

"Don't be foolish." His voice sounded annoyingly like Miranda's when she chided one of the children. "We will marry. I may not be English, but I understand what your rules demand."

Rules? She should have known. "Does it only matter what the rules say? What of your heart?" She tightened the laces of her nightdress and left the warmth of bed.

He flushed darkly. "It was not my heart I listened to last night, much to my regret." He frowned and undid the cravat he had tied badly. "I acted the fool; I am prepared to pay the price even if my father should choose to disinherit me for it."

Beneath his composed surface she could plainly see the pain and regret. "I think you have a soul as melodramatic as you claim mine to be. Disinherit you? Why should your father do such a thing just because you choose to marry me?"

"We Americans see such things differently than you English. I am in business. I need a wife to work by my side. You—" He looked away. "My father might worry that you could not take the strain."

"You mean he might find me as useless and frivolous as you do?" She pushed away the hurt that threatened to bring tears to her eyes. "Why, then, can we not simply solve the dilemma by agreeing not to reveal last night's events to a soul?"

"Juliet!" Why did he look at her as if she spoke nonsense? He added, in clipped tones, "There could be a child."

"Impossible." But, of course, it was not.

He did not answer, merely raised his eyebrow quizzically until she turned from him in frustration. His implacability on the matter made her frantic. She could not marry him. She could not leave England for America. She would not. She must convince him that he was not honor bound to marry her.

But how? She reviewed all the careful rules Miranda had drilled her in before she came to London to be brought out into society. If she had not been a virgin, he would not feel this obligation to her. She said firmly, to make the lie more convincing, "You are not obligated to marry me. You are not the first man in my bed."

"No?" In his eyes, shock was quickly followed by naked hope. "You have had another man in this room? In this bed?"

"More than one," she said a bit angrily. His eagerness squeezed at her heart. He had wanted her last night. She was sure of that. But this morning he was humiliatingly willing to consider any excuse that would allow him to escape her bed without a wedding.

He advanced toward her. Outraged, he asked, "More than one? Two? Three? A dozen?" Was this something so dire that he would strike her for it?

She closed her eyes and answered quickly, "Yes."

She waited for a blow. Instead, he commanded, "Open your eyes. Look at me."

She opened her eyes and gazed at him with reluctance. There was no hint of violence in his manner as he asked softly, "Tell me the truth, Juliet. You have had another man kiss you as I did last night?"

She forced herself not to waver in meeting his eyes as she answered, "Yes."

"And touch you here as well?" His index finger touched ever so lightly the sensitive crest of her breast through the thin covering of lawn.

Her response was a surge of desire. The answering flare in his eyes was quickly suppressed. "Yes." She reached up to capture his hand.

He gently disengaged her fingers from his and clasped his hands behind his back, out of her reach. "No, Juliet. You have not."

"How can you be so certain of my virtue?" She did not know whether to be insulted or flattered that he believed she had not allowed another man the liberties she had allowed him.

He regarded her closely for a minute, until she felt like a specimen on display in a museum. "The look in your eye when I touched your—" He broke off abruptly. With a swallow, he continued without inflection or emotion, to her great disappointment. "When I touched you just now I could see that what you told me was not true."

"How could you see such a thing?" Yes, he was definitely gazing at her in much too dispassionate a way for a man named Romeo.

For a moment she thought she glimpsed a spark of what had been in his face under the full moon. "Last night, when I kissed you, when I touched you, you had the look of a woman who was not certain what she wanted."

"So?" This was tedious. Why must he treat her like a student struggling with a difficult lesson? She much preferred the man she had gone to bed with than the one she had awakened to find in her bed.

"This morning you have the look of a woman who knows very well what happens when she is touched by a man."

"I do?" Was he just guessing? Could one see that kind of knowledge upon a face? "Can anyone tell, do you think?" Would Miranda? She could not bear it if her sister knew what she had done.

Leaning in toward a looking glass, she examined her face carefully. She looked no different to her own eyes. Perhaps there was a pink to her cheeks that had not been there yesterday. And, oh, goodness, there was a red mark on her neck that corresponded to a delicious kiss she remembered down to her toes. But that could easily be covered.

He sighed. "The truth is not visible to anyone who does not try to bed you, Juliet. Do not worry that any casual acquaintance will see it."

"Do you mean that if I choose to marry . . . or rather, when I choose to marry, my husband will know that I—that he is not the first man to take me to bed?" She did not like the idea of having anyone know such a thing about her. Most especially not a husband. "How could he bear knowing that I . . . ? Can a man forget something like that?" Or forgive it? She looked at him in dawning horror.

"I will never mention a word. I swear on my honor." He sank onto the bed and buried his head in his hands for a moment. "I was as foolish as you, but I knew what would happen. You did not know—at least not until I showed you. How could I ever hold you to blame?"

"We cannot marry, Mr. Hopkins. We barely know each other."

He raised his head and gave an exasperated laugh. "My name is R.J. I see no reason for you to call me Mr. Hopkins any longer, do you?"

"It would not be proper . . ." Juliet's protest died as she recognized the folly. If one did not know a man who had—the heat of memory took her—who had touched her breasts, who had pushed a part of himself inside her . . . Who would have thought so much pleasure could be had from what they had done that she could forget for a moment how little she knew him? "I don't want to call you R.J." She fought back the tears that threatened. "I don't want to marry because I made a mistake. I want to marry for love."

He regarded her sternly. "Living under the duke's protection, you may have thought you were answerable to no one. But I assure you that for our actions last night, marriage without scandal is hardly a great price."

"I could go to a nunnery."

He raised a brow. "I don't believe there are any in England. But if you are serious, I'm sure I can find an American convent for you."

Had she truly made the choice of husband without knowing what or whom she chose? Perhaps, if she made herself forget what they had done, it would not show on her face when she did choose a man to marry. "Would any man who wished to marry me be able to see that I . . . that we—"

"For some women, I believe the answer is no." He rose from the bed and came over to take her face in his hands. "But for you, Juliet? I am certain he would see it clearly in the way you looked at him."

"He would?"

"I'm afraid so. Unfortunately, you are now vulnerable to other men who would take advantage of you as I did last night. Men who would not offer marriage but only disgrace."

She gazed at him in dismay even as his hands on her skin made a shiver of pleasure course through her. "Then why would any man marry me?"

"I should not mind." He hesitated, and then said quickly, "But I would expect you never to do such a thing again." He added, "Except with me, of course."

THIRTEEN

At first she thought she had not heard him properly. And then outrage flashed through her like lightning. He could not have hurt her more if he had slapped her face instead of cradling it between his hands. She pulled away from his grasp and moved to the window. "How dare you? Of course I would not cuckold my husband."

"I am sorry if my words impugn your honor, Miss Fenster." He seemed almost as horrified as she had been by his words. "I do not know what to say. I can assure you I have never been in this kind of situation before."

The absurdity of being addressed so formally by a man who had taken many more liberties with her than the uninvited use of her first name made her laugh ruefully. "I do not know whether to be grateful or unhappy that you have no experience in dealing with such things."

He came to the window and looked out upon the balcony, which had been the cause of their downfall. "It is almost full morning. I must go." He tightened the knot of his cravat, straightened his jacket, and said briskly, "We will settle the details later."

Settle the details! Of a lifetime bound to each other. She did not like the businesslike sound of those words. She grasped his arm. "Promise me one thing."

"What?"

"Say nothing to Simon immediately."

He shook his head. "I am set to leave tomorrow. I must—"

"I want to tell my sister first. She deserves that from me, at the least."

"I see." Apparently he could think of no further objection. Juliet wanted to weep with relief.

She pressed further. "Let us tell my family of this together."

"Are you certain? I know confessing such a thing can be difficult. I would be happy to spare you."

Must he play the gentleman now? Could he not simply agree to her request. "Promise me."

"Of course." He paused beside her and looked somberly down upon her. "There is no excuse for my behavior, Miss Fenster. Juliet. I promise I will never bring this night up in condemnation of you. I will always treat you as a wife should be treated."

"I believe you, Mr. Hop—R.J." Juliet would have been more pleased if there had been even a hint of the man who had climbed her balcony last night. But she saw not a sign. Gone completely was the passionate man of last night, to be replaced with the cool-blooded R. J. Hopkins.

She opened the bedroom door a crack to peek into the hallway. No one, servant or guest, stirred yet. She gestured to him. "Hurry, before someone comes!" She pushed him out the door and leaned against it with a rush of fury at her own foolishness.

How had she ever let herself forget his true nature? They would make each other miserable within a month, never mind a lifetime.

She knew only one thing for certain. She must return to Anderlin at once, before he spoke to Simon and consigned them to a mismatch of tragic proportions.

To his great relief, R.J. managed to make his way back to his room without being seen. He undressed quickly, his mind racing ahead to what he must do. Talk with the duke—or should it be Juliet's brother? Valentine Fenster was not here, and there was no time to waste with a visit to him, so he would have to settle for the duke and see what Kerstone advised about the formalities involved. He had promised Juliet to wait until she had told her sister. But he must impress upon her that she needed to do so today.

He settled himself into the bed, which had been turned down the previous night. The bed warmer had grown cold, and he pushed it out of his way with his feet as he deliberately mussed the sheets and blankets so that no one would suspect he had not spent the night in his room, where he belonged.

He threw his head back to leave a good-sized impression in the feather pillows just in time. The manservant assigned to him arrived to lay out the clothes that had been cleaned and brushed for this day's use and take up yesterday's discarded clothing for cleaning. He lay still as the wiry man fussed a bit over his preparations and then left to see to the same function for yet another guest in his care.

He hoped that Juliet was taking similar precautions. No doubt she did not fully understand the scandal they could rouse. She had been spoiled in the duke's household and with such powerful protection would not realize that not all sins were easily forgiven.

He knew that Juliet would take persuasion before she accepted the idea of marriage to him. He wished she would be sensible, but he held out little hope for such an outcome. Her nature was not the sensible sort. Perhaps he should approach the duke immediately and ask for help in convincing Juliet this was best for all of them.

He was reluctant to do so, knowing that once he asked for aid, the duke would accept nothing less than the full story. R.J. would prefer that no one save him and Juliet ever knew the extent of their foolishness. He still burned with shame at his actions. He had blatantly ignored his common sense and run only with his emotions. Selfish emotions, at that. He knew the consequences. Juliet had not understood them.

But even she must eventually see that marriage was the only answer. He would simply hope that she did not hate him for what he had done. Perhaps she might even come to see that she had not made a bad bargain.

After all, a woman needed to become a wife sometime. Juliet had been long enough choosing, but the day had to come sooner or later. If she was not the type to hold on to her grievance, she would have nothing to object to about him once they were married.

He would be a tolerant, reasonable—if not indulgent—husband.

No doubt the biggest obstacle to her willing agreement was the daunting idea of leaving England. He wondered, briefly, whether they could marry and she could remain here, with her family. He did not think the duke, his wife, or Juliet's brother would object to the idea.

However, there was more than just her family to concern him here. The thought of what his father would say about such an idea made him shudder. He had been disappointed enough that Annabel had borne him no sons. He would not easily accept the idea of never having grandsons.

Of course, there was the possibility that she was carrying a child. If so, he would not allow his child to be raised an ocean away from him. A father needed to take a hand in guiding a child to adulthood. Without his own father, who could know how quickly he might follow in his mother's footsteps to self-destruction?

He sighed. All the reasons he had listed were compelling. But what kept swimming to the top of his mind was how she had felt in his arms. The sweetness of her breasts. The curve of her waist. Her delighted sighs of pleasure that had encouraged him beyond reason.

No matter how he tried to reason his way into a calm acceptance of his fate, R.J. found a certain rather primitive satisfaction in the thought that he would be free to make love to her every night once they were married. Perhaps the same thought might sway her.

He hoped so. For good or ill, they had chosen each

other last night. Best if she understood that from the very first. If she had not wanted him, she had only to say so last night. He wished that she had. Or that his common sense had not deserted him so completely.

He rose and paced the small guest room restlessly until a decent hour had arrived and he could breakfast without comment. Fortunately, neither Annabel nor Susannah were about. He had no desire for polite conversation or the latest sally in Annabel's attempts to find a lord for Susannah. He was feeling particularly disinclined to feel sympathy for his sister's wish to avoid marriage. After all, he had not managed to avoid the trap, why should she?

The looks he got from the ladies as he breakfasted were as frequent as they had been last night. But more guarded. There were several older women who looked at him as if they wanted to slap him. For a moment he had the foolish notion that everyone knew what he had done last night. He comforted himself with the reassurance that he was only feeling the aftereffects of his guilt.

Fortunately, Juliet was not about. He did not yet know what he would say to her. How he might even look at her and not reveal the intimate nature of their relationship to all who observed them.

He exchanged a nod with several gentlemen who entered the room in a group. They had done business in the past, and he had found them nothing but friendly. Today, however, their nods were cool. Within a few minutes, he could no longer put down his observations to his own guilt.

The gentlemen's attitude had changed as subtly as the ladies' had. The envious looks had grown sharper. A few of Juliet's more ardent swains seemed to consider him a serious rival this morning. But underneath the tension in the room was a suppressed amusement. A sense of dread began to gnaw at him. One that only grew as he began to hear the whispers and the quickly hushed laughter. And the name: Romeo.

Though no one said anything directly, he could no longer convince himself that he was reacting to his own guilty conscience. His suspicions were confirmed when Freddie cornered him as he left the breakfast room, his meal mostly untouched. "R.J., is it true that your given name is Romeo?"

He bit back the impulse to lie. "Yes. But I am never called anything but R.J." If the worst gossip causing the titters was his given name, he would have to live with it. After all, he would be returning to Boston soon.

"I can understand that." Freddie, too, seemed faintly amused. And then he said, with more concern in his tone, "For some reason, that and another, more vicious, rumor has been circulating the house."

"What are the gossips saying today?" R.J. hoped it was another matter as innocuously humiliating as his given name.

"Not that I believe it, of course. But you know how some gossip takes on a life of its own."

"Indeed I do." With the last of his patience, R.J. asked, "What is being said?"

"It hardly seems worth repeating." Freddie twisted

nervously, obviously wishing he did not have to repeat the gossip aloud.

"What rumor?" With great difficulty, he kept himself from grabbing the man by the collar and shaking the news out of him.

"That you were seen climbing up Miss Fenster's trellis last evening." Freddie's face was pale, reflecting the seriousness of the allegation.

"How absurd." R.J.'s heart sank. Was it idle gossip caused by the play? Or was there more to the rumor? Had he been seen in the garden beneath Juliet's window? Perhaps they had not avoided a scandal, after all.

Neither Annabel nor his father would ever forgive him if his foolishness ruined Susannah's chances of a titled marriage. The thought that his sister would thank him was scarce comfort.

"That is what I have said to any who mentioned it to me." The man clapped him on the shoulder. "It makes a pretty story, with the play and all. Romeo and Juliet. But I couldn't credit it. You warned me about her yourself, after all. You would be the last man to chase after a flirt like Miss Fenster."

"The very last," he agreed dryly.

A footman appeared with a request for R.J. to speak with the duke privately in his office.

Freddie looked at him anxiously. "Would you like me to speak to Kerstone on your behalf, R.J.?"

"No, thank you. You are a good friend." As he watched Freddie walk away, he realized that he was now suffering the fate he had tried to save his friend from. He tried for a moment to imagine Freddie climbing up the trellis. Never.

He could not help but wonder, though, whether he should have let Miss Fenster have him, after all. He would much rather it was Freddie facing the duke this morning than himself. How did one adequately explain the complete loss of reason to a peer of the realm?

The duke sat impassively behind his desk, his hands folded in front of him. He did not rise, nor did he offer his hand as R.J. entered the office.

Instead, he nodded to indicate where R.J. was to sit. "I have sent my wife to fetch her sister, Mr. Hopkins. They will join us shortly."

"I understand, your grace."

"Before the ladies return, however, I must have the truth from you. Is this rumor I hear buzzing around me true? Were you fool enough to climb Juliet's balcony last evening and kiss her while she was wearing only a nightdress?"

"I regret to say that the rumor is true." He bit back the excuses that came readily to his tongue. In the end there was not one worth speaking aloud. "I was indeed fool enough to do that."

"Did it end with a kiss on the balcony, then, Mr. Hopkins?" The duke's voice was deceptively quiet, but R.J. saw that his hands gripped each other tightly enough for the knuckles to whiten.

He did not want to answer directly. So he settled for saying, "I intended to ask for her hand today, your grace. I thought I would do so after you had breakfasted."

Kerstone sighed. "That is not what I asked you, but I suppose it is answer enough, considering Juliet's penchant for following her heart rather than her head."

R.J. knew, from a lifetime of dealing with his own father's disappointment whenever he had not behaved as he should, that the best way to handle such a matter was a straightforward acceptance of responsibility. "We were wrong, your grace. I know that my behavior cannot be forgiven, but I hope you will not hold Juliet to blame."

Kerstone looked at him with upraised brows. "I am well acquainted with Juliet and her nature, Mr. Hopkins. I assure you that she has never been loose or malicious before. No doubt the play brought you both too close to emotions you were not ready to realize."

R.J. stiffened in his seat. Did the duke mean to imply that he had developed an interest in Juliet before last night? Nonsense. "It was simply a foolish impulse. There were no emotions."

"No? I did see the play, Mr. Hopkins." Kerstone's gaze was piercing. But he had not yet suggested a duel.

"We were simply reading Mr. Shakespeare's lines."

"Indeed." The duke sighed. "I know Juliet likes to pretend to other than the way she feels. I had hoped you would be a more honest sort."

"My honesty has never been questioned." Now it was R.J.'s turn to wonder whether he should request satisfaction.

"I apologize for my careless use of the word. I can see by your manner that your intentions are honorable and that you are prepared to deal honestly with Juliet.

I suggest, however, that you examine why you, without any emotions involved, found yourself climbing a trellis last night."

"The moon was too bright . . ." R.J.'s voice trailed off. His words sounded foolish to his own ears, and he didn't want the duke to laugh aloud at his feeble excuses. He just wanted to get the damned marriage over with and go home to Boston.

"I see. The moon is at fault." The duke's mouth did not twitch even a hair in amusement. Still, R.J. felt the formidable will suppressing the smile.

Ignoring the humiliation that swept over him, he asked pragmatically, "If you have already heard the rumors, I suppose everyone else has as well?"

"As you suggested, the moon was full of mischief last night." Kerstone lifted the note in front of him and held it out to R.J. "Unfortunately, you were seen."

"Seen?" He felt sick as he remembered the abandoned kiss he had indulged in while the moonlight shone full on the balcony. Anyone could have seen them. And apparently had.

The note was an elegant but obviously disguised scrawl. A woman's handwriting? He wondered who, fleetingly. In the end, though, who had seen them was not important. The note was damning enough. And the gossip would see his sin exposed.

Kerstone repeated the words of the brief note. " 'I saw Romeo Hopkins climb the trellis onto Miss Juliet Fenster's balcony. Miss Fenster, clad only in her night clothing, allowed her suitor a most unsuitable kiss.' "

R.J. said bitterly, "I like the signature better than the message: 'A concerned party.' "

"Nevertheless, the information is accurate."

"So there is no help for it? We shall have to make a hasty marriage. I had hoped for a few weeks, at least, to give the appearance of a courtship." He sighed. Annabel would be furious with him.

Kerstone seemed surprised. "Has Juliet agreed to a marriage?"

"She is reluctant. But I will make her see reason."

"I remember feeling a similar sentiment once, years ago. I don't recall that reason swayed my wife at that point." Kerstone again raised a skeptical brow. "I confess, I'm not certain anyone can make a Fenster woman see reason if she does not wish to."

R.J. was astonished. Did that mean the duke would not insist on the marriage? Did he not care about the reputation of his wife's sister, then? "I will convince her."

A nod. The duke stood and held out his hand. "I will leave it up to the two of you, then. You will convince her to marry, or she will convince you to give up your suit."

"What would happen to her if she did not agree?" He did not like to think of the shame and humiliation to which she would be subjected.

The duke shrugged. "She must marry. I imagine the number of willing suitors would decrease, but no doubt one could be found to marry her."

"Why would you do such a thing?"

"As you have freely admitted, you hardly know her. I am not likely to send her to America with a stranger if she is set against it. I would allow her to choose an English husband if she so wished."

There was a wordless cry from behind him. Juliet. He turned to see her standing next to the duchess. If not for her sister's steadying hand at her elbow, he was certain she would have already fled the room. Considering the depth of the dismay on her face, possibly even the house.

FOURTEEN

Juliet heard Simon's words in horror. Marry Mr. Hopkins and exile herself to America or choose an Englishman? An Englishman who would know, just by looking at her, that she had. . . . She would not.

Why had Miranda not warned her of what business the duke had with her? She looked at her sister with a mute plea for support and saw that she was white with shock. Apparently she had not known what the duke would require any more than Juliet had.

Miranda said, "Simon! Surely that is extreme."

"I'm afraid it is not, my dear."

Miranda, with an expression that indicated she was ready and willing to do battle for her sister, put her arms around Juliet. "For one kiss?"

Simon shook his head and, looking directly at Juliet, asked, "Is that all it was? A kiss?"

Juliet did not answer, though the heated flush that rose up her neck and covered her face probably revealed the truth. She glanced at Mr. Hopkins sitting quietly in the chair. What had he told Simon? She should have realized he would not keep his promise to her.

Miranda took her by her shoulders and, watching Juliet's expression closely, asked, "Tell me? Was it not just a kiss?"

Juliet, knowing that if she did not have Miranda's support, she had no chance of avoiding marriage unless she ran away from her family forever, whispered, "I don't want to marry anyone."

Miranda pulled her into a tight embrace. "Oh, Juliet! How could you—"

"I didn't mean to—" Juliet fought back tears and pulled herself out of her sister's embrace.

Simon, never all that comfortable with feminine tears, said dryly, "Mr. Hopkins seems to think the moon shares a large part of the blame."

Miranda gave R. J. Hopkins a suspicious look and asked Juliet in a hushed voice, "Did he force himself on you?"

Juliet stared at her oldest sister and then at R. J. Hopkins. "Force himself on me?" Had he? Was that what it was called when a man pushed inside you as he kissed and caressed your body until you wanted to scream with pleasure?

Miranda said sharply, "Did he do you violence?"

"Violence?" How could anyone think of what they had done as violence? She had noticed some soreness this morning as she dressed. But surely that was natural. For a virgin. Which she was no longer, she realized with a sharp pang of loss.

Her sister sighed. "Did you willingly make love with Mr. Hopkins? Or did he coerce you into doing so against your will?"

Coerce her? She glanced at him before she answered. He looked so miserably guilty, no wonder Miranda had asked. "Of course not." She tried to reassure him with a smile. "He would never do such a thing."

She could not help smiling through her tears as she confessed, "He was wonderful. So romantic—" To her surprise, he blanched at her compliment.

Miranda gasped, and Juliet realized that had not been the answer her sister was expecting. Hastily, she added, "But it was a mistake. I will never do it again until I am married; I swear it. We just—"

Miranda said softly, sadly, with a slow shake of her head, "Juliet—"

"The moon . . . the play . . ." Juliet could see that neither Miranda or Simon were swayed by her words at all. Mr. Hopkin's expression spoke for all of them. They intended that she be married. One way or another. Mr. Hopkins or whatever Englishman would have a woman who was no longer a virgin, Simon had said. Intolerable thoughts, both. The term *ruined* was not as much a misnomer as she had first thought. What would she do?

R.J. crossed the room to take her hand. With a gentleman's aplomb, he helped her to a seat and then sat next to her. He took her hand. As if they did not have several pairs of eyes focused on them, he said, "Miss Fenster, please do me the honor of agreeing to be my wife."

His face was so close to hers, she could see the nick on his chin from this morning's shave. She could smell the faint scent of peppermint again. Did the man bathe in it? "I do not even know you." She added bitterly, "Besides, you do not keep your promises."

"You will come to know me." He bent his head, the peppermint odor growing more defined. He said quietly, "We were seen last night. Someone sent a note to the duke this morning. You will do no good to continue to protest."

"Seen?" she whispered in disbelief. She blushed scarlet at the thought of what someone might have watched them doing on the balcony. "We have created a scandal?"

He nodded reluctantly. "I believe we have created a singularly large scandal. And it will only grow if you refuse to marry me."

Stubbornly, she did not want to believe such a thing. There must be a way to salvage the situation without marriage. There must. She would have protested further, but the door came open again unexpectedly, bouncing with a forceful bang against the wall.

Annabel Hopkins entered the room in a fury greater than any Juliet had ever seen. Ignoring her host and hostess completely, the woman crossed to confront her stepson. She positively hissed when she saw Juliet. But her words were directed to her stepson alone. "R.J., I forbid this marriage."

Simon stood. "Mrs. Hopkins."

R.J. stood as well, holding on to Juliet's hand and bringing her up to stand beside him. He said calmly, "The matter is decided, I am afraid."

Annabel Hopkins's nostrils flared with indignation. "I speak for your father on this matter. I hope you know what that means." The woman seemed to consider those words a grave threat.

R.J. tensed beside Juliet, as if he, too, feared his father's wrath. She glanced up at his expression, but the dratted man appeared as cool as if he were discussing the weather on a sunny day. Still, his grip on her hand was almost painfully tight, and she had to believe he was worried. How could that be? Surely a father would forgive his son an indiscretion. Wasn't it only women who were supposed to be tediously virtuous?

R.J. said quietly, his expression grave, "I understand what I have done and what the consequences must be, I assure you. Father will find Juliet to be an acceptable wife for me. Even if my method of choosing her did not meet his exact specifications."

"Scandal! Do you know what is being said about the two of you at this very minute? Romeo and Juliet! What a story! And you must believe the news will reach London within a day."

Annabel's scorn was scalding as she glanced dismissively at Juliet. "She is not a suitable wife. You need someone sober and serious. Someone who can grace your table, not someone who will seduce every eligible man in the city of Boston for her own amusement."

Juliet remembered, belatedly, that he had said his father would disown him for causing such a scandal. For the very first time, she understood that her life was not the only one turned upside down by their madness.

She sighed. Though she didn't like the fact much, she knew it was her responsibility to protect Mr. Hopkins—R.J.—from the worst of the consequences. If she must be married, at least she could choose a man who would never be able to lament the loss of her virginity before marriage. She said forcefully, "I may have been a flirt. But I know the duties of a wife, Mrs. Hopkins. And I will meet them so that R.J. has no cause to complain."

Everyone, including Miranda, turned to look at her, mouth agape. R.J. was the first to snap his mouth closed and smile at her with bemused approval. Sadly, there was no sign of the hunger she would have preferred to see in his eyes.

Simon moved to stand next to Miranda and said with finality, "We shall have the wedding in two days' time." He raised a single brow as he inquired with a glance at Juliet and R.J., "If you think you can manage to keep yourselves apart for that long."

R.J. said solemnly, "You have my word, your grace."

Juliet would have preferred that he hesitate a bit longer before answering. When Simon gazed at her, waiting for her answer, she sighed. "I promise, Simon. I will not so much as look at the man until I am his wife."

"Excellent." The duke turned to Miranda for approval. "If we can manage everything in such a short time." His gaze was warm, and Juliet realized with a little shock that they probably had experienced the same pleasure with each other that she had had with R.J. last night. Or maybe more, she reflected sadly, because they loved each other.

Miranda threw Juliet a troubled glance. "You are certain of this?"

"Yes," Juliet lied. She could not let R.J. be disinherited simply because she had seduced him and refused to marry him. Such a thing would ruin his life. She did not want that on her head.

Miranda smiled bravely at Simon. Well, then"—she nodded—"of course we can. We can work miracles here. You, of all people, should be aware of that, Simon."

The smile she directed at her husband made Juliet ache. She had lost the chance for a strong bond of love like that of her sister and the duke. Or had she? She glanced at R.J., so proper, so calm, and remembered him as he had been last night.

The question was, who was the real Romeo Hopkins? She would soon find out. And spend a lifetime living with the answer.

Two days. Forty-eight hours after she had agreed to the marriage, Juliet found herself standing in front of the minister exchanging vows with R. J. Hopkins.

She found herself accepting a new name, a new husband, and a new home in another country.

She looked into R.J.'s eyes as she recited her vows, searching for a glimmer of the fire she had seen the night she had tossed her future to the winds of chance. He had wanted her once, only days ago. Where had his passion gone?

She tried not to fear for her future as she listened to his steady voice, with his odd American inflection, reciting his own vows. Her mind reeled, unable to assimilate all that had happened since she opened her mouth to defend R.J. to his stepmother and found herself volunteering to be a dutiful wife.

What was she doing here? For a mad moment she considered running from the room, from the marriage. Only the knowledge that she had brought this on herself kept her standing here. No, not true. The man facing her kept her here as well. She wanted to see him look at her again as he had that night. He would. He must. Tonight.

As the minister pronounced them man and wife, her stomach clenched. He would kiss her now. Surely she would see the spark in his eyes then. How could he not remember what they had shared? He *must* hunger for what they would share in the future, just as she did.

As he bent to kiss, her she thought she saw an ember of desire. But his kiss was a mere brush of lips, dry and businesslike. As if he were sealing a deal rather than greeting his bride, the woman who must be by his side for the rest of their lives.

If only she could see a little of what she felt reflected in his gaze, she would not worry so much—despite the fact that the marriage, the wedding, the scandal had been so very different from what she had envisioned for herself.

"R.J." she whispered, hoping for reassurance.

"Only a few more hours, Juliet." His smile was bracing, but not sympathetic as he took her arm and led her away. Husband. Wife. Strangers. "Let us try not to create yet another scandal before the first has even spread itself to London."

She stood numbly at the head of the reception line, accepting congratulations from the few guests who had attended the ceremony and the supper to celebrate the marriage. She had dreamed of her wedding ever since she had been old enough to understand that she must one day marry. She had dreamed, and she had planned for the day.

The man himself had been a shadow. Handsome, she knew. But dark? Fair? She had not cared. But the dress. She had designed it in her mind. The palest, pearliest pink. Satin. A flowing train that the twins would bear in a solemn procession behind her. And the flower she would carry—a single white orchid. She had planned for a hundred guests. Family and friends around her.

Only one part of her dream had come true. Family. Her sisters had shown nothing but kindness to her. Her brother Valentine was here despite the haste of the plans. His wife, Emily, had needed to stay home at Anderlin with her sons. Juliet wondered sadly whether she would see Emily or her little nephews ever again.

She did not know how she would live without her family. America was so far away. How could she bear not to see her brother and sisters for years at a time? They were everything to her. She loved them all. And they loved her; she knew it despite their often exasperated reactions to whatever she chose to do. Including making love to R. J. Hopkins on a moonlit night. Valentine had even, sweetly, subjected R.J. to a four-hour interview last evening to ensure that the man was not an unsuitable husband.

"Juliet, are you well?" R.J. was regarding her with concern.

"I'm fine." She smiled, although she would have preferred to sob out loud.

"You look sad."

"I am. I miss my family."

"We have not left yet," he said reasonably, as if such a fact should counteract her feelings of loss. "You will not have to say good-bye to them until we return to London tomorrow to board the ship for Boston."

"I am aware of that, R.J.," she grated, trying not to let her annoyance with him show to any casual observer. "However, I am contemplating the final parting tomorrow. And that makes me sad." Why must she explain her emotion to him as if he were a backward child who had never been sad himself?

His lips pressed together, the only sign that he was not happy with her response. "Don't let your sorrow show, then."

But that is how I feel. She wanted to shout at him. His stuffiness exasperated her so.

He glanced about the room. "We must pretend that we are happy about the marriage or the scandal will be even worse."

Stung, she said sharply, "What does it matter what we *pretend*? People will say what they wish whether it is true or not."

"Juliet." His voice was cold and meant to quell.

She did not like being silenced. Especially not by

R. J. Hopkins, who had not looked once upon her with desire since. . . . "Very well, then. I will visit my sisters in the schoolroom. I know they will not gossip about me just because I am sad today."

Glad, she watched as he suppressed a flicker of dismay. "You cannot do that now. We are about to go in to supper. What will people say?"

She smiled as sweetly as she knew how. "Why don't you tell them that I am too nervous to eat, as I am in virginal terror of my wedding night." She gave a gasp of false horror, widening her eyes.

"Juliet." He seemed unable to say much more than her name. His expression was as unexpressive as a marble statue. Why didn't he get angry? Why didn't he shout at her? Why didn't he *want* her now that she was his wife?

A few curious guests glanced her way, so she lowered her voice when she added, "Oh, but you cannot do that, can you? Everyone knows I have already had my wedding night—unfortunately, not in anticipation of any proposed marriage." Unable to bear his coldness one moment more, she turned on her heel and fled.

What had he said? R.J. had only pointed out the necessity to keep one's private thoughts private. From Juliet's reaction, he might have told her she needed to lop off all her hair and wear sackcloth and ashes forever. He considered following her up to the schoolroom. But then the gossips would sharpen their tongues over the absence of both bride and groom from their own wedding supper. What would they think?

Heat flushed through him as he realized what would be suspected if they were both absent—that they could not control themselves and had stolen away to consummate the marriage. He closed his eyes briefly, fighting the surge of longing to follow Juliet, carry her bodily to his room—to their room—and show her that they need not regret the future.

Would she want him to? He didn't know. She had enjoyed making love. She had called it wonderful when the duchess questioned her. He had wanted to kiss her then, in front of the duke and duchess. Only his force of will had prevented him from making a fool of himself there.

He had kept a tight rein on his desire these last two days, knowing what he could have with her, needing what he would have with her tonight. And not able to act on his need until they had exchanged vows. Selfishly, he could think of nothing but tonight and the pleasure he would give her. But would the pleasure diminish for her now that she had no choice in the matter? She had wanted to make love to him that night. She had not wanted to marry him.

He pushed the difficult thoughts away as he saw his sister approaching. He hoped she would not notice that Juliet was nowhere about. Although he would have to find some excuse for Juliet's absence unless she returned before dinner began. Somehow he did not think she would.

Susannah hugged R.J. warmly. "I'm sorry that

Mama is being so miserable. But she did so hope that I would become Lady Blessingham."

Another regret to add to the pot. "I have made that virtually impossible, I fear. Unless you wish me to see—"

"No. Lord Blessingham is not for me. There is no one here." His sister's expression clouded for a moment, and then she smiled at him. "I am so happy that we are going home."

"So am I." R.J. answered. "I do apologize, though, that my foolishness should cast a shadow upon your life."

"Don't be silly." She laughed. "I am delighted to have a new sister. I am praying she can make you smile more, dear brother."

"Still, I am sorry for it." Though she seemed not to realize the damage he had caused to her reputation with his foolishness, he did. Annabel was right to be furious with him. He could only hope that the taint of scandal did not follow them back to Boston.

FIFTEEN

Susannah made a sound of exasperation. "I don't care a bit that my connection with you and your scandal make me an unsuitable bride for an English lord."

He could see that she meant every word she said. In some ways, his transgression had diverted Annabel from her plans for Susannah in a way that nothing else could have. "You got your way without having to tip your hand. I think you owe me a favor. Perhaps you can say a word in my defense to Father." He tried to hide his own misery under affectionate teasing.

"Of course I will," she promised before flitting off to say farewell to yet another friend she had made during her time in London. He expected she would be sending shiploads of correspondence across the ocean. His father would complain about the unnecessary cost, no doubt.

Father. R.J. would not want Susannah to know how much he dreaded the coming meeting between Jonathan Hopkins and Juliet. True, Juliet was not a dark-haired Italian woman, but her flirtatious behavior was akin to his mother's own behavior toward his father. He could only hope he could curtail her vibrancy enough to make living in the household together bearable.

He already knew he did not have Annabel's support in this effort. His stepmother had made it abundantly clear that she had no patience, for either his new bride or his foolish lack of discretion.

Curtailing Juliet's impulsive nature was already proving to be troublesome, he thought, as he remembered their last conversation and her abrupt departure. He reminded himself she had a loving nature, if a bit impetuous.

Surely his father would see her good points. After all, she had been one of the most courted young women in London. He sighed. If Juliet, who had won the hearts of so many suitors, could win his father's respect, perhaps the damage could be repaired.

Perhaps his father would trust him again. Perhaps.

But what a task it would be.

The duchess approached him with an air of concern. "Have you seen Juliet?"

"She went to visit the schoolroom one last time, I believe." He saw no reason to lie to her sister. Surely she knew Juliet better than he. She would know what to make of his bride's odd mood.

She nodded. "I remember how sad I was to leave my sisters and brother behind when I married Simon." Sadness shadowed her gaze for a moment. "Of course, I did not go an ocean away."

"We will visit, I promise." R.J. determined, even as he made the promise, that he would convince his father to further his interests in England. Juliet must see her family at least once a year. "And certainly you and the duke will be welcome in my home."

She smiled. "You must think me silly to worry about her. But you are strangers, after all." Her gaze was steady and searching as she watched him. "I trust you will treat my sister well. She is worried about being so far from family."

"I am her husband. I am her family."

As if she had not realized that until he spoke, the duchess blinked. "You are. But you do not know each other well."

He did not know how to reassure a worried older sister. What would ease his mind if he spoke to Susannah's husband in such a way? "I hope to curb some of her more exuberant habits, but otherwise we should get along well enough."

"I have no reason to think you will harm her, Mr. Hopkins."

"Please call me R.J., now that we are related. And be assured that I mean no harm to my bride."

"I know." She laughed. "R.J., I have questioned poor Lord Pendrake until he wishes never to see me again. He has nothing but good to say of you." She paused a moment, and he sensed she wished to say something more. "I do worry, though, that you know my sister so little, you may misjudge her heart to be frivolous. I assure you it is not." She hesitated, as if about to impart a great secret and not certain if she should.

Then she leaned toward him. "You cannot tell her that I told you this. In fact, if anyone in this room with the exception of our family knew, Juliet would not be welcome here."

His heart jolted against his ribcage. "Something worse than the scandal we have generated?"

"Oh, yes." As if she had recognized his worry belatedly, she held out her hands and waved them in front of her face as if to erase her words. "You see, scandal in matters of the heart is not unusual for our family."

"No?" He had heard rumors to such effect, but he had not thought it wise to pursue them. After all, he would be far from this family once he was back in Boston.

"Yes. Unfortunately, our family has generated even more scandalous situations." She looked at him speculatively for a moment, and he had the uneasy feeling she was imagining him upon the balcony with Juliet. "Well, perhaps not quite so traditionally scandalous. Why, Valentine was accused of murder, and his wife had to announce their clandestine marriage on the eve of her wedding to another man. So if you find it any consolation, you and Juliet have a rather run-of-the-mill scandal."

"Then what is it she has done that is so much worse it cannot be spoken of outside the family?" He wished he had heard this information before the marriage.

It seemed convenient that she waited until it was too late to tell him. Was there madness in the family?

"The buttons you find so foolish?" She waited for his nod before she continued. "They are her business."

"Her business?" He tried to sort out her meaning.

Certainly a well-bred London society woman would not be conducting business. She would be shunned.

"Yes. In fact, those very buttons are responsible for the dowry that she brings you."

"Buttons? She makes buttons?" He pictured her, for a brief moment, calmly carving buttons. The absurdity struck him almost as soon as the picture formed in his mind.

"No. She discovered one of the tenants at Anderlin, my brother's estate, had lost his legs and was not able to farm but was good at carving."

She was watching him carefully as she told him her fairy story, and he did not know what reaction she sought, so he was careful to give her none at all. "She brought him some ivory, and he turned out beautiful buttons for her to wear."

Miranda continued when he said nothing to encourage or discourage her tale. "She recognized that his talent, given adequate stone supply, would help Anderlin's financial situation. She convinced Valentine to allow her to travel to London to supply some of the more fashionable modistes with these uniquely carved buttons."

He found himself impressed despite his original skepticism. "That was well thought out."

"Yes." The duchess nodded, pleased that he understood. "Her simple wish to help a tenant has done much to bring Anderlin back to solvency, although it can never create a fortune to match yours."

"Why have you told me this?"

Her lips pressed together in disappointment for a

moment. "Because you have said that you value those who work for their living."

Did she equate making buttons with hard work? "I realize that seems a trivial thing in your society, working for one's living," he said. He was pleased, though, that Juliet would not need to have all the principles of good business explained to her.

"On the contrary. I do not consider the matter trivial in the least. I wanted you to see that Juliet is capable of more than posing beautifully in your parlor or singing tears to your eyes."

"Thank you." Juliet an entrepreneur. The idea would take some pondering. "I will keep your words in mind."

She said in stern warning, "But do not tell her that you know. She wants no one to know."

"I can see no reason to keep this a secret. It is admirable enough. Though she doesn't do the work herself, she did manage to make a man without a leg a useful part of society—given that buttons are a necessary evil."

A flash of dismay crossed her features, and he was certain that she wished she had not told him. On a sigh, she said, "Consider—if you allow her to tell you this in her own good time, you will know that she has come to trust you."

Come to trust him? "Why should she not trust me? I am her husband."

"Because you do not trust or respect her." She paused. "Yet."

He did not like realizing she was correct. "Your sister was beautiful enough to lure me to break a long-standing habit of acting with common sense. She is more than capable of earning my trust and my respect."

There was a touch of sadness in her voice as she answered: "Beauty is no protection against heartbreak."

"I hardly think she has anything to worry from me in terms of harm."

"You will be her husband. You hold her happiness in your very hands. Just as she holds yours."

Happiness? Better safety or health—those he thought he could manage. But happiness? "I will do my best to make her life all that she could wish."

"I'm certain you will. And Juliet will do her best to be a good wife to you. She, as I said, has a giving heart. I know she will try not to hurt you."

R.J. could attest to one aspect of her giving nature. He had yet to see her heart, however. The very thought made him uneasy. "Fortunately, despite my recent indiscretion, I am a very reasonable man. I do not think that reasonable men are vulnerable to the emotional storms which cause one to be hurt."

"I hope that you find you are wrong about that, R.J." She glanced at her husband, who was standing across the room, with great affection. "Sometimes I think it is when we learn how deeply it is possible to hurt one another, and then to trust each other, that we find the most satisfactory pairing of souls."

"I'm afraid I am not interested in pairing my soul with Juliet's. If she creates no more scandals, graces my table, and bears me a son, I shall be well pleased with her."

His words did not please the duchess. She shook her head as if he had said something foolish. "There is more to marriage than well-pleased, Mr. Hopkins. I hope one day you realize that."

Juliet stood for a moment in the doorway, trying to imprint the sight of her sisters at their daily routine into her memory to serve her until the next time she might see them. The air of gloom in the schoolroom surprised her. Had her mood transmitted itself up two entire floors into this usually sunny little room?

All their movements were listless. Rosaline had her paints, Helena, her sketch pad. Kate was curled up in the window seat with a book, and Betsey worked at her needlework.

She leaned against the doorjamb as the sorrow flooded through her. She would never see them this way again. They would grow into women while she was living in America.

Kate looked up a moment before Juliet regained her composure and saw her. With a little cry, her youngest sister leaped up and hurled herself into Juliet's arms, sobbing loudly. "I don't want you to go. Why can't you stay with us like Emily did when she married Valentine? They made a scandal, too, but they didn't have to go to America."

Rosaline threw her brush across the room and ignored Helena's appalled sound of disapproval. "Valentine and Emily didn't create their scandal because they went all crack-brained for each other, Kate. No. *They* had to deal with a murderer. All Juliet and her

Romeo"—her emphasis was not entirely kind—"had to do was fight some romantic claptrap that made them moon mad for an evening. And they failed miserably at it."

Helena said moderately, "Rosaline, you don't ever wish to be married, so you don't understand—"

"Of course I do. Juliet actually believes she can live one of Miranda's silly fairy tales."

Juliet said sharply, "I most certainly do not. And who has been filling your heads with scurrilous gossip, anyway?"

Rosaline raised a brow. "Do you mean now that you are not around to tell us the latest juicy news?"

Helena sighed, closed her sketchbook, and put it down. She rose to move over to Juliet and hugged her swiftly and hard. "I'm going to miss you. We are wasting our last few minutes with you squabbling. Shame on us."

Rosaline, as if realizing how rude her words had been, said, "I'm sorry. But Juliet, you don't even know the man. Not to mention that he is an American."

Kate stopped her sobs to look up into Juliet's face and ask, "You wouldn't marry him if you didn't love him, would you, Juliet? I hate him because he's taking you away. But you don't, do you? Miranda says never to marry without love."

Juliet felt more awful than she had earlier. Should she allow them to believe she was happy with her marriage? With her husband?

Or should she tell them the truth? That sometimes to do something reckless, no matter the pleasure, creates more heartache than it is worth?

"Of course I love him." She was surprised to realize that she did not lie.

She did love the man who had allowed his passionate nature to show.

It was the rest of him that she was unsure of.

Rosaline made an unladylike sound of disgust. "Love. Who needs it? If a man ever dared climb in my window, I'd run him through."

She hugged Kate to her and smiled at them all. "I am marrying a fine man. And America will be an adventure for me."

Rosaline frowned. "I do envy you the adventure. Boston. Do you suppose they are civilized there yet?"

"Of course they are." Look at poor R.J. Only civilization could do that to a man—pinch back the adventurous spirit that had allowed him to climb her trellis that night; to kiss her so that her mind ceased to function and her body came fully awake for the first time in her life. Even now he was ashamed he had done it; she could see the shame in his expression as he said his vows earlier.

"But it is so far."

"You will come for a visit. After all, the dowager duchess lives in America as well. No doubt Simon will bring you all to visit your American relatives very soon."

Tears began in Kate's eyes, and Helena stepped up to take her gently by the hand. "Look, Kate. I have the next best thing for us. If we cannot have Juliet, we can have this sketch of her." She held out a quick drawing she had done of her sister in her wedding finery.

"You are a marvel with your pencils, Hellie." Juliet saw herself from her sister's eyes. Beautiful. Happy. Had she looked so? Or had Helena been influenced by her own dreams of fairy tales?

"I have one for you to take with you as well." She paged through her sketchbook and paused to rip out a sketch.

Helena had none of her twin's brash nature. Her concern that her work would not measure up was written in her expression as she handed the paper over, careful not to crinkle or mar it with her fingers.

Juliet kept her expression blank as she studied the paper. The drawing had obviously been worked on with love and care. Juliet could not suppress her gasp.

Helena had sketched all of them, Juliet centermost.

In the drawing, Miranda sat upon an enormous toadstool, a book of fairy tales on her lap. Valentine stood sentinel over the family, just to her left.

Kate curled up against a window, her hair ribbon askew, a smile upon her face that suggested that she had just committed some mischief or another. The twins, Rosaline and Helena, posed by a tree, Rosaline high on a branch, Helena sitting with her back against the trunk, her sketchbook open in front of her.

Juliet herself was not only central but slightly larger in the foreground.

She stared at herself, surrounded by her family, seen through her sister's loving gaze. Helena had captured her, singing, in mid-note, her head thrown back more than was proper to do justice to whatever music she heard.

Juliet gathered the sketch to her chest, her throat

tight with tears she didn't want to shed in front of her sisters. "I am going to miss you all so much. Hellie, this is wonderful."

Looking at her sisters with tears in her eyes, Juliet tried to lock them in her memory forever.

Suddenly, the awful possibility loomed that she might never see them again. Even as she struggled against the awful realization, Miranda and Valentine entered the schoolroom together.

Miranda said softly, "Your guests are asking after you."

Juliet rolled the precious drawing that Hellie had done into a tight tube. "I would rather be here."

"Nonsense. You have an obligation." Valentine said sternly, as if he felt he must play the role of father, since their own was no longer living, "You must be a good wife, Juliet. It is time to put the impish games you played in the past aside. You have a husband, and you must behave responsibly."

She could not hide her fear. Not from them. "I don't know if I can."

"Of course you can," Miranda said quickly. "You and Hero ran Anderlin quite well after I married Simon. You are more capable than you know."

"I can certainly manage a household well enough." That only required a good housekeeper, after all. And R.J. must be able to afford such an expense, considering the gossip she had heard in London and the number of willing females vying for his attention despite his very uninterested and uninteresting nature. "But I don't know if I can be a good wife. What will he expect from me?"

Valentine treated her question seriously, much to her surprise. "He will expect you to behave yourself. He will expect you to think before you act now. He will expect you to treat him with respect and obey his wishes."

Juliet wondered miserably if she could do that. "As long as they are reasonable, I will."

Her brother nodded and kissed her cheek to comfort her. "I know you are frightened of the future, Juliet. But I have spoken to your bridegroom. He is a good man and means to be a good husband." His tone was bracing, as if to ward off further tears.

His words comforted her. She knew, however, that neither of them could answer her most important question. "What if I love him and he does not love me?"

"That would be most unfortunate." Miranda hugged her. "But other women survive such misfortune. He seems a good enough man. I don't think he will make your life miserable." Her sister linked arms with her. "Now, come down to share supper with your guests and show them you are not afraid of being a wife."

Juliet would not allow herself to cry at the less than comforting words. She did not care if he made her life miserable. She wanted what Miranda, Valentine, and Hero had with their spouses. She did not want a marriage that made do. She wanted one of passion.

She closed her eyes and made herself remember how it felt to be held in his arms. The passion she had seen in his Romeo. She squared her shoulders and allowed herself one sigh.

He might have the ability to be the husband she wanted and needed. But there was no doubt it would take work for her to mold him. She was not certain she was capable of such a daunting task.

SIXTEEN

R.J. was grateful that her sister and brother had managed to retrieve Juliet from the schoolroom in time for supper. To his eyes, she did not seem happy. Though she managed to keep a smile on her face during supper, he sensed the effort required to appear a happy bride. Politely, she assured everyone who asked—some solicitous, some curious, and some spiteful—that she was delighted to be traveling to America. He could tell she lied, but he did not think anyone else looked closely enough into her eyes to see her misery.

R.J. was no happier than she. He longed to comfort her, but what was he to say? She would be leaving her family. She might not see her sisters again for years if business in England did not prove profitable.

As the last of the dishes were cleared, the supper guests grew expectantly quiet. All eyes focused on him.

The duke stood, drawing the attention of the guests to himself, and said quietly, "It is traditional for us to celebrate a toast to the happy couple before they leave us." There were a few knowing smiles from the gentlemen and titters from the ladies. They would retire to their wedding bed tonight, after all.

The duke's rich voice rolled over the gathering, his gaze focused on the newly wedded pair. "As my wife would be the first to note, your meeting and your wedding have followed the fairy-tale tradition that seems to bedevil our family."

Juliet stiffened beside him as her brother and sister both chuckled softly at the duke's unfortunate remark. "But now you two must make your own happy ending. Just as Miranda and I, Valentine and Emily, and Hero and Arthur have had to do."

Simon gave his wife a warmly wry smile and then met R.J.'s gaze squarely. "I cannot say my determination to give my bride a happy ending has always been easy. But I would not change a day of my life since I met her." He raised his glass. "And I sincerely wish you two, no matter what it takes, make as happy a life as I have found with my own fairy-tale bride."

R.J. glanced at Juliet. Her smile was brave and sweet, but he was caught by the look in her eye, one that echoed the dread settling in the pit of his stomach. He forced the feeling away with an effort of will. Susannah had told him she hoped Juliet would make him smile more. He could only hope that life with him would not erase his bride's smile completely.

And then it was time for them to retire for their first night as a married couple. The duchess took Juliet away to prepare her for her wedding night. R.J. sat restlessly amid the jovial conversation of the gentlemen for a time, until the duchess returned and gave him a tentative smile. Permission to join his bride.

He made his way up to their room in a fog, with well wishes following him. Fighting an overwhelming sense of unreality, R.J. opened the bedroom door, not knowing what to expect.

The bed was empty.

For a moment he thought that she had refused him, had decided not to share his room tonight. He could not blame her. They were strangers, after all. He had even meant to suggest that they take more time to get to know one another before—but he had not. He had not wanted to wait.

"Does this feel as strange to you as it does to me?"

He saw her then. She stood at the window, staring at him. She wore nothing but a simple nightdress and wrapper, and he could not help but remember his first sight of her dressed so, on the balcony.

"R.J.?" She crossed to face him, and he caught the faint scent of roses.

He did not want to talk. Did not want to think. But he must. With heroic effort, he forced himself to say casually, "Yes. I do feel as if I am still playacting." He forced himself to move calmly about the room. To undress with his usual evening routine despite the fact that she was here with him.

She said nothing, but he felt her gaze follow him as he undressed and carefully folded his clothing into his trunk, ready to be loaded for their trip tomorrow. How would she want him to treat her? As if he had never touched her before? As if he knew the pleasure he could give her? She was his wife now. He must treat her as he had meant to treat Lucy Matthews. With respect and kindness.

As he closed the trunk, he heard her sigh behind him. He heard the sounds of the bedclothes rustling as she climbed into bed. The light went out.

He made his way to the bed in the dark. To his surprise, when he brushed against her, he could feel her trembling. He pulled back. "Are you afraid?"

"No."

"We can wait if you like."

"No!" It was the answer he had wanted to hear. But her tone strongly suggested that she wished to get an unpleasant chore over with rather than that she anticipated their lovemaking as eagerly as he did. He paused, listening to her even breathing in the darkness of the room. Absurdly, he found himself unsure of what to do with the woman in bed beside him.

Juliet wondered why he asked if she wished to wait. Why did he not take her in his arms and show her that the passionate man of the other evening had not completely disappeared? Did he no longer want her?

How could she tell? The sound of his breathing filled her ears. Even. Not the ragged breath of passion she remembered from before. Could he be back to the taciturn dry bones she had first met? Was the passionate man who had swept her off her feet a mere figment of her imagination, conjured up one night and never to be seen again? If so, she had only herself to blame.

Why had she not governed her emotions that night for once? If only she had told him to go when he asked. Told him she did not want his kisses, his lovemaking. Did not want his arms wrapped around her.

Did not want to feel him—She would make herself mad if she continued like this.

She would not.

He seemed to know how she felt, for he touched her gently beneath the covers and pulled her to him for a warm embrace. An embrace not of passion but of consolation.

Pressed against his chest, she could almost imagine that life might one day come back to normal. And then he kissed her.

She tried to push him away, her hands against his bare chest, the little hairs brushing against her fingertips. "What are you doing."

His puzzled laughter tickled in her ear. "Making love to my wife."

All of a sudden she changed her mind. Perhaps they should wait. "I don't know." She pushed harder at his chest until he released her. "We hardly know each other!"

He laughed, pulling her back into his embrace. "This is why we are married. Should we deny ourselves?" He showered a gentle rain of kisses upon her neck and shoulders. Did you not enjoy . . ." He stopped the delicious little kisses. There was a dawning apprehension in his tone. "I thought you . . ."

"Of course I did." As soon as she made the admission, she wished it back.

"Yes. I remember. *Wonderful.*"

She flushed to her toes. How had she ever said such a thing to Miranda—in front of both the duke and R.J.? Would he think her wanton? She stammered nervously. "I just thought we should get to know each other first."

"Get to know each other?" There was a bit of outrage underlying his question.

"Yes." She wanted to distract him, but how? "What is your favorite color?"

He sighed. "Blue, the very blue you favor in your dresses, as it happens." And then his kisses began again, and he murmured in her ear, "We have a lifetime to get to know each other. Don't tell me you want courting now?"

Courting. Was that what she wanted? She had been courted by dozens of men since she was seventeen years old. But never by R. J. Hopkins. He had not courted her, he had merely climbed her balcony and changed her life without the usual string of compliments and dance of temperaments that marked a courtship.

Perhaps she did want courting, then. "Is that too much to ask?"

His answer was much too practical for her liking. "What difference will it make now? We've married, and we must make the best of it."

The best of it. Did he not want her as he had wanted her that night? "So I am never to have a sign from my husband that he cherishes me because the marriage papers are signed?"

He made a sound of impatience and tightened his arms around her. "Juliet, you must understand. I cannot promise you poetry and chocolates. I cannot promise you the romance of your fairy-tale princes."

She protested, "I am not asking—"

His kisses grew less gentle and more insistent. "All I can promise you is that I will do my best to be a good husband." His mouth took hers, demanding a response.

Not the most romantic declaration. But if he tried, she must as well. "And I will promise to do what I can to please you." She touched him, tentatively at first. Despite his words, his body told her what she needed to know. His desire for her was not to be doubted. Not now. Not here in the darkness.

He groaned as she stroked him with surer purpose. "This pleases me more than you can know." His hands were warm on her breasts. She shivered as he pressed his lips to her neck. His restless hands spread a heat through her that she did not want to deny.

"I suppose it is a start." She gave herself up to his touch until they were both breathless and weak from pleasure.

After he slept, she found she could not. What did it mean that he could make her feel such things? Again, in his arms, she had felt the magic of the moonlight. The same magic they had shared that night he climbed the balcony.

But there was no moonlight here. Only darkness.

Simon's toast echoed in her memory. Had they somehow, unwittingly, found each other because they were fated to be together? When he made her feel like this, she could not help but think him her fairy-tale husband.

But in the cold light of day could she hold on to that belief?

* * *

Miranda, Simon, and Valentine came down to the docks to wish them a safe voyage. How odd it felt to her to stand with R.J., Annabel, and Susannah when she wanted so much to stand with her brother and sister. She did as she knew she must and hugged them all and promised to write often. Her heart screamed to her to leave with them, however, rather than staying here with R.J. and his family.

R.J.'s stepmother, having finished supervising the loading of their trunks, approached her. The woman had avoided her since the day in Simon's study when she had fruitlessly forbidden the marriage. But Juliet still remembered the bitter declaration that she was not a suitable wife for R.J.

Annabel watched as the carriage bearing the duke and duchess made its way through the crowded, hazardous dockside. "You would be wiser to stay here in the bosom of your family. I can see you recognize that." Her tone was all sympathy, but her underlying message was clear. She did not welcome Juliet to the family.

Juliet wished R.J.'s stepmother had continued ignoring her, right up until they reached Boston—and possibly even then. "A wife belongs with her husband. They know that, and so do I."

"Even when the marriage is so hasty and the husband and wife virtual strangers to each other?" Annabel stared at the departing carriage disapprovingly. "I would never allow Susannah to go to a strange country alone."

Juliet could not help herself from remarking, "If she had married a lord, as was your intention, you would have had to leave her with her husband when you returned home. How would that situation have been different from mine?"

Annabel stiffened visibly at the question. But she did not answer it. "Your family has been most kind and forgiving," she said snidely.

"They love me. They trust that R.J. will take care of me as he promised Simon. And that I will make him a good wife." She thought, for a single moment, that Annabel would kill her, would simply lift her white gloved hands and wrap them tightly around her throat until the breath of life had left her.

But then the brittle smile was back in place, and all she said was, "He needs a wife of stern mettle, my dear. I fear you will find yourself tested to your limits before long."

No doubt Annabel intended to be the one who set the tests. Juliet thought of the long voyage to Boston ahead of them and wondered if she could possibly survive it?

R.J. took his meals with her assiduously every day as they traveled. Between meals, however, he conducted his business continuously. Two secretaries followed him, taking notes, scribbling figures, and nodding their heads when he spoke. Juliet rarely saw him unless he passed through on his way from one meeting to another.

Not that she was bored aboard ship. No. There were plenty of amusements provided to the first class passengers. And R.J. did not mind that she spent a great deal of her time playing cards and walking upon the deck, either.

He himself would not consider indulging in such idleness. Although there were many other gentlemen who did not seem to disdain amusements, as R.J. and his father chose to.

There were times when the gentlemen surrounded her, plying her with compliments, that she could almost forget that she was a married woman. She recognized the danger in such forgetfulness. If she did not behave in a dignified manner, she was certain that there would be nothing but unhappiness for everyone.

Every time she chanced to glance around, no matter whether she was dancing, taking a stroll, or playing a game, she would see Annabel watching her. No doubt R.J.'s stepmother thought that Juliet would have an affair with one of the men who seemed to enjoy her company. But Juliet was determined to be a good wife. She had promised herself. She had promised R.J.

Annabel made R.J.'s father seem like a veritable monster. Sometimes Juliet hoped that R.J. would be disinherited by his father in a quick, but not too painful, scene upon the Boston docks. Then they would be free to return to England.

She knew it would be an enormous blow to his ego. But Simon would offer him a job somewhere. The man had proved himself to have a good head for business. Half the lords in London had sought out his financial advice. And half the gentleman on the ship seemed to do so. But those gentlemen, she noticed, were not so busy that they could not spend some time paying attention to the ladies.

To her great chagrin, despite their compatibility in the bedroom, all her compliments since the day of her marriage had come from gentlemen other than her husband. R.J. seemed insensible to what she wore, did, or—sadly—thought.

Mr. Handley-Brown was the first gentleman to remark upon her looking well each morning. She was certain R.J. took note only of the cost of the materials of any garment she wore. If pressed, she doubted he could name the color or style of cut.

However, Mr. Handley-Brown always made mention of how well the color complemented her complexion. Or how the lace at her throat made the delicacy of her neck evident. Annabel would sniff and mutter over her needlework, but Mr. Handley-Brown took no note. Juliet would not give her the satisfaction of appearing to be ashamed of speaking to a gentleman other than her husband. After all, they were in public. Annabel sat not five feet away.

At first, she had not known how a married woman should react except that she could not encourage him as a suitor. There would be no more suitors for her. She settled for treating the gentlemen as she did her brother and her sister's husbands. Not that Annabel appeared any more pleased with her behavior. R.J., however, said not a word to her. She supposed that meant that she was doing nothing untoward for a newly married woman. But she did not dare ask him outright. She would not want him to tell her that she should shun the attention she received. Not unless he was willing to spend more time with her.

Some of the men, she noticed, tired of her when they realized that she would not entertain more than friendship and went on to the courts of other ladies aboard ship. Mr. Handley-Brown remained faithfully friendly. As they chatted about their homes and their families and the flowers he raised, however, she learned Mr. Handley-Brown's secret. He harbored a secret fondness for Miss Tincton, a single lady traveling as companion to a wealthy widow.

In only a few days, Juliet had his confession. She teased him, hoping to push him out of his timidity. "Why do you spend so much time with me when you prefer to hear another's dulcet tones?"

He blushed, then looked to ensure that no one else had heard her comment. "She has been nothing but proper toward me."

"Don't you know a lady can show her favor by the utter unwavering attention to the propriety of her actions?" Juliet herself had rarely had the self-discipline to use that tactic. But she had seen many young women do so successfully.

"How so?" He leaned toward her eagerly.

She laughed. "If she calls you by name often, it is a sign of affection."

He straightened in indignation. "She would never use my Christian name."

"Of course not. But how often does she manage to say Mr. Handley-Brown when she speaks to you?"

His eyes lit up. "Quite often. At least twice, even in the shortest exchange of pleasantries."

"Well, then!" Juliet leaned back with a smile of encouragement.

His glow of pleased comprehension faded slowly as he contemplated what she had told him. "But what . . . How can I be absolutely certain she wishes my attentions? That I am not being forward?"

Juliet did not wonder how Mr. Handley-Brown, no matter how sweet or well-off a man, had attained the advanced age of thirty-four without a wife. "I suggest you ask her to stroll upon the deck."

He seemed shocked by the idea. "How forward. And what if her employer does not favor my request?"

"Choose a time when her employer has gone below for the evening. She does settle in for a nap about this time of day, and Miss Tincton comes back to the deck for a cup of tea and a little fresh air before her employer rises again. That would be the perfect time."

"What if—"

"She may say no, Mr. Handley-Brown, there is no doubt of that." Juliet sighed at his look of dismay and hurried to add encouragingly, "But remember that if she does so, it may mean nothing more than she is tired or that she has much on her mind. Take courage, man, and offer her a stroll."

"I shall." In a burst of affection, the man leaned down and planted a brotherly kiss upon her cheek. "I must thank you, Mrs. Hopkins. I have not known how to begin, and I feared the voyage would be over before I found a way to speak to her."

"Good luck, Mr. Handley-Brown." Juliet watched him go as she struggled not to laugh. Poor man, such a tizzy over a simple enough conversation. She would not like to see him when he decided to propose marriage.

She hoped her advice would give him the push he needed to be happy. If not with Miss Tincton, then

someone else who would appreciate a man who knew
how to worship the ground their loved one trod on.
Unlike R. J. Hopkins. She sighed.

SEVENTEEN

Juliet pushed away thoughts of her own discontent as she sipped her tea and watched the progress of Mr. Handley-Brown's courtship.

For a moment, as he stood before the stiff-spined woman who had captured his heart, she was afraid she had sent him into the lion's den by mistake. But then Miss Tincton's cheeks pinkened in shy pleasure as she rose to join Mr. Handley-Brown at his most politely delivered invitation.

One good deed done on the voyage, at least.

"My dear, I think you forget you are a married lady." Annabel never made a comment that was not thought out, so Juliet knew that she was to take the words as warning. But warning of what?

She turned to greet her husband's stepmother and sister. "I have not. I have my husband to remind me every day."

Susannah, stepping in with alarm, added, "R.J. has made no complaint, Mama."

Annabel frowned at her daughter until the girl looked away with a blush. Then R.J.'s stepmother turned her glare on Juliet again. "The way you encourage those gentleman, you would think you were looking for a husband rather than newly married."

Juliet could see nothing in her behavior that might deserve such criticism. "I am simply being friendly."

"Too friendly, I fear. But I can well believe that you do not understand how unfortunate your conduct has become."

"I believe I know what proper behavior is."

"Of course. Kissing a man upon your balcony for all to see. I find that behavior completely innocent."

Juliet knew defeat when she saw it. And her own defeat was implacable in Annabel Hopkins's features. But she was certain her behavior during the voyage was nothing to talk of. The gentlemen surely knew she was merely teasing them.

In London a lady was not expected to cease all friendly conversation with the opposite sex upon her marriage. Was America so very different? She sighed. Being married was much harder than she had thought it would be. Miranda and Hero made it look so easy. Just do what you would normally do during a busy day—kiss your husband several times a day, laugh at his jokes, blush when he looked at you with adoring eyes. Unfortunately, she did not know what to do when her husband didn't look at her at all.

Unlike the dozen or so gentlemen eager to spend time with her, her husband kept himself busy with matters of business rather than pleasure. Only at night did he become the man she had been swept away by. Only when they were alone in their stateroom did he treat her as if she made his blood sing and his heart fly.

"Gentlemen do not always make such fine distinctions. That is why a lady must unfailingly conduct herself with decorum," Annabel said with a tight smile. "Accepting a kiss on the cheek from a man who is no relation is in no way decorous."

"He meant nothing—"

But Annabel was not interested in Mr. Handley-Brown's courtship of Miss Tincton. "I'm afraid I must tell R.J. of this. Perhaps your husband can explain the dangerous waters you tread," she said smugly.

"I think more likely he will tell you that there is no need for me to wrap myself in mourning cloth simply because I am now married." Juliet forced herself to be calm. He would understand. Wouldn't he?

R.J. had been waiting for this moment, although he hadn't realized he had until the moment came.

"Thank you, Mama Annabel. I will speak to her at once." He could not bear to look into his stepmother's triumphant face any longer. She knew how her unwelcome news would affect him. He would be damned before he would allow her to see she was right.

"I cannot answer for your father, R.J., if you ignore—"

"I will speak to her. Never fear. I will be vigilant against any further scandal." He rose and took her arm, sweeping her out of his cabin.

He rubbed his hands into his temples as he decided what to do.

Juliet was bored. Had she tired of the game of being his wife so soon? Annabel had practically accused her of having an affair. He did not believe it. Not when she came to him so willingly, so passionately, each night. But he could not ignore the matter, either.

When she returned to the cabin to dress for dinner, he took her aside. "I have ordered dinner in the cabin tonight."

"Must we discuss Annabel's poison?" Her expression was mutinous, as if she might refuse dinner if he insisted on having the conversation.

He sighed. When might he have a discussion with Juliet without her temper? "She is concerned about the family, as she should be. None of us are served by gossip."

Begrudgingly, she admitted, "Mama Annabel does not like the way I converse with the other gentlemen."

His stomach knotted. Had he been mistaken in her? Surely it was too soon to worry about her conducting an affair. They had hardly been married two weeks.

He spent a moment struggling with his own sudden doubts. Surely she could not be so passionate with him if she had already developed an affection for another man. No, he refused to believe that. She did not have that kind of heart. "Have you been flirting heartlessly, my dear?"

"How can you ask me that?" He was surprised to see that his words had wounded her.

"If you have, I do not mind. I know that you do not intend to do anything to jeopardize our situation any further. Now, tell me. Why was Mr. Handley-Brown kissing your cheek?"

To his relief, there was not a speck of guilt in her

eyes when she said shortly, "Because I showed him how to approach the woman he is interested in."

He laughed with relief. "Matchmaking? I should have known." As he had suspected, he had nothing to fear. "Still, you must be careful. Even an innocent kiss of thanks can become a stain of scandal too large to blot up with explanation."

She did not seem at all chastened. In fact, her truculent attitude suggested he was at fault somehow. "Well, perhaps there would be no gossip that I am casting my eye on another man if only you paid me some attention."

"Pay you some attention? Like this?" He followed her suggestion, bestowing the attention of his lips to her neck. When she moved away, he followed and took hold of her waist so that he could nibble at her ear.

But she had fixed upon her idea and would not be shaken from it no matter the kisses he pressed to her neck or shoulder or breast. "Couldn't you put your business aside just for the span of this voyage?"

He closed his eyes. So like her to ask such a thing. "That's impossible."

"We could consider this our wedding trip. Men don't work on their wedding trips, do they?" She put her hand on his mouth to stop his kisses while she spoke.

Her argument was not unreasonable. But if he were to give in to her now, he would spend a lifetime catering to her whims, and he would not have that. So he avoided answering her directly. "What has brought this on? Are you bored already?"

"If you spent more time with me, then no one could gossip, not even Mama Annabel—"

"Juliet, you must understand." He sighed. "That is impossible."

"But—" He stopped her words with kisses. At least for a time, until they both lay side by side, exhausted from their lovemaking.

She ran her hand lightly along his ribs. "R.J., could you not spend just a little more time with me?"

"I'm sorry that I can't give you the kind of marriage you wished, Juliet." He gathered her into his arms and rubbed his cheek along the top of her head. "But we both must compromise. You must find your amusements without me. And I must do everything in my power to make my father see that I am not completely irresponsible."

"Surely he will not—" Shock robbed her of words.

"He will." His father was a hard man to explain, especially to a woman like Juliet. R.J. had no intention of doing so. He added, "I have to show him that one mistake doesn't mean I can't be trusted."

He could see that she intended to continue the conversation no matter his wish, so he released his hold on her and turned his back. He would pretend to sleep until he did, no matter that he missed holding her more than he thought he could bear.

But he must begin as he intended to continue with her. Juliet would twirl his will around her little finger if he allowed her to do so.

When R.J. moved away from her, Juliet was stunned. She had to bite her lip to keep from crying. Surely in a moment he would turn around and take her into his arms again. They had slept entwined every night of their marriage. But he did not turn back to her.

At last, she was so cold, she pulled the covers up to her neck. But the chill didn't dissipate even then.

At last she thought of a response. "So I am a mistake?" She was furious. No one else thought of her as a mistake.

There was no reply from him, and his breathing remained so even that she could not tell if he had fallen asleep or was merely pretending. She turned her back to him in a temper.

She would show him that she did not need him to entertain her during the day. And then, perhaps, he would regret choosing his ledgers over his wife.

Before she slept, she heard his quiet, even breathing and fumed. He slept like a babe, without even knowing how deeply he'd hurt her. So much for making a marriage work. Apparently that meant that he had no obligation except to please his father. And she must amuse herself without consideration for her heart or her boredom.

Well, she could take care of herself, and he would see that soon enough. If he didn't mind her flirting with the gentlemen, she wouldn't mind it, either.

Annabel's disapproval would give her a good enough indication as to whether or not she was on the verge of creating another scandal. She would not, she vowed, do that. R.J. worked hard so as not to be disinherited, she would not allow her behavior to cause him trouble with his father.

She would keep Susannah by her side at all times

so that she could not be accused of conduct unbefitting a married woman. Susannah would agree. She understood that Juliet meant no harm. She just liked to laugh. And she enjoyed making others laugh as well. Even if she could not do so for her own husband.

In the ship's drawing room, she did as she pleased. And she pleased the men. They enjoyed her laughter, her amusing tales of her sisters, her erstwhile suitors, and London life in general.

After a while, she was comfortable again, feeling as if she had recovered some of herself. Unfortunately, R.J. did not seem to notice how the other gentleman fawned over her. And he seemed immune himself from her persuasions. Except at night in the privacy of their bed.

No matter how she tried to divert him from his work, he would return again to his books, totting figures and making plans for the future growth of his father's company. Once, she had a taste of triumph when she convinced him to take a walk with her by arguing that it was good for his health to walk daily. After that, he joined her at least once, sometimes twice, a day. But it was her only victory against her biggest rival—his work.

One night, up on deck under the full moon, he took advantage of the empty deck to kiss her as the breeze caressed them lightly. In his eyes was the same passion and hunger that had made her throw common sense and caution to the winds.

She shivered at the sight and felt the dull ache in her heart when, the next morning, the moonstruck Romeo was once again gone without a trace. She would have given every pretty frock and jewel she owned to see that look in his eyes again. In the daylight.

The ache in her chest was a shock. Somehow her husband had won her heart, and she did not know how or when he had done so.

Now what was she to do?

Boston was a noisy city. The sounds seemed profoundly different from those of London. Juliet stood on the dock, absorbing the odors, the sounds, the sights, of this young and ambitious country.

The people spoke loudly, harshly, their accents sometimes difficult for her to understand. She tried to think of it as her new home. To think of it in terms of adventure, as she had told her sisters she would. The noise and bustle, however, seemed anything but welcoming.

A woman who resembled Miranda in a way that made a wave of homesickness wash over Juliet greeted her returning husband with a sound halfway between a laugh and a cry. The embrace they shared radiated their joy to be reunited.

Juliet wanted desperately to turn on her heel and reboard the ship. Unfortunately, R.J. stood behind her, blocking her path. Besides, she thought as her moment of panic subsided, her family would only send her back to face the marriage she had made with her own disregard for consequences.

She scanned the crowd, looking for a man with features similar to those of R.J. or Susannah. "Which man is your father?" she asked.

Annabel turned to look into the crowd. "I see Norton and the carriages." She pointed toward where two stiffly formal servants stood in front of two fine carriages. "Your father does not appear to be here." She frowned and turned to R.J. to say coldly, "No doubt your father does not wish to show his displeasure with your public display. How unfortunate your sister and I must delay seeing him again because you have lost all reason."

Without allowing him time for a retort, she swept forward to supervise the loading of their luggage onto the second carriage.

R.J. stared after her for a moment and then shared an eloquent glance with his sister that Juliet could not interpret. Was he hurt by his father's absence? Was he worried?

Could this snub be her fault? Juliet whispered, "Would your father truly have been afraid to meet you publicly?"

Susannah smiled at her in comfort. "No. Father does not often have the time to gather us from the train station or the dock. I have not known him to do such a thing ever before."

"True enough." He sighed. "I suspect Annabel just wishes to grind her heel into my sinful heart one more time before she must behave herself in front of Father."

Juliet tried to imagine Annabel curbing her use of sharp words and criticism. "Do you mean she does not say such things to you in front of your father?"

Susannah shook her head. "She would not dare. Father does not like recriminations or excessive displays of feeling." With one glance of resignation, she hurried to follow her mother to the waiting carriages.

A heartening thought at last. Someone who would not bow to Annabel's whim, as R.J. and Susannah both did. As they walked toward the carriages themselves, she stopped him for a moment to catch his gaze and hold it. "Is what Susannah said true? Does Annabel guard her tongue around your father?"

He nodded.

"Then I am looking forward to meeting your father no matter what Annabel has said about his intentions to disinherit you because you married me. If he knows better than to listen to Annabel, he cannot be a true monster."

He smiled. For a moment there was a look in his eyes that made her think he would bend down to kiss her, even in this public hustle and bustle.

Instead, he contented himself with saying, "I think he will be quite pleased to meet you, Juliet."

With a touch of pique, she asked, "Even though, as Annabel says, I caused a scandal and ruined you?"

"Even then." He took her elbow to hurry her along, and she wished instead that he had gathered her into his arms for a reassuring hug.

His words, however, were pleasing to her ears. "You have a way about you with men, Juliet. I don't think my father will be any more immune than the rest of us have been."

Possibly Annabel was wrong. Perhaps Juliet's behavior would not have to be perfect to prevent father and son from being divided.

* * *

R.J. knew that his words to Juliet on the dock were too optimistic. But she had been looking into his eyes with such hope. He had not wanted to see the relief on her face dissolve back into dread when he explained that Annabel did not criticize and complain in front of her husband. No. Her words were much more tempered. But they were just as deadly accurate at delivering her assessment of a situation.

Annabel did not even change from her traveling clothes before closeting herself with her husband. Before R.J., Juliet, and Susannah had removed hats and gloves, before he had finished issuing orders for baths and refreshments to be prepared for the travelers, a footman was informing him that his father awaited his presence immediately.

The command specifically ordered Juliet to go to her room to freshen up. Which meant his father wanted to say a few things for R.J.'s ears only. That could not be a good omen. He sighed.

He hoped his own abject apology, combined with his sensible and swift handling of the situation, would allay his father's fears.

As to the business he had conducted while away, he could not help but be proud of what he had to report. London was ready for their goods. And he had made many contacts his father had been hoping to make these last few years.

Who knew so many businessmen traveled to England? But then he realized that his father most likely had known and had been testing R.J.

When would his father decide that he had passed all his tests and need not be examined for failure any further? Probably not much longer, now that he had acquired Juliet for a wife in such a scandalous manner.

Then again, his father was a practical man. He would no doubt agree that the scandal, having been born in London, could be buried without comment here in Boston. As long as Annabel agreed not to say anything. He tried to imagine Annabel spreading gossip that would hurt her daughter's chances for a good marriage and could not.

He doubted that Susannah was likely to announce the scandal, since she had developed a distinct fondness for Juliet. Much to Annabel's chagrin.

He thought of his sister with a niggle of worry. She had been unusually quiet on the trip home. There was something bedeviling her; he could see it in her eyes. At first he had thought it was his own situation. But now he believed there was more.

He sighed. He must find out, of course, for he could not bear to see her hurt. But he must first deal with his father and with Juliet. After he had seen to reconciling his family to his marriage and his wife to her duties, then he would set himself the task of straightening out his sister's life.

EIGHTEEN

As he entered his father's study, his worries ceased. For now he would have to trust that Annabel would not let anything dire happen to her own flesh and blood. No doubt Annabel would be able to handle whatever it was. Poor Susannah if her secret was anything her mother did not approve of.

Jonathan Hopkins's expression was grave. "R.J., I am disappointed." He smoothed a note in front of him, as if by running his palms over the paper he was absorbing the words written there. "I thought I had taught you enough to know when to avoid the trap of a pretty face and a moment's impulse."

"Father, I was completely wrong." The words hung between them. He had expected his father to respond. Apparently his father required more apology.

In light of his behavior, R.J. had been prepared to grovel. Looking at Jonathan Hopkins's serious face, however, made him balk. He was the one forced to marry, after all, not his father. "I should never have allowed my impulses to lead me into an unexpected marriage. Still, I do believe that you have no cause for concern. I think you will find that Juliet will make a fine wife for me."

Jonathan Hopkins did not accept such assurances without question. "She is the sober woman you were looking for? The helpmate for a good businessman?"

Sober was not a word he would use to describe Juliet. But he did not want his father to get the wrong impression about his bride. "She is beautiful, true, and used to laughter. However—" He could not use Juliet's button enterprise to impress his father without breaking his word to her sister.

Or worse, letting Juliet know that he knew what she had done. "However," he continued, "I have found her to have good judgment." At times, he added silently.

"Good judgment," his father said mildly. "Remarkable, then, to think she allowed you to climb up to her balcony and make love to her when she barely knew you."

R.J. flushed. "No—"

His father asked quizzically, "She is a gold digger, then. Who calculatingly lured you into her seductive web so that she could enjoy your fortune?"

"No—" How could he explain Juliet to his father? "Once you meet her, Father, you will see that you have nothing to fear. She will be an asset to me. To my work. To our family."

His father sighed, a single sigh, heavy with disappointment. "I know the story, R.J. Annabel provided me with all the details I need."

R.J. began to protest, but his father raised a hand

to halt him and said, "I will welcome your bride." R.J. subsided with a nod. He could not ask for more.

His father continued: "I have little choice, given the circumstances. You are fortunate that Annabel feels we can hide what happened in England. Given that you went with the express intention of finding a bride, no one should question the fact that you brought one home."

"I hoped you would see it that way."

Jonathan looked at his son sternly. "But I tell you this. If your bride causes any scandal for our family, I will hold you responsible." He sighed, as if bearing a heavy burden. "Just so you understand what hangs on this momentous decision which you made without use of your common sense: I will not only disinherit you, but you, your wife, and any children she bears you will be out of my life as if you never existed."

"Father!" R.J. could not mask his unhappiness at his father's cold statement.

Jonathan Hopkins, ever uncomfortable with emotion, shook his head as if to deny that he had said anything that should upset his son. "Enough. We need not have shouting in my office."

"I—"

"Calm yourself, R.J. We are merely discussing what must be. I had hoped you did not inherit any of your mother's more unfortunate traits. But I see that was a vain hope."

"It is not."

"Good. I hope that is true, that your baser instinct has not led you into ruination." His father had not looked so sharply at him since the time he broke a vase running through the hall to show off a new kite. "If it has, I will not tolerate you taking our family business with it."

"I married hastily. I had one lapse in judgment." R.J. wondered if a description of the moon would soften his father. Somehow he suspected it would only add to his father's disappointment. "I will never allow it to happen again."

"Very well. Then we will talk of it no more." With a much lighter manner, Jonathan Hopkins asked, "How did your business go?"

Briefly, he updated his father on the most pressing business news he had. The tension in the man across the desk from him gradually abated as they spoke.

At last, with the closest approximation to a smile that he could manage, his father waved him away. "That is enough for now. Go up to your bride and show her around so that she might be comfortable. I will meet her before dinner."

R.J. bowed. The meeting had left him more shaken than he would have his father know. He had no more room to make mistakes. Not that he made allowances for his own failure.

But with Juliet now, still accustoming herself to Boston ways . . . He must make certain that he convinced her to take Annabel and Susannah's lead in making her way.

He hurried up to his bedroom, grateful to be home at last. He stopped short in the open doorway, however. The room was—well, there was no other word for it but chaos. Trunks sat open, and brightly colored clothing rioted on every surface, including his bed. Juliet.

With his father's warning ringing in his head, he had somehow managed to forget that his wife would be here waiting in his bedroom. Her bedroom. She sat at a small dressing table, before a mirror that he had used for draping his cravats.

He closed the door, admiring his wife in her wrapper, fresh from her bath. She slowly worked some cream or other into her cheeks, chin, and forehead. He suspected her mind was elsewhere, for she didn't seem to notice that he had arrived. He was content to lean back against the door and enjoy the sight.

After an amount of time that could have been seconds, or hours, she glimpsed him in her mirror. He saw in her eyes a reflection of his own surprise at the idea of sharing a bedroom. A reflection of the same pleasure at the idea. And then she frowned.

As she turned, he saw her struggle to hide her sudden anxiety from him. "How is your father? Has he disinherited you?"

Juliet's concern jolted him back to reality from the pleasant fantasy he had been enjoying. "Of course he has not disinherited me." Not yet.

"He is well? He did not let you refresh yourself after our travels before he summoned you."

"He is hale and hearty and eager to hear how my business prospered." Should he tell her what his father had said?

No. He did not want to see the smile on her face dim—or disappear. He had sensed her fear as they had left the ship and traveled to what, for him, was home. No doubt, to her this house, Boston itself, was as strange as all of London had been for him. She needed time to settle before he burdened her with his father's fears.

"He could not wait for that?" She raised her comb, her expression disapproving. "Your father is as impatient as you if he could not let you change before he had the business details from you." She ran the comb through her hair, leaving order where there had been tangles.

He moved to stand next to her, his hands on her shoulders. "My father is all business." He lifted her sweet scented hair to his nose for a moment. "Time is precious in business. A few days' lead on the competition can make all the difference."

"So he is not as furious at you as Annabel expected?" She lifted another pot of cream from her dressing table and began to stroke it into her neck. The scent of roses wafted up to tickle his nose.

Better to give her a compliment than a warning right now. "You are beautiful; you don't need all these little jars of . . . whatever these are."

She smiled at him, distracted, as he had intended. "What do you know, silly man?"

"I know you are the most enchanting woman I have ever seen in my bedroom."

Her laughter was music to his ears. She had not laughed as freely since their hasty wedding. "And just how many women have you had in your bedroom, sir?"

"Only my wife." He bent to press a kiss to her

damp hair. "Who is much too beautiful for pots and potions."

She leaped up and threw her arms around his neck. "I must do all this"—she gestured to the little table of creams and beauty ointments—"so that I remain beautiful in your eyes."

He remained quiet, enjoying the feel of her pressed against him. Idly, so as to keep her there, he raised his hands to circle her neck and stroke up the straight column.

His thumbs skimmed lightly, but still he could feel her pulse accelerate. Her response redoubled his until he could hear the blood rush like a pleasurable waterfall inside him.

She sighed in pleasure and gave herself up to the caress, her eyes half-closed in contentment. The slim, straight neck bent for him, offering him access to the most sensitive place under her ear. So fragile under his hands. Almost as fragile as his hold on his father's respect. He could lose everything he held dear with one mistake. But he would not.

Pushing back any fear, he bent to kiss her neck and paused to allow the sweet scent of her to waft over him. He would do no good to worry now. He would be on guard for them both. He would make certain that nothing went wrong.

She brushed her cheek against his chest and then recoiled with a small sound of distress. "Oh, look what I've done." She dabbed at the cream she had rubbed onto his jacket.

"Don't worry. Mrs. Marlberry is a wonder at getting

stains out of clothing." He tried to bring her back into his arms.

She resisted him with a teasing laugh, pushing him toward the dressing-room door. "Hurry and bathe or the water will get cold. Your father kept you quite some time."

Reluctantly, he moved to the dressing room. The humid air promised a still-warm tub as he worked his cravat loose.

She peeked around the doorframe. "You need help," she declared with a wicked smile. And then she was helping him off with his clothing.

He stood motionless under her ministrations, marveling at this new facet of his wife. She had never offered such a service aboard the ship. But then, although they shared a single bed every night, she had had a separate room in which to dress and bathe. They had come together only to make love. He had never known what he missed not to share quarters with her more intimately.

Her hands were as deft and skilled at undressing him as any servant's ever had been. But no servant's fingers would have trailed along his ribcage or caressed his hip in order to push his trousers down. Nor would a servant's hands have skimmed his legs as she bent to remove the trousers from around his ankles.

She folded the trousers neatly and put them on the rack meant for them. She reached to unfasten his shirt, and he loosened the tie to her wrapper. Pulling her close against him, he sighed. "Dinner is in only two hours, Juliet."

"Then let me assist you in the bath." She reached into the tub and splashed a little water on him.

He divested himself of the remainder of his clothes and reached for her with a laugh.

There was no point worrying her with his father's ultimatum. Juliet would not be the final wedge between R.J. and his father.

Perhaps she would even bring a measure of happiness into this grim household. Funny, he thought, as her hands slipped wet and warm over him, he had never realized how stultifying his life had been until this moment. Until Juliet had turned his bedroom into a place of colorful, joyous chaos.

Juliet wondered what kind of family she had married into. R.J.'s father was truly formidable. As soon as she entered the dining room, she saw him sitting at the head of his long oak dining table almost as regally as the duke ever had.

He waited, watching them gravely and enigmatically as R.J. led her to his right.

R.J.'s arm was tense as a harp string under her hand. "Father, may I present my bride, Juliet."

Jonathan Hopkins stood and took her hand briskly in his for a moment. "Welcome to our family, Juliet." He said nothing more, but she had a feeling there was more he wished to say.

His expression was impossible to read. He could have been furious to have to greet her. Equally, he could have been pleased. She did not know how to interpret the calm, neutral lines of his mouth and chin.

"Thank you." Juliet didn't know what else to say. For once, she could not find a response she thought would put a smile on the face of the person who addressed her. Silence hung for an awkward moment.

R.J. stepped in to say, "I'm sorry we are late for dinner, Father. I'm glad you did not wait for us. I would not have liked to interfere with the household routine."

Juliet glanced up to see if he had meant his comment to sound bitter. He had not seemed to think it an unusual rule when he had explained it to her up in their room.

Of course, she had been tickling his ear with her tongue at the time. His face, however, she was dismayed to see, was as inscrutable as his father's.

Jonathan Hopkins, with a glance down the length of the table, said sternly to his son, "Dinner is at eight sharp. You know Annabel deviates from the schedule for no one, not even myself."

"Indeed I do, Father. And I have informed Juliet as well. I do not expect we will be late again. Do you, Juliet?" Again, Juliet could not see any emotion at all in the features that had become so familiar to her.

She said quickly, "Of course not. I would not want to disrupt your schedule here."

Annabel raised a brow at this assurance, but Jonathan Hopkins merely nodded and said, "I'm afraid we must wait until after dinner for a better chance to get to know each other, my dear, since you were unable to come down for a drink in the parlor before dinner."

Again, she sensed a tension that was at odds with his bland expression and regret in his words.

"As I said, I'm sorry, Father." R.J. led her away from his father, toward a seat at Annabel's right hand. "Dressing for dinner was more complicated, given that we have just arrived home. I assure you we will be on time tomorrow."

There was no indication from R.J. that the delay had been a pleasant, passionate one. If Juliet did not have her own warm memories of the pleasure they had shared not long ago, she would have refused to believe that R. J. Hopkins knew such emotion existed.

"I'm certain you will not disappoint us tomorrow." Jonathan Hopkins did not precisely smile, but Juliet felt that was the meaning of the small movement of his lips. To her surprise, he moved to where she was about to sit down, took her by the shoulders, and leaned over to peck her cheek. "I very much wish to get to know your wife now that she has joined our family."

Juliet sat in the chair R.J. held out for her, pleased to see that he then moved to sit opposite her. She needed his reassurance that she did indeed belong here. The tension in the ornately decorated room was palpable. Even Susannah, normally an easy companion, bore a strained expression.

Was this not a simple family meal? Is this how they dined each evening even without a new daughter to greet? Or had her presence added this?

To Juliet's surprise, as she glanced around the table, she saw that there were guests on their first night at home. Jonathan Hopkins introduced them briefly as the first course was served by maids in starched uniforms of black.

Dr. Phineas Abernathy and his wife, Drusilla. A more mismatched couple Juliet had rarely seen. She smiled politely in greeting. What had they been told about R.J.'s marriage? About his new bride? She felt unaccountably nervous and knew that she was likely to feel this flutter in her stomach for weeks to come. The best she could hope for would be that the stories told to explain R.J.'s hasty marriage treated her kindly.

"What a beauty you caught across the sea, R.J." the doctor said with an appreciative survey of Juliet that made her flush warmly.

Dr. Abernathy was handsome to the point of sin. Dark curling hair, warm green eyes, and an expansive nature that made one feel as if he had been a friend since childhood. She smiled a genuine smile at him, prompted to an almost natural response by his open, approving gaze.

"I'm afraid I ran off with the toast of London, Phineas." R.J. did not noticeably take offense at the compliment to his wife by another man.

Dr. Abernathy's wife, on the other hand, was clearly not pleased. "How nice it is to meet R.J.'s new wife." She spoke "wife" with her mouth pursed small and the word a mere exhalation of breath, as if she might say plague.

Juliet did not like the cold glance she received from the woman's small eyes, even though the welcome was properly phrased. She wondered again what stories had preceded her arrival in Boston. Did this woman know the true story behind the marriage? She hoped not. Those eyes were not friendly, and the woman seemed to be a harsh judge of others.

Drusilla Abernathy was somewhat older than her handsome husband. A portly woman with none of the warmth of some women of a certain age, her small, round eyes gazed out upon the world with suspicion, following every movement in the room. Perhaps the obvious age difference between herself and her husband had led to the air of jealous watchfulness that permeated the atmosphere around her.

Juliet was certain the doctor's wife could have accurately recited the type, color, and number of each flower in the elaborate flower arrangements placed around the room. As well as each dish served and any tiny infraction of etiquette a servant might commit during the course of service. Again, she thought, a more mismatched couple than these two she could not imagine.

NINETEEN

As the conversation flowed around her, the tension lessened considerably. She learned that Dr. Abernathy was a physician of repute in Boston.

Drusilla had met him when he attended her dying mother. They had been married for ten years and had no children.

Apparently, judging by the conversation and swiftly exchanged glances of understanding between them, Drusilla and Annabel were friends from girlhood. The easy communication between the two women made Juliet homesick once again for her sisters.

Deliberately, Juliet did not try to force herself into the conversation. Though Susannah and R.J. made polite attempts to involve her, she knew that she would find out far more by just listening to them speak to each other than she would if they spent their time questioning her about London and English society in general.

She was grateful, though, for Dr. Abernathy's witty asides to her, which as a rule required no more than a smile or a laugh. The oppressive air of respectability and responsibility seemed to lift with someone else in the party who knew how to smile long and often. Dr. Abernathy's charm and engaging personality lightened everyone's mood—even, to Juliet's astonishment, Annabel's.

His laughter was not completely unrestrained, she knew. His wife's reproving sniffs saw to that. She saw the shadow that crossed his expression whenever his wife served to dampen the mood he had strived to lift. But he said nothing to her, did not even give her a glance of reproach.

Still, Juliet thought that sometimes he flirted a little overmuch with her just to provoke a sniff or a "Phineas!" from his wife. She did her best to ignore her suspicions, however, for it was so pleasant simply to enjoy his company.

Unfortunately, as the evening progressed, the warm attentions of Dr. Abernathy only increased her unease. Each time he flirted with Juliet, his wife's mouth pinched in more narrowly. Juliet was not unfamiliar with the reaction and had rarely troubled herself about such foolishness before. If Drusilla Abernathy could not recognize the difference between amusement and seduction, she was likely to frown herself into a prune face within the next decade of her marriage.

Juliet was quite sure that Dr. Abernathy flirted from natural temperament, not attraction, as he shared his attentions equally between Juliet and Annabel, who giggled like a schoolgirl once, to Juliet's dismay. If he also took a little pleasure in his wife's disapproval, that was only to be expected.

The woman found little pleasure in anything. Even the dishes she consumed to the last crumb were dismissed with comments like "Too salty." "Too dry." And, most outrageously, "Too tender."

The only restraint Dr. Abernathy showed in his behavior was toward Susannah. He treated her more like a child than a young woman who might soon be married. At first, Juliet thought nothing of his treatment of Susannah. Any family friend might think of a daughter of the house in such a way.

Her heart sank, though, when she observed Susannah's reaction to such treatment. She laughed too loudly at his jokes. She watched his every move. She listened to every word he said as if they were each a pearl of wisdom she must not miss. The girl was obviously smitten with the good doctor.

As she watched the pair, Juliet doubted her own supposition that his restraint was due to his certain knowledge that there was no hope of a dalliance with a young, unmarried daughter of friends. Gradually, she became certain that more was at work.

Whenever Susannah would attempt to gain his attention, he would divert the conversation back to a safe topic in which they could all converse. His actions were deliberate, and his ease in changing the subject suggested to Juliet that he had grown used to doing such a thing.

Juliet knew from experience that it was not easy to change the flow of conversation to avoid flirtatious exchanges when someone as persistent as Susannah was involved. Nor was it possible to remain unaware of the tender feelings of the other party. Apparently, the two of them had been engaging in this little conversational dance for quite some time.

That he still went to great trouble to keep Susannah from unwittingly revealing her feelings to her family raised a warning sign to Juliet. The man obviously cared for her. She only hoped he would do nothing about his feelings. The tragedy of Romeo and Juliet would be nothing compared to their agony should they reveal their feelings to each other.

No wonder Susannah had been so relieved to escape London without a husband. She had focused her admiration on someone here in Boston. Someone dashing and admirable. Someone she was perhaps too young to understand she could never have.

Juliet allowed herself a moment of regret for Susannah's inevitable heartbreak. Phineas Abernathy and Susannah Hopkins might have made a good match—if Drusilla Abernathy had not already married the man when Susannah was still in the schoolroom.

She wondered briefly what had made Abernathy choose a woman who took such pains to dim his natural charm. The answer, she realized with a pang of sorrow for Susannah, was as old as time. Money. Wealth.

She glanced at R.J. There was another age-old reason for a mismatch. Did he regret the night he had climbed her balcony? He had not complained as they cavorted in the bath earlier. But he spent so little time at home that she sometimes forgot she was married for hours at a time. Until he came into the bed and she remembered what bound them together—forever.

Remembering the feel of him, warm and slippery from his bath, she caught his eye and smiled. Apparently he could read her thoughts, because a distinct flush crept into his cheeks as he returned her smile.

R.J. had to look away from Juliet's frankly appreciative glance. Clearly, she remembered their last few hours as well as he did. To distract himself, he turned his attention more fully on the conversation around him.

"How is your work with the poor faring, Dr. Abernathy?" Susannah asked yet another question of the man. R.J. watched his sister, wondering why she found Phineas's work so fascinating. She asked after his charity practice every time the Abernathys visited.

When Phineas beamed with pleasure and began to expound on his favorite subject, R.J. had his answer. She was simply practicing the skills she would one day need to be a hostess for her husband.

She listened so intently, he could almost believe she was interested in what the doctor had to say as he laughed ruefully and said, "At times I wish there were a dozen of me. There is a great need for physicians to help the poor."

"I hardly see why the poor should be in more need of a physician's aid than their betters." Annabel did not understand Phineas's charity work, and it showed in her contemptuous tone.

His stepmother had made it clear through the years that she felt her friend Drusilla had married beneath her. Sometimes, though, R.J. wondered if she compared the handsome, charming Dr. Abernathy with Jonathan Hopkins and felt a prick of jealousy.

Phineas treated the question as if it were seriously meant. "Disease seems to hit those living in poverty with more virulence. Sometimes I despair of ever turning the tide of death among the poor. Still, I feel I am making a difference in the lives of those who are not too afraid to see a doctor when they are ill."

Apparently Susannah's tender heartstrings were touched by his comment, for she leaned forward to say passionately, "Why would they fear you? Don't they understand that you can save them."

"I cannot save them all, Susannah." Phineas seemed nonplussed at her vehemence. R.J. decided he should counsel his sister later not to become so emotional during a conversation that it made her guest uncomfortable. "For many of them, all their experience tells them the sight of a doctor heralds death. I cannot blame them for fearing me."

"Surely they have merely to look at you to see that you are a wise and capable doctor?" Susannah's naive compliment brought a flush to Phineas' cheeks. R.J. suppressed a chuckle of amusement. The man was so handsome that he was subjected to the most outrageous compliments on his looks and charm; he took them without thought. But a compliment to his medical skills—that still brought the man to a blush.

He glanced at Juliet, wondering what she was making of this first dinner with his family. Would she be angry with him for allowing time to slip away from them so that they arrived like errant children late to dinner? He saw no sign that she had such thoughts.

His wife did not return his glance, however. She was avidly following the conversation that Susannah had initiated with an odd expression of worry. He hoped the topic of poverty had not distressed her. He considered Phineas's passion for medicine and helping the poor his Achilles' heel. He would discuss it forever, which Susannah well knew.

Phineas was arguing with Susannah's contention that the poor should consider him a god. "My dear Miss Hopkins, these people see that I am well fed and healthy. They see that I charge a fee."

"Not enough," Drusilla put in tartly.

Phineas's eyes flashed with anger. "I charge what my patients can afford." This was an old argument between them.

Susannah, oblivious to the tension between husband and wife, said blithely, "It is a shame that you can't just give them the help they need."

R.J. interrupted her, hoping to calm the antagonism between husband and wife. "A man doesn't value what he doesn't pay for, Susannah. Dr. Abernathy is right to charge whatever the patient and his family can afford." He turned his head to catch Juliet's gaze and smiled. "Everyone deserves to keep whatever dignity they can."

Juliet chimed in to help him ease the situation. "A man does not like a handout nearly as much as something he has earned, Susannah." R.J. felt a jolt of possessive pleasure. For the first time, he felt that the two of them were a pair, allied against any forces that might threaten their harmony.

"He should charge for supplies and his time, at the very least," Drusilla Abernathy said sharply, unwilling to let her point be lost.

R.J. sighed, wondering if he could avert the coming storm. His father would be displeased, but he did not think there was any way short of dragging one of them from the table. On any other matter, Phineas would have deferred to his wife, allowed her the last word, and considered the matter no more. But not when she attacked his practice of medicine. "That is why I charge my wealthier clients more for my time, Drusilla. They can better afford to pay the obscene rates we physicians charge."

R.J. watched his father grow more and more distant as Drusilla continued the argument. "The more your fee, the more you are respected." He wondered why Annabel had not stepped in to calm her friend.

"Yes." Phineas at last seemed to realize that he was not being a good guest. He added mildly, though it obviously cost him effort, "For my wealthy clients I have conceded that truth to you years ago, my dear."

"You should do the same for all your clients."

Juliet came to his defense in an ill-timed attempt to calm things. "But who is to say that a patient returned to good health by Dr. Abernathy for a low fee will not then become able to support his family better, to make more money for himself, and to afford to pay more of a fee the next time his family has need of your husband's services?"

To his relief, Annabel, after a short shocked silence, remembered her hostess duties and said sharply, "Perhaps this subject is better left to the men. They understand the business so much better than we women, after all." Her smile was brittle, and her glance at both Juliet and Susannah scalding with disapproval.

Juliet said nothing, although he knew that she

wished to argue by the stubborn way she pressed her lips together and flared her nostrils slightly.

Susannah, however, did not remain silent. "Why can we not discuss such things? Father and R.J. admire hard work. They have said so numerous times. They expect us women to understand that sentiment. Why should we not speak of Dr. Abernathy's worthwhile toil?"

Jonathan Hopkins at last stepped in to say quellingly, "No one is saying that Dr. Abernathy does not do admirable work—"

For the first time in his memory, Susannah interrupted her father to continue arguing her point. "In fact, I wish I could do more than speak of it. I wish I could do something to help those people myself."

"What, with all the wisdom of your eighteen years, would you do?" Annabel's question was obviously meant as a sharp scold. Her intention no doubt had been to reduce Susannah into chastened silence.

Susannah, however, fueled by some frustration he could not comprehend, uttered the unthinkable. "I would become a doctor myself."

There was a stunned silence that even R.J. welcomed. What sensible thing was there to say about his sister becoming a physician?

Annabel broke the silence with a nervous laugh. "What an absurd idea, my dear."

"Why?" Susannah, who had always been a touch high-spirited for her quiet family, turned unexpectedly belligerent. R.J. watched his sister in astonishment as she challenged her mother. Hectic color burned in her pale cheeks as she gazed at each of them in turn, saving her most furious gaze for her mother. "Why should R.J. and Father work hard and we not carry our burden as well?"

"But we do." Annabel's fury made her voice extra quiet and extra reasonable. R.J. knew the repercussions of that quiet voice much too well. He suppressed a shiver as Annabel continued: "We provide them with a comfortable home and pleasant company."

"Exactly, my dear. And we men understand that to do so is woman's honest toil." Jonathan Hopkins spoke calmly, his voice an instrument to quiet the stormy seas of the conversation.

R.J. glanced at his father, wondering if he had any awareness of what fate his wife's soft voice portended for Susannah. But other than the faint twitch at the corner of his father's mouth, he saw no emotion at all.

He sighed. As usual, it would be up to him to protect his sister as best he could. Susannah would pay for her outburst in private. He would see if he could step in later, when matters had calmed. He did not like to think of his gentle sister at Annabel's mercy. Nor did he wish to give Annabel any further reason to be angry with Susannah. Perhaps he could suggest that her unusual behavior was a result of a great disappointment in losing her chance at a titled husband.

Though the idea was ludicrous, Annabel would most likely consider it reasonable. And then her anger would be aimed at R.J. and his scandalous marriage to Juliet. He sighed again. He must ensure that Annabel did not take out her redirected anger upon Juliet.

Juliet, with a frown at Susannah, said, "Not to mention children. They are quite a deal of work for women as well."

Unfortunately, her words roused Drusilla, who turned three shades of plum before she asked, "And how would you know that? Have you any children yourself?"

Juliet turned to him for support, but all R.J., horrified, could do was wish that he had warned her of this trap ahead of time.

Without his support, Juliet stumbled on to say, "I had charge of my three younger sisters." Her eyes begged him to help her rescue the conversation.

Juliet was not quite certain what she had said wrong. But she knew that she had said something dreadfully wrong. Dr. Abernathy's gaze darkened with sorrow, and his wife put down her fork without finishing the last of her meal. Belatedly, Juliet realized that the Abernathys were childless still after ten years. Apparently it was not a situation that suited either of them, though imagining Drusilla Abernathy as a doting mother was impossible.

Juliet could certainly understand the quiet heartache of childlessness. Miranda and Simon bore their own despair with grace, but she had seen the sorrow in her sister's eyes as Valentine and Emily added two children to the family in three years of their marriage and Miranda remained barren after six years with Simon.

She could not refer directly to such a thing, however. So she said, hoping that R.J. agreed with her, "R.J. and I are hoping to be blessed with children, of course."

Afraid to stop talking and hear the awful silence that would greet her, Juliet babbled on. "But the future is not always certain. Why, the duke of Kerstone, my sister's husband, had his mother make him a brother again when she was over forty."

There was no response for a moment. She prepared to launch herself into more inane confidences about her family and the children they wished for or had. Fortunately, R.J. said, "The dowager duchess had a daughter, I heard. From her second marriage to an American."

Juliet nodded. She could not stem her nervous words, however. "Yes. It was quite a shock to the family when Simon's sister was born, as you might imagine. But a wonderful one." *Stop talking,* she commanded her tongue. Afraid she would never stop, she took one quick breath and finished: "So I am content to wait for my blessings."

"I trust you will not make R.J. wait a score of years for a child." Dr. Abernathy spoke with a bright smile that did not completely erase the shadows of his personal grief.

"We will do our duty," R.J. said somewhat stiffly. There was a smile on his lips, though, she saw with relief.

"Duty, eh?" Brow raised, the doctor teased her directly, "I believe a younger man is better able to cope with the exuberance of children." Then he laughed, obviously making an effort to shake off his own sadness. "I well remember my own father playing the horse for my brother and me."

He turned to R.J. and said with mock severity, "And

you must make time for your children when they arrive. A man who neglects his family for business deprives himself and his family of great joy."

R.J. glanced into Juliet's eyes with a spark of warmth that brought an answering heat to life within her. "I am eager for the day when I come home to my wife and as many children as we are fortunate to be gifted with through the years."

"Two children is most sensible." After the tense conversation of moments ago, Jonathan Hopkins was almost smiling again, "One boy and one girl, as I have."

"I want a dozen," Susannah said forcefully. As her gaze was directly upon Dr. Abernathy, Juliet expected both her parents, and perhaps even R.J., to recognize the depth and passion of her infatuation.

"You will change your mind after you have the first," Annabel said sharply. "Perhaps you should wait until you are married and a mother to make such pronouncements. Unless you want to be seen as a foolish child."

Juliet was astonished to see that Annabel's indignation seemed to be entirely for her childless friend. Again the girl's mother showed no sign that she recognized Susannah's infatuation with the handsome Dr. Abernathy. Perhaps she had blinded herself, since he was the husband of her childhood friend.

A glance at R.J. and his father confirmed that they were also oblivious to the signs that Susannah had given away her heart.

TWENTY

Boston society was much like shipboard society. The ladies had little to do with her but snipe. And the gentlemen were much too attentive for Annabel's approval.

Juliet sang the last few notes of her piece and smiled at the stiff young woman who was accompanying her rather poorly. She received no answering smile and was not surprised.

"Lovely, my dear. You must have applied yourself to your singing lessons," Mrs. Vandeventer said perfunctorily to Juliet.

She swallowed the scathing comment that threatened to reveal exactly how infuriating she found Mrs. Vandeventer's lukewarm appreciation of her voice.

That she sang like an angel was the other thing beside her beauty that she was certain of. Even her sisters, who had always teased her mercilessly about beauty being fleeting, had always given her her due when it came to her voice.

Mrs. Vandeventer, however, either did not recognize a good voice when she heard it or, more likely, would not acknowledge it in a woman who had scandalously trapped R. J. Hopkins into marriage. And apparently that was how she was known in Boston society despite all of her attempts to behave circumspectly.

Turning to the pianist, the older woman said, "Phoebe, what improvement you have shown in your playing, my dear. I quite imagined myself in a concert hall listening to a virtuoso."

Juliet did not show her astonishment at such a prevarication. Poor Phoebe, beaming at the compliment, could use it more than Juliet, after all. She not only had no ear for musical notes; she had no chin to speak of.

Mr. Darnell came forward to offer a compliment. "The birds have become silent in awe of your talent, Mrs. Hopkins," he gushed.

"More likely because of the drapes over their cages." Juliet laughed.

She had meant to attempt a bit of dry wit so that she offended none of the ladies and Annabel would not accuse her again of unseemly encouragement of a gentleman. But Mrs. Vandeventer's expression tightened, and the woman's three chins lifted in affront.

Susannah, trying to rescue the situation, leaped to her feet. "Poor things. Mr. Darnell, please help me uncover them so they can see daylight again."

Juliet watched as the pair whisked the covers off the birdcages and the birds came to life again. Or as much life as Annabel allowed them.

They were beautiful birds, and all could sing pleasantly enough when they wished to. Why they would wish to was what Juliet could not understand.

Annabel had not only caged them; she had ordered their wings clipped so that they would never again fly.

Appalled at the discovery, Juliet had asked R.J. why such a thing had been necessary. His expression had been particularly blank as he told her of the time he, as a thirteen-year-old boy, let one of the birds free.

Quite naturally, for a youth, he had wanted to see the bird spread its beautiful wings and fly around the room. He had intended to see it back safely into its cage once the bird landed again.

Unfortunately, what he had not noticed was that a careless maid had left one of the large conservatory windows open at the top. The bird escaped. R.J. confessed and was punished. The careless maid was dismissed without reference.

Annabel, however, did not rest merely with punishing the guilty. She then decreed that she would have no birds without clipped wings in her home again.

R.J. had told the story so vividly that she could picture it. Dark-haired, solemn-eyed R.J., watching with a broad smile as the bird took wing. Running to the window, too late to stop the bird's escape. Taking his punishment without tears.

But what had struck her to the heart was his last admission. That he had found the beautiful songbird two days later, lying broken and bloody on the ground.

He had no doubt that one of Annabel's two Persian cats had done the damage, Juliet nearly wept when he confessed that he'd buried the bird and told no one else of his discovery. He'd made up a story for Susannah, telling her that the bird had flown home to some warm island and was now safe and warm among other birds of its kind.

When he first told the story, she had felt for him. Now she also sympathized with the bird's plight. At times she was afraid she would share the same fate as the unlucky songbird. There were moments when she thought that if she found an open window, she, too, would fly.

But the cat's claw of scandal would bring her down if she fled her husband, there was no doubt of that.

In all honesty, she did not want to leave R.J. Only cold and unfriendly Boston and this dark and over-decorated mausoleum that served the family as a home.

If R.J. could be convinced to return to England with her, she would leave everything here behind without a glance over her shoulder.

But his family was here. His business. His heart. Sometimes it seemed that she had merely joined him in his cage. A pair of lovebirds on display for the amusement of the Boston ladies and gentlemen. And the ladies didn't even appreciate her song.

She could live like this no longer, Juliet decided.

After a month of finding conversation silenced when she happened to approach, she was ready to find an answer.

She asked Susannah for advice, but Susannah could only bite her lip and shake her head when asked. "I don't know, Juliet. They have all known me from birth. They do not treat me as coldly as they do you, but still I am a child in their eyes, and I have not been able to change that."

"No doubt that will change when you marry," Juliet comforted her absently. "There must be some way to change the way one is seen in society. I know there must."

A sudden silence was her only answer.

She looked up and forgot her own problems completely for a moment.

Susannah's eyes brimmed with tears despite the struggle not to break into sobs evident in her carriage and expression.

Juliet reached a comforting hand out, realizing her error too late. She alone understood why Susannah would not let herself marry. But the girl evaded her touch and said quickly, "Excuse me, please."

Susannah was in love—with a married man. Worse, the husband of her mother's dearest friend. The potential for scandal was unbearably high.

Juliet had no intention of allowing Susannah to be ruined, as she had been. The thought of what would have happened if R.J. had been married—or had not been willing to marry her—made her shudder with sudden, dreadful understanding.

She must find a way to explain to R.J. the danger his sister courted so openly, so openheartedly, by loving a married man with a humorless, jealous wife. Instinctively, she knew that Annabel would not confine herself to a scolding. Susannah could find herself married to the first eligible man Annabel could manage to wrestle to the altar. Juliet would not wish that fate upon her worst enemy.

Or perhaps she should do the duty of an older sister and counsel Susannah herself. It was, perhaps, time she took on a measure of responsibility, much as she had always hated the idea.

Watching as the girl fled the room, Juliet wondered if they were all not caged birds in one way or another. She recognized her own tendency for melodrama and quelled it by thinking of her brother and sisters and their happy marriages.

Knowing what Miranda's advice would have been, she sighed. Yes. It was time to find out how she could throw open the cage doors and still avoid the cat's deadly claws.

R.J. listened with only half an ear as Juliet described the latest tribulation she had suffered as she tried to find her place in Boston society.

He did not catch more than a few words—"humiliating," "foolish," "trouble," and other such negative adjectives.

He had a basic understanding that no one appreciated the beauty of her voice. Which struck him as ridiculous. How could any but the deaf not hear the extraordinary quality of her voice and appreciate it?

But his attention was fully drawn when she burst into tears and he could no longer ignore the deep unhappiness of his wife.

He gathered her into his embrace, pressing her to him until her sobs quieted. "I thought you were doing well, Juliet. I expect you are just impatient. It may take years for you to be fully accepted, you know."

"Years?" Her voice was strained from her emotional storm. "How can you say such a thing? I will go out of my mind if I must endure years of this behavior."

"What is so awful?" He stifled his alarm at her upset. She tended to feel things a little strongly. She did not mean what she said. His hand stroked her spine to soothe her.

He did not want to lose her; that he knew. His life was so much more pleasant with her company. He knew, guiltily, that he did not spend as much time as she would like with her. But the time he did spend gave him such joy. Perhaps she did not find as much joy with him. Or perhaps she only needed to find her place and then she would be busy with her day while he worked.

He knew that, as it was now, she believed he preferred time at work to time with her. That was not true. But it was also irrelevant. What she did not understand, and perhaps he should make her see, was that if he wanted his father to trust him, he could not even give the appearance of neglecting the business for his wife.

"Juliet. Hush." He took her in his arms. "I am working for the both of us, you know."

"I do know it. But why can I never see you?"

He thought of a carrot he could offer to help her see that there was a reward for their patience. "Don't you want your own home to run?"

"Yes. Are we to move?" She brightened at the thought.

"One day."

The happiness in her eyes dimmed. "When I am old and gray, no doubt."

He laughed. "Sooner than that. As soon as I have convinced Father that I am worthy to be his heir and successor."

"Who else would he choose?"

R.J. stopped for a moment, his argument fleeing his brain. Who would Father appoint if he did not turn his businesses over to R.J.?

Seeing his puzzlement, she asked, "Has he trained no one else?"

"No."

"Has he spoken of anyone else he trusts to take over for him?"

"No."

She smiled as if she had made a telling point. "Then perhaps you should worry less about pleasing your father and more about pleasing yourself—and your wife."

For a glorious moment his hopes soared. Perhaps she was right, after all. Perhaps his father did trust him and hesitated to tell him so only from caution.

"Not yet." No. He must not change his commitment to working long hours for success. He and Juliet would simply have to enjoy the few moments they could snatch out of the day. And the nights, of course. They would always have the nights together.

Her disappointment resulted in more tears. As he wrapped her in his arms, he knew he needed to find a way to ease her despair. Annabel had already mentioned twice to him that she was flirting with the gentlemen again. He could not risk another scandal, not even a small one caused by an unhappy bride.

Feeling out of his depth but realizing that if he did

not help her she might do something foolish, he said quickly, "We shall ask Annabel for advice. Surely she can help you settle."

Annabel had been delighted to be asked her advice on Juliet's less than rousing entry into Boston society. "You'll have to prove yourself, my dear."

"But how?" She knew she would be better hiding her frustration and anxiety, but she could not.

"You consult an older, wiser, more experienced head, of course." The advice itself was sound. Still, Annabel had not been a friend to her in the past, she would have to weigh her advice carefully.

"Why is it that I am treated so coldly here?" In company she often felt as she had when R.J. had forbidden her Susannah's company, only a hundredfold this time.

"Your ways are different." Annabel said briskly. "Which is to be expected considering you were raised in England." She smiled encouragingly. "I find your willingness to understand that you must change yourself in order to be accepted a hopeful sign."

Change herself. Juliet sighed. "How much do you think I will need to change?" Ever since she was a child, everyone had always wanted her to change herself. None of the changes, however, had pleased her critics.

Annabel paused and then said, tactfully, "Until you are accepted, I suppose."

Since R.J.'s stepmother was in such an agreeable mood, Juliet pressed further. "And you do think that possible?"

"Of course I do." Annabel walked a circle around her. "With my help you cannot fail."

"Thank you for helping." Juliet wished she could put some warmth in her thanks. Whenever she talked to Annabel, though, she found herself waiting for the woman to pounce, claws out.

"I just want to keep the Hopkins name one to be proud of, Juliet. If you remember that and keep yourself aimed toward that goal, you will have accomplished much."

Claws. Juliet was surprised to feel a touch of relief to see them at last. "I will."

"Good." Annabel could not completely mask her doubtful expression. She added with a tight smile, "I am certain you will make the family proud."

Trying to imagine Jonathan Hopkins with an expression of pride, she answered a trifle tentatively, "I hope to."

Annabel, as if sensing her doubt, patted her arm. "R.J. has chosen a beautiful English girl. All you need to do is adapt yourself to our ways."

A little of her frustration bubbled to the surface, making her response more heated than she would have liked. "I *have* been trying—"

Annabel backed away a bit and held up one hand to halt Juliet's words. "I'm sure you have, dear. You only need a little guidance."

More than guidance. Drastic change seemed a likely necessity to her. "Tell me honestly, Mama Annabel, how much do you suppose I will have to change?"

"Not much. Just a nip here and a tuck there." Annabel's reassurance was not convincing. "Don't worry;

we shall have you acting the proper Boston wife before you know it."

Juliet could not suppress an inarticulate sound of distress. Annabel had said *acting* the proper Boston wife. Did no one think her able to *be* a proper wife?

Annabel smiled. Her voice was almost a purr. "Of course, it would be a shame for you to wholly lose your charming English ways."

"If learning to speak the language as you do in Boston will allow me to enter a room without feeling as if I were wished instantly back across the sea, I will be a good student." Juliet hoped that she could be. She had never been the best at studying.

Her own governess had thrown up her hands in dismay at times, claiming Juliet would learn nothing she did not wish to learn no matter what incentive she was given. "Where do we start?"

"I will make an appointment with my seamstress."

Juliet was astonished at how quickly Annabel was able to get her in for a fitting at the exclusive establishment. She did wish, however, that Susannah had been able to accompany them. Annabel's uninterrupted scrutiny made her uneasy. R.J.'s stepmother, in consultation with the seamstress, looked her up and down as if she were a piece of furniture in need of refurbishing. The two of them did not consult Juliet at all as they discussed color, cut, and ornamentation of an entire new wardrobe.

She made one protest, early, when a particularly hideous shade of forest green was paraded before them. Annabel merely shook her head and said, "You must learn not to make a spectacle of yourself."

A spectacle? She suppressed her urge to argue with Annabel. "How do I do that?"

Annabel said promptly, "Don't solicit compliments from other men."

Juliet could not hold back a protest at that unfair remark. "I don't solicit them; they just offer them."

Annabel raised a brow in disagreement. "My dear, no man offers compliments to a woman he knows will not accept them."

"But I—"

"The way you dress, carry yourself, the tone in which you speak—all contribute to the way you are perceived. Surely you understand that? You are no green girl, after all." Annabel stepped back and crossed her arms over her chest. Sternly, she said, "I thought you wanted my advice."

Juliet calmed herself and said meekly, "I do."

"Very well." Annabel nodded her head once sharply. "If you want to be accepted, you will dress more soberly."

As if Annabel had known exactly how to strike at her heart, Juliet heard the command with a gasp. "R.J. has not complained about the way I dress."

"R.J. is a man. He has no idea of what is right in these things. You are a matron now."

"A matron?" Juliet could not completely hide her horror at the word.

"You might be a mother soon enough." Annabel looked at her with a speculative eye.

"Not too soon, I am sure."

Annabel smiled condescendingly. "Nature has a way of making a mockery of our expectations."

So that Annabel would not realize how badly the conversation had rattled her, Juliet said breezily, "I try not to have too many expectations for nature to mock."

Annabel poked at Juliet's middle, pinched in tightly by the corset. "I hope you do not have as fickle a womb as you have a spirit, my girl."

Juliet was astonished. It had never occurred to her to wonder why she was not yet carrying a child. She had been pleased the last two months to find that she was not. She had been rushed into marriage with R.J. To add a child would only make the strain between them worse. But now it seemed that she was failing in yet another duty to be a good wife. She sighed, looking despondently at the drab colors and sober designs that Annabel had chosen for her transformational wardrobe.

Would R.J. be pleased? Had he disliked the way she dressed before? Did he worry that she would fail him in some crucial manner? Nonsense. R.J. wasn't worried that she wouldn't have a child. Was he?

TWENTY-ONE

R.J. surprised Juliet in the middle of the afternoon. He knew he was being irresponsible, but the blue of the sky had called to him, reminding him of Juliet and the day she had crossed the gardens to hand him the script that would change his life.

The room was strewn with dresses, much as he had found it the first day they arrived. A quick rush of memory engulfed him. Perhaps they could while away this afternoon in a bath, as they had that day.

She smiled when she saw him, but she was obviously distracted.

"What is all this?"

"I've a new wardrobe. Annabel suggested I should appear more matronly if I wanted to be taken seriously."

"Sounds like a wise course of action."

"But I find I cannot part so easily with these." She waved her hand to encompass the colorful garments strewn about the room.

He lifted one, a bodice with a vee-shaped design made of dove-shaped buttons. "Will you keep your buttons?"

"No." Sadness slowed her movements as she carefully packed a garment into the trunk that lay open before her. "Annabel says they are the mark of a young woman trying to attract a man. As I am married now, I have no need for showy dress."

"So where are your new clothes?"

She turned, a smile on her face. "Would you like to see?"

She held up a rather brown skirt against her waist. He could not picture her in it. Perhaps it would be a practical color for when she took her afternoon stroll.

"I can't picture you." He reached up to run his finger around the collar of her gown. He was pleased to note the way her breathing quickened. "Why don't you let me help you out of this so you can show me."

Though they spent a pleasant half an hour in a state of undress, eventually she began to try on her new wardrobe for his approval.

He did not know what to say. "They're all so— lovely," he lied, knowing instinctively by the unsure way she stood before him in her new clothes that she did not feel completely comfortable in her new look.

"Are you certain?" She gave him such a look of trust, he was afraid to answer. "Annabel says this will make me fit better into your society. Do you think if I added a few of my buttons I would spoil the effect?"

"I don't know what to tell you, Juliet. Perhaps you would do better to consult Susannah or Annabel on whether ornamentation would be acceptable." He did not ask her why the new clothes were all in sober colors—gray, brown, navy, and maroon.

He supposed it was inevitable. Juliet was no longer

a young woman looking for a beau. She was a wife and must be responsible. Although she did not look more responsible in these clothes, just more miserable.

"I confess I miss your buttons." He still remembered what Miranda had told him—that if London society had known Juliet was conducting business, she would have been immediately ostracized. Thank goodness that kind of prejudice did not exist in Boston.

"You will be there tonight? All night?"

"I promise." He had promised to attend Annabel's dinner party with her tonight, to give the new Juliet an introduction: a woman completely transformed from the flirtatious and vibrant young woman he had married. Would Boston society more readily accept her now? Perhaps. After all, he realized with a shock, she now closely resembled the woman he had thought to marry before he had had his life turned upside down in London. Lucy Matthews.

He firmly tamped down his disappointment in the changes Annabel had wrought with Juliet. After all, if she would find a place in society dressed like this, then it was worth losing a bit of color. He consoled himself with the comforting knowledge that he would be able to peel away the drab colors and reveal the true Juliet any time he wished.

The new Juliet did not seem to be accepted any more easily than the old. He had realized there was something wrong the moment they stepped into the room together. All eyes were on Juliet. Though many complimented her on her transformation, there was no sincerity in any of the voices.

He wondered if Annabel had known that this new

look would be unsuccessful. Would she have deliberately . . . No. His stepmother had simply erred when she chose the severe hairstyle and the maroon gown of silk and satin that would better have suited Susannah. The color washed out Juliet's pale beauty until she appeared distinctly unwell.

"Good evening, Mrs. Hopkins. May I get you a drink? Some refreshment?" One of his father's business associates had made the offer. R.J. had never seen him smile so widely before.

He looked at his wife, surprised that her new look could still elicit such attention. For the first time, he understood why she was having so much difficulty being accepted in society. No matter that she was now dressed more soberly, her smile still shone brightly.

The gentlemen were drawn to it; the ladies, infuriated by it. Poor Juliet. He remembered how he had thought of her that first time. He had not seen beneath the beautiful exterior to the strong and kind heart beneath the ornamental buttons or yards of silk and lace.

But what could he do with his new insight? He was only a man. He could not help her. He must have Annabel and Susannah do more for Juliet. Surely there must be some way to bring her into society without stripping her of all that made her Juliet. After all, he thought as he glanced around the room and saw Phineas Abernathy surrounded by his usual coterie of admiring ladies, some charming people had no trouble being accepted.

He wondered if there was some secret that Phineas could whisper to Juliet to help her gain the acceptance she wanted and needed. Although R.J. was certain

Phineas had never betrayed his vows to Drusilla, the man was daily given the opportunity. As he guided Juliet toward the doctor, he heard one of the women cooing. "Poor things. How kind of you to take them in." To his surprise, he saw that the woman was Susannah.

He asked, "Who have you taken in now?"

Phineas looked up and shook his head. "No one."

"Of course you have. You are so modest, Dr. Abernathy." Susannah appeared to be his biggest supporter.

Phineas sighed. "I have merely agreed to run the orphanage temporarily. Otherwise it would be shut down, and I will not have that."

"How good of you."

"It must be a great deal of work to run the orphanage, Dr. Abernathy. Will your regular patients suffer?" R.J. knew the questioner to be among Phineas's well-to-do patients. No doubt her interest was personal.

Juliet ignored the jealous looks the women around Dr. Abernathy shot her and just clutched tighter to R.J.'s arm as she heard the news of Dr. Abernathy's appointment with interest. And watched Susannah with trepidation.

"Why have they threatened to close the orphanage?" Susannah was asking. Her skin was flushed. Juliet hoped that everyone would put down her fervor to indignation over the orphans.

"Expense." Abernathy spoke as if the one word said it all. And, in a way, it did.

"I will help you." Susannah, her heart in her eyes, declared herself before everyone.

Juliet stepped in quickly to cover her importunate offer. "Yes. We must all help." She glanced at R.J., and he gave her a nod of encouragement.

Drusilla Abernathy gazed at her narrowly. "I did not know you wanted to take an interest in a charity."

Juliet improvised quickly. "Parentless children are close to my heart. My own parents died when I was a child. Though my brother and sister did their best to raise us well."

Annabel, with a glance first at her daughter and then at Drusilla, turned to Juliet. "Perhaps you might find supporting the orphanage a good cause to champion."

Did she understand her daughter's feelings? Juliet wasn't certain. "Yes, I would."

"Excellent. I can teach you how to organize teas and benefits. Susannah may help us as well."

"Thank you, Mama Annabel." Juliet hated calling her that insipid name. She hated even more having to thank the woman. But for once the idea was good. She could hardly be accused of flirting while doing good deeds. And she had begun to feel as if she were one of Annabel's birds, clipped wings and all.

The idea of giving a tea or a benefit was worthwhile. But Juliet could see from Dr. Abernathy's harried features that the orphanage needed more than future funds. It needed help immediately.

She was not averse to rolling up her sleeves. She imagined how proud R.J. would be of her for embracing hard work in a good cause. "I would like to make an appointment to speak with you about what you need for the orphanage." She thought of the frightened, parentless children who might now lose their only home because they cost too much to feed and clothe.

"Tomorrow would not be too soon." Dr. Abernathy smiled broadly. "You are a godsend, Mrs. Hopkins."

Susannah shot Juliet a jealous look. "I will be there as well, Dr. Abernathy."

Oh, dear. This would be more complicated than she had expected. She would never admit that it was simply missing her sisters that compelled her to offer to help the orphans. For the first time, she began to realize how deeply Miranda must regret not having had children in all her years of marriage.

True, she had had her sisters to raise. But an heir for the duke. A child of her own. A child born of her love for Simon.

She glanced at her husband, deep in discussion with Dr. Abernathy about the finances of the orphanage. Would R.J. be happy if Juliet were to find herself expecting a child? Would some of the life she had seen only brief glimpses of be reflected in his eyes when he looked at a child of his own?

Valentine and Emily glowed when they looked at their own offspring, even when the little devils were covered with grass and mud.

Perhaps that would be the key to unlocking the true heart of Romeo that was caged deep within the perennially sensible R. J. Hopkins? A son. Better yet, a daughter with her father's dark hair and her mother's laughter. He could not ignore a child of his own as he ignored his wife. Or could he?

And would she want to bring a child into the world to be ignored by a father? Her own father had often been away from home. He had spent most of his time when he was home with Valentine. His daughters he had had little part of except to name and to discipline.

He had called Juliet his little beauty. But those were almost the only words he ever spoke to her when she would be brought down to greet him when he was home.

No. Somehow she must convince R.J. that he needed to find time for her, for the family they both wanted.

She had not really realized what an orphanage was. She had imagined small clean faces, neatly brushed hair, well-fed smiling faces. Not this. Not this dark place with its shadows and drafts.

"Might I show you around, then, Mrs. Hopkins?" Dr. Abernathy smiled at her, but she knew that he had somehow sensed her shift in mood. He seemed almost predatory in his attention, watching with a hawk's keen eye instead of the flirtatious appreciation he had shown her last night.

"That would be very kind of you." She had hoped for a nurse or some maidservant to do that honor. He made her nervous the way he was looking at her. "Are you certain that you have the time? I imagine you must be very busy here. You are the only doctor on the premises, are you not?"

"Yes. But I have made my rounds, and there are no pressing matters waiting for me." He glanced behind her. "Annabel and Susannah did not come?" He did not manage the casual air he attempted.

"No. Annabel felt that Susannah should not be exposed . . ." The battle had been quite unsettling, but she would not share such a detail with Dr. Abernathy. There could be no doubt now that Annabel knew her daughter's heart.

"Good." There was unmitigated relief in his face.

Juliet said quickly. "She is young. She will—"

He interrupted with a brisk nod. "Of course she will."

For some reason, though they had said very little about the matter, Juliet relaxed. He had just very discreetly assured her that he had no intention of allowing Susannah's infatuation to become anything more.

He took her through the wards. Through the kitchen with a temperamental stove belching smoke into the air. Through the laundry, where children labored, faces red from the steaming water used to wash linens and the dull institutional clothing that appeared to be standard—dove gray for boys, a washed-out blue for the girls.

Juliet wondered if they longed for brightly colored clothing just as she did now that she must be satisfied with a matronly wardrobe of sober colors.

She found it easy to talk with him, to discover the needs of the orphanage as she followed him around. Her notebook rapidly filled as she traveled from room to room. The institution lacked everything from furniture to linens. She could see why he spoke of the need with urgency.

What affected her most was the nursery. Babies lay in their cribs, crying. No one rushed to pick them up. No one even seemed to notice their cries, though the sound was enough to break a dozen mothers' hearts.

"They'll cry themselves to sleep soon enough," one frazzled nurse told her.

But Juliet could not bear it. She lifted one child from his crib and began to sing her favorite lullaby as she rubbed her finger along his smooth cheek.

All the babies slowly silenced. When the nursery was blessedly quiet, Juliet put the sleeping baby down gently so that he would not awake. Looking into the cribs of slumbering infants, she was filled with a peace she had never felt in her life.

Phineas Abernathy, who had been called away to attend to a sick child, came to collect her from the nursery. He paused a moment, a look of puzzlement on his face. He peeked into a crib and then methodically checked each one. He glanced at the sleeping babies and murmured, "You are a miracle worker."

"Nonsense. I have been singing babies to sleep for years. My nephews are very fond of my voice, and my sister-in-law is even happier when I put them down for their naps."

He smiled in appreciation of her humor. "You can see the need we have is great."

"Yes, indeed I do."

"Whatever help you can give would be wonderful." He smiled as he stood and held out his hand to her in dismissal.

"I shall be back tomorrow, then."

He blinked. "Back? Is there more than you wish to see before you make a donation?"

"You need more than money here, Dr. Abernathy. You need willing hands. At least until you have the funds to hire adequate staff."

"You are offering to . . . to work here?" His voice had a horrified undertone, but there was a spark of admiration in his eyes as he realized that she did indeed mean to return.

She smiled, thinking of the lessons she had given her sisters and Betsey in the schoolroom. They had only been four students. Here were five times more. Could she do it? She smiled at Dr. Abernathy and said with confidence, "Of course."

"The work is not easy."

She raised her brow at him, tilting her head at the children sweeping the carpet outside in the hallway. "Is it any easier for the children?"

His smile chased away the exhaustion in his features for a moment. "Welcome to the Wellburn Orphanage, Mrs. Hopkins." And then he frowned. "Perhaps you might want to make certain that R.J. does not object."

Juliet looked at him coolly. She did not like the thought that R.J. could tell her what to do, but it was a reality that all married women must accept sooner or later. She sighed. "Surely you know my husband better than to believe he will object to my putting myself to good use."

He nodded. "As you say, Mrs. Hopkins. Your husband does admire and appreciate hard, worthwhile work."

Indeed. All she needed to do was make him see that this was worthwhile work. And that she needed to do this particular worthwhile work herself.

TWENTY-TWO

R.J. crept guiltily into their room. His business had kept him exceptionally late tonight. He expected that she would be asleep. But she was not.

He undressed quietly in the dressing room and turned out the light before he made his way to the bed. Halfway there, he heard the movement of the bedclothes as she sat up. He braced himself for complaints over his late hours.

Instead, her voice carried softly across the darkened room. "I have discovered a purpose today, R.J."

"A purpose?" He wondered for a heartbeat if she might be carrying a child. But it was too soon to be sure of such a thing. She would have to miss her courses for more than a few weeks before they could even begin to hope.

"I went to the Wellburn Orphanage today."

Ah, the orphanage. He climbed under the covers and pulled her close. "The one Phineas has saved from imminent demise?"

She nodded, her hair sliding along his chest quite pleasantly. "The same one. Although salvation will be short-lived if we do not find a way to endow the venture."

"What does Phineas say?"

"He is so exhausted, R.J. I have never seen him like this, not in the short time I have known him."

"He is the kind of man to throw himself into his charity work. Drusilla and Annabel lament his generous nature continuously. How many children does he have?"

"Twenty-five. They are so helpless."

"Write him a generous draft at once." He paused. "Or have you already done so?"

"No." She prodded him to turn over and began to massage the tense muscles of his neck and shoulders. He groaned in pleasure as she continued: "I wished to speak with you before I made a decision about the donation. How much do you think we could manage?"

R.J. had little idea of what would be reasonable. "A hundred dollars?"

"Not a thousand?"

He was shocked and half-rose, but she pushed with the palms of her hands under his shoulder blades, and he sank back down to enjoy her ministrations. "A thousand!" He shook his head. "Perhaps. But wouldn't it be better to have some event to raise money for the orphanage among the wealthier of our citizenry?"

"Yes. But the need is immediate. And desperate."

"Then a thousand is not too much."

She hesitated. "I also plan to volunteer my time helping out at the orphanage."

"Does that seem wise?"

"Imperative."

"Do you think it wise to spend time in that neighborhood?" He thought her vulnerable to any cutpurse. And then he realized that her motivation might be more than simply helping the orphans. "Will this get you accepted in society at last?"

"Probably not," she admitted. "But does it matter? The children need me."

He turned and took her into his arms so that he could bury his face between her breasts for a moment and just inhale the scent of her. "I don't think you should do this. Phineas can hire help."

"No." She cradled his head in her hands. "I need to do this. Why can't you see that?"

"There are others who can help. It is not your responsibility."

"No, my responsibility is to please the harpies of your society so that I can give teas and dinners while you spend all day in business. And that is not even until we get our own home. Sometimes I don't believe that day will ever come."

"It will."

She sighed. "Come with me tomorrow. I'll show you why I cannot turn my back on them. At least not until Phineas has the funds he needs to hire adequate help."

"I can't, Juliet. I have a very important meeting. But I will trust you to make the best decision on how much it is wise for you to do." He kissed her. "You will discuss this with Annabel, will you not?"

"I will speak to Annabel."

He was not reassured, somehow, by the clipped

agreement. But it was easy to forget his worries when he held her in his arms. She smelled warm and soft, like sleep. But her kisses made him anything but sleepy.

The child slept soundly on her shoulder. Her throat ached from singing, and there were tears in her eyes at the thought of leaving them here tonight. Little lambs innocently asleep, safe now. But tomorrow would come. Harsh, cold morning. No one to hold them and love them. Just a quick cold wash of the hands, face, and neck and a familiar bowl of porridge and a lukewarm cup of tea.

She had to find a way to do more for them than this. These children needed parents to love them, to protect them. But how could such a thing be possible?

"Let me put her to bed, Mrs. Hopkins." Dr. Abernathy came from behind her, and she just barely suppressed her start of surprise. He walked like a cat.

Which was probably a good thing here: no doubt he managed to come upon mischief in the making and put a stop to it all the earlier.

She relinquished the child reluctantly. "She was crying for her mother."

"She is new here. She will soon learn that will do her no good." His voice was flat with exhaustion. A month trying to get the orphanage to succeed had worn him down.

"How can you be so heartless?" She knew the accusation was not fair even as she leveled it. After a week, she could see for herself that the work here was never enough and never done. She taught children their letters, singing, and simple addition and subtraction. She sang them to sleep at night. And every day they struggled for enough money to keep food in the cupboards and coal in the stove.

"You needn't worry, Mrs. Hopkins, it is not your concern. You have done more than your family or this orphanage—or I—could have hoped. You may go home with a clear conscience."

"The state of my conscience is not your concern. The happiness of these children—what I can do for them—is my concern." Juliet said no more.

He would not believe her words until she proved it with action. He was a man of action himself and judged others accordingly.

"Susannah has asked to help. I will bring her tomorrow."

He looked up, and she saw a flare of objection die in his face. "As you wish."

"I will watch her."

He smiled. "I would be too tired, I assure you, Mrs. Hopkins, to begin an affair with an energetic, enthusiastic, idealistic, young woman like Susannah."

She thought of how she crawled into bed exhausted at night, glad to wrap herself around R.J., to make love in a sweet, dreamlike fog until she slept. No, if she allowed Susannah to help, she would have to be vigilant, for all their sakes.

"Annabel is concerned that you are spending too much of your time at the orphanage."

"The children need me."

"Unfortunately, because Phineas Abernathy is such a handsome man—"

She stopped stabbing the grapefruit she was ostensibly eating and stared at him. "You are not accusing me of improper behavior, are you?"

He had not been. But Annabel had in no uncertain terms. "I don't believe you are conducting an affair."

"Well, thank you. I most certainly am not. I am washing children's faces and their clothes and teaching them their letters, and there even are two children that I am working with who sing like angels. Dominic has a voice that would make an Italian opera lover weep."

"Juliet. It is not enough that you work hard. You must also avoid putting yourself into situations which appear . . . unsavory. Consider the way your actions look."

She gave up trying to eat the grapefruit and dropped her spoon with a clatter that expressed her irritation. "What difference does it make? I have transformed myself to no effect. No one likes me. The women whisper behind my back. They go all pinch-faced when I come near, as if I smell like rotted fish or dried dung."

"Nonsense. You are just having a little trouble settling into the ways of a society which is very different from your own."

She gazed into his eyes, the intensity of her emotions visible. "The children at the orphanage know my name. They smile when they see me. And they *need* me."

"You must take Annabel's counsel. She understands—"

"I have done everything Annabel told me to do." Her frustration showed in the tapping of her fingers upon the table. "I dress as if I had no need for color or beauty."

He did not know what to say. He could not tell her she was wrong. He had seen with his own eyes that the women in his mother's circle would rather burn her at the stake than offer her a cup of tea. "Perhaps a pretty bonnet would help." Even as he offered the suggestion, he realized how feeble it sounded.

She sighed. "I have worked so very hard, and no one seems to see that I am different from the girl I was when I let you climb my balcony. And now you tell me to stop going to the orphanage and helping the children who smile at me. Who hug me, even if their hands are sometimes sticky with jam. I can see the good I do there. What good have I done in society itself?"

"Give it some time."

"I'm tired of giving it time." She stood up from the table abruptly and then came around to hug him fiercely. "I've found something that makes me happy. Don't take it away from me. Don't take me away from those children. They need me, R.J."

"When we have children of our own—"

"These children will still need love, R.J."

"I need you at home." He did not like coming home and sometimes finding that she had not yet returned from the orphanage because the children had required an extra lullaby.

"Why?" You are not home until late most nights. Why should I come home early from the orphanage when the children need me so much and you do not?"

"You are my wife." He thought that all the answer necessary. But apparently she did not.

"Your prisoner, you mean. You stay in your cage if you like it so much. I intend to do more than that."

"I am not asking anything unreasonable from you—"

"I enjoy my charity work. Everything else makes me want to scream, R.J."

"I can see that." He wrapped his arms around her. "I hope I don't have that same effect."

"Well, you do. Only I don't mind screaming for you." She smiled. She kissed him softly. "I will not go unless Susannah is with me. Then the gossips will have nothing to gossip about."

He thought of her precarious social position and felt an unnamed dread begin in the pit of his stomach. The gossips wanted to feed on her. Would anything keep her safe except his locking her in her room and throwing away the key?

Her work at the orphanage was satisfying. She and Susannah worked well as a team. If Susannah had been born a man, Juliet would have thought her well suited to become a physician. But she was a woman, and that profession was barred to her.

But her work with the children didn't fill the growing void within her. She wanted more. She wanted

R.J. He did not even listen when she spoke of the children.

Annabel, after having failed in her attempt to make R.J. lay down the law, had told her directly that she was going much too far spending so many hours with the poor of society. It almost seemed as if the woman thought poverty were a disease that could be caught if one spent too much time among those suffering from it.

There was no way Juliet could create a scandal just helping children who had no one else in the world to look after them. She shook her head. Annabel didn't understand. And there was little point trying to convince her. At least not until Juliet could prove that she had made a real contribution. One that could not be laughed off as frivolous.

The children haunted her nights. There must be something more than what she was doing for them now that she could do.

She decided to raid the attic for discarded furniture. The maids helped with true pleasure. "It's good to see that this will be used for a good purpose," Mary said.

"A very good purpose," Juliet answered. "The children have no possessions to speak of, and they have only hooks to hang their clothing on.

"Even their Sunday best, ma'am?" The maid was shocked.

"They share a trunk for anything they own other than their daily clothing." The girls had only one trunk per five girls to store their clothing and what little of value they had from their previous lives.

She surveyed the dressers and wardrobes in the at-

tic. How many could she take? At least three. Maybe
even a mirror or two for the girls' room? The boys
would not care so much. And perhaps something with
glass in it would not be wise in their room, considering the way they seemed to only be able to storm like
bulls despite all her attempts to teach them how to
walk, not run, jump, or leap from place to place.

No, no mirror for the boys. But the girls. How could
they grow up without ever seeing themselves? Without
ever trying to tie hair ribbons in different ways? She
determined to fetch a length of ribbon material for
the girls' hair.

She could teach them to cut and tie as they looked
into the two large and sturdy mirrors she directed
brought down and loaded onto the cart of things for
the orphanage. Missy, especially, with her beautiful
choir voice, would look well in a bright blue ribbon
to catch back her wheat blond hair.

It was as Juliet was delivering the furniture and trying to find the money to buy things to brighten up
their days that she realized what might help. And it
was the children themselves who had given her the
answer.

She was not completely surprised to find Phineas
Abernathy opposed to her changes at first. She tried
to be patient.

He was struggling to keep the orphanage open, and
he could not bother himself too much with more than
keeping the children fed and sheltered.

But she could. If she could convince him.

She outlined the changes she would not only fi-
nance but oversee as he listened. The fatigue slowly

lifted from his shoulders. At first he argued. "These children need more than a little music and some colorful pictures on the wall, Mrs. Hopkins."

"Do you mean to say they must never have beauty because they are poor?" She knew he would never agree to such a harsh assessment of the children's future.

"Of course not. But they need food and warm clothing and a roof over their heads much more."

"I agree. I will pay for every suggestion I have made." She did not mention her plan to oversee the changes as well. He might have a moment of male pigheadedness. Better to have him fully endorse her idea. Then she could tell him she would implement the ideas.

"Is R.J. aware of this offer?"

Chagrined, she knew she would be out of luck if he spoke to R.J. before she did. But she would not be stopped now. "He is in full support of my idea." Or he would be, once she explained it to him. How could he not be?

"But even with your generous funds, the bills for feeding, clothing, and caring for twenty-five children will hardly leave money for the frills of life."

"I agree." Juliet could feel herself beaming, and she was pleased to see a genuine broad, answering smile on Phineas Abernathy's face. "We must raise additional funds to create a trust for the orphans."

"And how shall we do that?"

"We need to have a charity benefit."

"That is a common practice. It has worked before."

A little of the joy went out of his eyes, and his shoulders sagged slightly again. "Who would we invite?"

"All the richest people, of course." Juliet thought that should be obvious. "I will have to rely upon Annabel and Susannah for that, you understand." But she was determined that this event would make her the most envied hostess in Boston. "Everyone who is anyone will be present. We will fund an endowment that will allow the children not only food and shelter but music and art and dance." Since quiet persistence and behaving like a pious nun did not gain her entrée into society, she would try to take the city by storm.

There was open skepticism in his gaze, but the tired air had left him completely. "Why would they come?"

She smiled. Once he heard her idea, he would understand. But would he agree to allow the children to participate? "To hear Dominic and Missy sing, of course."

"Our little opera singer and that angel who has a voice almost as beautiful as yours?" He nodded slowly. "I think you may have had a brilliant idea, Mrs. Hopkins."

TWENTY-THREE

"I am going to run away."

Juliet did not know what to say. Susannah had been very quiet as the carriage brought them home from the orphanage. But she had supposed it was just their natural tiredness at the end of an exhausting day.

"Will you help me?" Susannah spoke calmly, with the same rational tone that R.J. and his father used. But what she said was not sensible at all. "I wish to be a doctor, Juliet. Mama will not listen to me. And Father will not consent."

"You cannot do such a thing on your own. How will you support yourself?"

"I have saved my pin money."

"Susannah," she said gently, "medical schools do not accept women."

"Then I will pass myself off as a man."

Juliet could not help smiling at the thought. Susannah was tiny, under five feet tall. "You might pass as a boy in a dimly lit room, but you are not likely to pass as a man. You must think of this sensibly. You cannot succeed."

"Oh, Juliet! I expected you to understand. You and

R.J. You were so beautiful together in the moonlight. If you had done what was expected of you, neither of you would have ever—"

Juliet sat stunned. "You saw us . . ." She closed her eyes. "Susannah, did you send the note to the duke?"

"Yes." The girl squirmed under Juliet's glare. "And I am not sorry. You two were meant for each other. And I am meant to be a doctor. Like Phineas." She said his name in a near whisper, and the love she bore the man was fully evident. Juliet felt a sudden sharp sympathy.

"Even without your note, I think your brother would still have married me, so I will forgive you. But I think it best that you never tell him. He might not forgive you so easily."

"He would thank me." But Susannah did not speak with full assurance.

"Nevertheless, you are acting without knowing what the consequences of your actions may be. I have learned that matters sometimes do not end the way you plan them. What I did that night was act without thought. For that one lapse in judgment, I ended up in another country with a husband who has no time for me and a stepmother who despises me. And a society which delights in looking down upon me."

As the carriage pulled up to the front of the house to deposit them safely home, Susannah said stubbornly, "I am going."

"When?" Juliet could not let her go.

"Tomorrow. When we go to the orphanage. I will walk to the train station and go. I wish to be a doctor."

She put her hand out to stop the girl from jumping to the ground. "Do you? Or do you wish to be a doctor's wife?"

Susannah tried to disguise the naked hope in her eyes by leaping gracefully from the carriage. "That is impossible. He would never do such a thing to her. She is responsible for his own profession."

"Susannah, you are asking for heartbreak. You are begging for it, to be blunt."

"I cannot help it. If I cannot have him, I will have his profession." She turned toward the house.

Juliet pleaded. "Let me talk to R.J. Perhaps I can convince him to talk to your father. It is not so horrible to think of you as a doctor, attending medical school. After all, your family has pride in hard work, does it not." She sighed. "Perhaps there will be a medical school that will consider a dedicated woman student."

Susannah's expression was sad but determined. "I'm going, Juliet, and no one will stop me. Not R.J., not Father, not Mama. No one." She slipped into the house, leaving Juliet sitting in the carriage with the door agape.

She tried to imagine R.J. or his father agreeing to such a scheme and could not. Why would anyone wish to go to school to learn how to deal with people who are sick, perhaps dying? But life would not be as pleasant without doctors. Surely she could find some way to convey this to R.J.

Or maybe it would be better for her to suggest that they indulge Susannah in her whim now and let nature take its course. No gently bred woman was likely to survive the rigors of medical school that Dr. Abernathy had described to her. If they accepted her in the first place.

Whatever the case, she must find him. Now.

R.J. was shocked when his secretary let Juliet into his office. She had never come to visit him here, and he felt a little nervous that she, with her English prejudice against hard work, might look down upon him.

Her face was white with shock. He asked, "What is wrong?"

"Susannah intends to run away."

He refused to believe it. "You must be exaggerating."

"I am not." The drawn quality of her features, the whiteness around her lips, something in her face, convinced him. Susannah did intend to run away.

R.J. stopped only momentarily to tell his secretary to cancel all his day's appointments and reschedule for another day. He did not know what his father would say. "Perhaps we should enlist Father's help."

"Your father does not like trouble, R.J." Juliet considered for a moment and then shook her head. "This is more than girlish high spirits, R.J."

"How can you be sure?"

"Susannah knows the repercussions of her actions. Let us talk to her first. Perhaps we can salvage the situation so that no one but the three of us even know any problem occurred."

* * *

Susannah's plight fled their thoughts when they arrived home, however. Annabel met them at the door. "Dr. Abernathy's wife has been murdered, and he has been taken up for the murder."

Juliet spared a moment to note that Susannah, white with distress, was still safely at home when the girl began to protest her mother's statement. "He could not have done such a thing. I know it—"

Juliet held up her hand to silence the flood of words. "How was his wife murdered?"

Susannah said softly, "They say poison. But he would never do that."

Annabel was sharp, shaking her daughter more roughly than Juliet had ever seen her do. "Someone did, obviously. Who else but Dr. Abernathy himself?"

"He couldn't, Mama; he couldn't." Susannah was nearly incoherent. Juliet watched her sharply. More than grief made her stumble against her mother. Had Annabel given her a sleeping draft?

"Dr. Abernathy has been arrested? Who is at the orphanage?"

"I'm certain I don't know."

"I will go."

"No." R.J. was white. "Stay here with Susannah. I will go and speak to Phineas. Find out what needs to be done for the orphanage until he is—" He looked at her, and they both recognized the horrible possibility that the man would be hanged for murder.

He swept her into his arms—solid, warm, and safe—for just a moment. And then he was gone.

Juliet went into the parlor, where Annabel was tending to Susannah, who appeared deeply asleep now.

"Did you give her a sleeping draft?"

"Yes. And I have one for you as well."

"Thank you, but I don't need one." Juliet did not want to sleep. She wanted to understand why a man like Phineas Abernathy would ever murder his wife. Even one like Drusilla.

"Of course you do." Annabel said softly, soothingly. "You are going to go to sleep; nothing more, Juliet." Juliet glanced at her and then was caught in horror. The woman's face twisted, and her voice grew ugly for a moment. "You deserve worse, but you are fortunate to escape your true deserts, my dear."

Juliet's mouth went dry. "What is that?"

"Poison."

"Poison?"

"The same draft that brought poor Dr. Abernathy's wife to her death."

"You—" Juliet was horrified by the bald admission.

"Yes." She measured out a dose of the poison and poured it into the tea she had prepared for Juliet. "But due to your taking this and the note you will leave as well, everyone will believe you did the deed."

Juliet struggled to understand. "What motive would I have for killing her?"

"Why, jealousy, of course. Everyone knew that you were having an affair with him."

"I was not—"

"Of course you were. Why else would you spend so much time at the orphanage?"

"The orphans!"

"Nonsense. Any good society person would know that excuse is the weakest sort."

"Susannah—"

"Susannah will get over her distress shortly. I have seen to it that she will never, ever, repeat her foolish error again. I believe she fully understands how fortunate she is to escape."

"She loves him."

"So Drusilla was going to tell everyone. Could you imagine what that would have done to Susannah?"

"She will never forgive you. She loves him, Annabel."

Annabel frowned. "Love is nothing. Love weakens you. Do you know that R.J.'s mother loved her husband, too. But that didn't protect her from me, now, did it?"

"You?"

"Her mind was not as strong as it should be. And he is not the kind to put up with vaporish women."

"Do you mean you poisoned her?"

"No. She wasn't as stubborn as you. She saw her own inadequacy and took care of the problem for me. I didn't have to do more than help her see that she would never have her husband's love. That she didn't even deserve it."

"She had R.J."

"A son is never a substitute for a husband for that kind of woman. She used to cry for him at night. I used to have to comfort her."

Juliet could not mask her surprise.

"You could not know. Even R.J. does not remember that I was his governess before I became his stepmother."

"You were his governess?"

"Yes." She smiled. "But it would not do for Mr. Hopkins to marry his governess, especially not when his poor wife had thrown herself from a window and broken her neck under suspicious circumstances."

"What did you do?"

"I? I did nothing. Jonathan took care of it all so that there would be no scandal. He sent me away and then brought me back as a respectable unmarried sister of a friend. He introduced me into the society, and after a year of mourning for the wife he was well rid of, he married me."

"And R.J. doesn't know?"

"He was much too young."

Juliet's mind reeled. "So you know all about scandal and about covering it up, then? But Drusilla Abernathy was your friend."

"Yes." Annabel frowned, as if she were still puzzled by something. "I tried to explain. But she would not listen. I begged her."

Juliet pointed to the bottle of poison clutched in her hand. "You want me to be arrested for her murder?"

"No. I just wanted the suspicion. I'm not like you, my dear. I don't thrive on scandal. I avoid it."

"By murder and by feeding unhappy souls poisonous thoughts?" Juliet could not keep the anger out of her voice. "You will never do this again!"

"Who will stop me, dear? You? Not after tonight." She carried over the tea and held it out.

Juliet refused it. "I will not drink that willingly."

"Of course you will."

She must be mad. "Why would you think I would drink poison from your hand without protest?"

"Because if you do not, I will tell R.J. that you are having an affair with Dr. Abernathy."

"He will not believe you."

"Of course he will. After all, it is true, is it not?"

"No!"

"I saw you. It is why Susannah has been so agreeable."

"What is?"

"She saw you in his bed."

"I—" Juliet could not say anything. "I am not having an affair with Dr. Abernathy. Susannah knows that. R.J. will know it as well."

"He will not. Men are so jealous, you know. Their heads are easily turned. They call women fickle, but it is truly the province of men to change their minds and move their interests elsewhere. Why else would R.J.'s father have turned his attention to the governess when his wife was crying out for his attention?"

"Because he was a selfish fool." R.J.'s father had had enough of the conversation. Juliet nearly wept with relief as the man came into the room. Surely he could stop his wife's madness.

Annabel's fury burned through her for a split second, and Juliet thought she might die then, of a teapot cracked over her head.

R.J.'s father quickly took her by the hand. "That is enough, Annabel. I cannot believe what you have said here today."

"She was bound to cause a scandal sometime, Jonathan." Annabel's voice was oddly normal despite the unnatural things she said. "I was just trying to trap her—"

"Come with me." He led her away gently. "We will handle this without scandal, never fear. Your name will not be sullied, Annabel. And neither will mine."

"Not Susannah's, either, or she will never catch herself a lord and become a true lady."

"No, my dear, not Susannah's, either."

Annabel said softly, "Poor R.J. He will be so sad."

"We will not tell him of this."

Annabel laughed. "The police will tell him. I sent them a note to explain about the affair she"—her finger stabbed toward Juliet at the very moment Juliet understood what Annabel was saying—"the affair she was having with Dr. Abernathy."

Juliet let out a cry of outrage and dashed out of the house without a backward glance. She would leave Jonathan Hopkins to clean up the mess his wife had made. She must find R.J. before he spoke to the police.

TWENTY-FOUR

He was not at the police station. She ordered the carriage to go to the orphanage.

All the lights were lit in the windows as she pulled up. He must be there. He must be.

She leaped from the carriage before it had fully halted and ran to the entrance. To her surprise, she saw Phineas Abernathy standing in the open doorway.

"Phineas, Annabel is the one—" She broke off. The expression of grief on his face compelled her to embrace him tightly. "Phineas. Everything will be all right. I promise it. Annabel poisoned your wife. I will tell the police—"

"Juliet—" A strangled cry from within the orphanage. R.J.

She pulled away from Dr. Abernathy's embrace. "R.J."

But his gaze, disbelieving and then fiercely jealous, was brief. With one quick movement he turned on his heel and strode off.

Phineas Abernathy moved to follow R.J., but she held him back. "No. Let him be."

"He thinks we—" His look of distress was genuine. "Someone sent a note to the police—"

"Annabel sent it. I know what he thinks. But if he does not know me well enough to know it is a lie, then I should think he should ask before he condemns me for it. Don't you?"

"He is my friend. I must tell him—"

"Tell him what? That you love Susannah?" He blinked in surprise, as if he thought she had not seen his feelings clearly from the first.

"I never—"

"I did not say you had an affair with her. I said you love her. And she loves you. Do you think those are words any brother would wish to hear? No. Better to let him think what he does."

"He will never forgive you."

"He will if he loves me. I will tell him what he needs to know."

"And what is that?"

"That I love him."

She looked at the children peering between the posts of the staircase banister. Worried eyes, all trained on her. She summoned tremendous courage from somewhere and smiled at them all. "Everything will be fine, little chicks. Back to bed with you."

"Will you sing us to sleep?"

"I cannot tonight."

"I will sing." Dominic said proudly.

"You sing for the boys. I'll sing for the girls." Missy was not one to be outdone.

"Excellent." Juliet watched the children go eagerly to their beds for their lullabies. She wanted to cry—

with pride, with pain, with fear that her life would never be the same again. That she, like these orphans, would lose the anchor of her life.

She smiled at Dr. Abernathy. "I must go."

At home, before the carriage door was fully open, R.J.'s father appeared to block her exit. He did not seem happy. "R.J. told me he saw you embracing Dr. Abernathy. Do you understand the scandal that will surround you?"

"Annabel—"

"I will care for Annabel. But that will not erase the rumors of your affair. I will not have you in my house a moment longer. I warned R.J. And still this happens."

"What do you mean, you warned him?" Juliet could not believe this man would protect Annabel for having committed murder and would turn her away for a scandal that was not true no matter how likely it was that it would be impossible to disprove.

"I told him he was responsible for your behavior and if he did not keep you from creating yet another scandal, I would no longer know him."

No longer know him. How could a father say such a dreadful thing? "He did not tell me."

"He did not?"

"No." She frowned at the tiresome man. "No doubt he wanted me to come to like you. I never would if I'd known you'd said something so horrible to your only son."

"I beg your pardon?" He drew himself up to his full height. But she no longer found him intimidating.

"You are a bitter old man. A fool who does not

recognize the value of your son. You do know the tale of Romeo and Juliet, do you not?"

"Don't say that name."

"Why not? It is his name. It is a beautiful name. His mother, who loved him, gave him that name."

"Foolishness."

"No. Foolishness is not forgiving your son for one mistake. He tried to stop us from losing our heads that night. But I wouldn't let him. I've never let him." She grabbed his hands. "Please don't turn away from him."

"I gave him my word—"

"Forgive him."

"Forgive—" He looked as though forgiveness were a sin, not a virtue.

"Don't make the same mistake that Capulet and Montague made. The same mistake Annabel made."

"What mistake was that?"

"If she had not felt the need to protect Susannah when she didn't want to be protected, none of this would ever have happened."

"Perhaps you don't understand the scandal you have caused."

"I do." She closed her eyes against the tears that came, making it hard for her to speak. "It is all my fault. Place the blame on my head, where it belongs. No one in Boston will argue with you. Except perhaps Dr. Abernathy, who knows the gossip is not true."

"Abernathy—" He growled in anger.

"No. Don't blame anyone but me."

"How shall that erase the scandal?"

"It will not. But when I am gone, back to England,

back to ignominious disgrace, then R.J. will be free to be the son you want him to be. The son he can be."

"He may follow you if he wishes. I will have no more to do with him."

"No. I will leave. I will go back to England, and you will never hear my name again. But do not punish R.J. Please. He loves you. He is the best person to run your businesses. You cannot disinherit him because of me. It isn't fair."

"That means divorce, I suppose." He sighed. "Another scandal." But his tone had moderated. He was considering her offer.

"Not too much scandal, not when he is your heir and such a powerful businessman."

"You have a head on your shoulders, girl. Too bad you couldn't keep yourself out of scandal."

Juliet nodded and said firmly, "R.J. is not to be disinherited or I will come back to Boston and create a scandal such as you have never seen."

"What cheek!" He stood staring at her, spluttering as the carriage pulled away.

But he would keep his word. She could see it in his eyes. The very same color as R.J.'s eyes.

What had she done?

R.J. did not believe she had been having an affair. It had been a shock to see her in Abernathy's arms. If not for the note he would never have thought . . . but the embrace had not been loverlike.

Halfway home he had realized that she had simply,

as usual, offered her brand of kindness to a man in the throes of grief.

No. She had not been having an affair. But she had still become the focus of a scandal that would never go away. He would have to talk to her. Would have to let her know that she did not have to convince him of her love. No doubt she would try.

Perhaps his father would allow him to manage one of his factories. Perhaps he would have to use what he had learned to start his own business. R.J., watching for her return, glanced out the window in time to see his father send her off.

He raced down to stop her.

His father stood on the stoop, watching the carriage pull away with a disgruntled expression on his face.

"Where has she gone?"

"Home."

"This is her home."

"Not anymore. Interesting girl, though. She convinced me to give you another chance."

"Then why—"

"She's the one caused the scandal; she's willing to pay the price alone."

R.J. looked at his father in astonishment. "Did you think I would allow such a thing?"

"Can't have scandal stirring things up."

Annabel had murdered to protect Susannah from scandal. His father did not blink an eye. Juliet was the target of vicious gossips for something untrue . . . "I'm going after her."

"I'll have to disinherit you, then."

"Fine."

"Stubborn, are you? Very well. There is no way for her to live with her head held high here. Why don't I put you in charge of developing an English branch? You can bring her back there, and I'll keep my eyes closed to any and all scandals."

"Are you serious?"

"Just a good business decision." Blinking twice, the old man turned and went back inside, leaving R.J. to wish, just once, that his mother had lived.

His only consolation was that Annabel had not gotten away with doing to Juliet what she had done to his mother.

Ironic, he realized, that his father was more upset at the false scandal caused by Juliet's kind heart than the very real but hushed-up crime that Annabel had committed.

He supposed he could not expect all miracles. Not with a family like his. His fortune was his wife. Now he must go collect her.

TWENTY-FIVE

Boston dwindled to the size of a city enclosed in a glass toy as she stood upon the deck of the ship as it steamed away. How odd that it was only six months' time since she had seen it grow in her sights, full of promise and potential. No one could have told her then that people as deliberately and quietly cruel as Annabel existed. Or as foolishly afraid of the hint of scandal as Jonathan and R. J. Hopkins.

Well, she could not help what Annabel had accomplished to destroy her chance of a good marriage to R.J. And, after all, she had played a big part in that.

No. She had much to do. Perhaps after she had Dominic settled she would find the courage to return and try to make things right. She had spent the two weeks before her ship sailed thinking about what she could have done to prevent R.J.'s loss of faith. That hurt most. She had hoped he would follow her to the orphanage and beg for forgiveness for doubting her. But he had not come.

She sighed. At least she had gotten the children straightened out. Phineas had received a huge donation—he had claimed it came as a direct result of the scandal but would say no more. The orphanage was staffed well. And Missy had taken over the task of singing the children to sleep very capably.

Juliet had taken Dominic to be trained for the opera in Italy. But she had promised Missy that she would have training in Boston for her own voice. It was only her own life that needed to be sorted out. Had she done the right thing to leave R.J. to his father?

Should she have given him the choice, as she had hoped he would give her? All she knew was that she could not bear it if he were unhappy. Did he need Boston? Did he need his family? Did he need his father's business? She could not take them away. She could not.

The one thing she knew was that after a lifetime of believing there would never be a man for her, she knew there was. And his name was Romeo, whether he liked it or not. She sighed and rested her head on the ship's railing. What had she done?

"I have to say I admire those buttons of yours, Mrs. Hopkins."

She turned. He was there, but for a moment her heart was afraid to believe the evidence of her eyes. Breath caught, she held out her hand and touched the broadcloth of his jacket. On a cry of joy she inhaled the faintest of peppermint scent, and then she was wrapped in his arms.

"Did you think I would let you go?"

"You didn't try to stop me."

"How could I when some of the children explained what you intend to do for Dominic?"

"You went to the orphanage."

"I did. I told Phineas not to tell you." He said quietly, his lips pressed into her hair, "I knew you weren't having an affair, Juliet. I just didn't know how to convince the world you weren't."

"Have you figured out a way?"

"No. The world will have to think of Juliet however they will."

She closed her eyes. Would she never stop causing scandal? "I'm sorry."

"I'm not. Without you my life would be nothing more than business and duty. You brought me joy. You made me see there is more to life than reason."

She clung to him, hardly daring to believe he was here. "What about your father? His business?"

"He sent me to England with you."

"He knows? He allowed this—"

"I gave him no choice. If he wanted his son, he had to take his infamous bride as well." His mouth smothered any answer she might have had.

After a while, she broke away from him. It was only then that she noticed they were not alone on deck. "I'm afraid we're creating a new scandal, R.J. If your father hears of it, perhaps Simon will give you a job? I know he will."

He ignored the shocked stares of the other people on deck and pulled her back into his arms. "I can find a job anywhere, Juliet. But there is only one you. And I want you, scandals and all."

The trip to Italy was glorious. Sun during the day. An incredible moon at night. Dominic was accepted as a student. One day she hoped to see him onstage, his voice mesmerizing operagoers as it had the other orphans in Boston.

"Are you ready to face your scandalous past again in London?" R.J. took her hand in his as they stood quietly enjoying the sunset on their secluded balcony.

"As long as I have you, I can face anything," she said softly, squeezing his fingers. "Even gossipy old crows who will count months to see if our child comes too early?"

"There's no fear of that," he said softly. "We've been married a good half-year."

"Well, that's one scandal we won't have to live with, then," she teased.

He laughed. "The first time I saw you, I knew you were a remarkable woman."

"The first time you saw me, you thought I was a shallow, heartless flirt." Juliet smiled at him to show him that the knowledge no longer haunted her. "And I thought you a passionless man with a dried husk of a heart."

"You were wrong."

"I was fortunate. Perhaps more fortunate than I deserved to be."

"Never. Your heart always shone through. I've never known anyone with a heart like yours."

"Thank goodness we had the moon to show us the way."

DO YOU HAVE THE
HOHL COLLECTION?

Celebrate Romance with one of Today's Hotest Authors
Meagan McKinney

__In the Dark $6.99US/$8.99CAN
   0-8217-6341-5

__The Fortune Hunter $6.50US/$8.00CAN
   0-8217-6037-8

__Gentle From the Night $5.99US/$7.50CAN
   0-8217-5803-9

__Merry Widow $6.50US/$8.50CAN
   0-8217-6707-0

__My Wicked Enchantress $5.99US/$7.50CAN
   0-8217-5661-3

__No Choice But Surrender $5.99US/$7.50CAN
   0-8217-5859-4